Acclaim
of

"Remarkable...acute suspense...the tension torques up as the body count rises."
—*Houston Chronicle*

"The narration pulses with verve and threat, and through Payton's vividly rendered voice readers will know...sweat, lust, and fear."
—*Publishers Weekly*

"Edgy...terrific atmosphere and downtown attitude."
—*Detroit Free Press*

"The characters are quirky, the dialogue smart and fast, the action relentless."
—*Los Angeles Times*

"The entanglements and entrapments are sometimes as surreal as they are suspenseful. I had a wonderful time reading Russell Atwood's novel."
—*Ann Beattie*

"Good suspense, plenty of action, and great local color add up to a winner."
—*Kirkus Reviews (starred review)*

"[Atwood] keeps the story of this altruistic gumshoe moving at breakneck speed, cloaking everything in offbeat shades of noir."
—*Biography*

As soon as I saw her, I started bleeding again. She stood before me dressed in an airy, chocolate-brown silk blouse, a short pleated black skirt, and tasseled calf-high calfskin boots. She smiled at me and gave me a hungry look, and the cut in my forehead started to trickle. A droplet ran down and around my brow, then continued to descend along my left temple like a rivulet of sweat.

She must've seen it, but she didn't say anything.

I excused myself, turned, and headed for the bathroom.

I splashed cold water on my face and dried it. To be on the safe side, I put on a Band-Aid. It made me look tough, in a cartoonish sort of way, like Sluggo from the comic strip Nancy.

When I returned, Sayre Rauth was still standing on the threshold, hadn't come in yet.

She raised both her arms up over her head.

"Want to frisk me? I might be armed."

"Skip it. I've softened my stance on deadly force. Come in, nunchucks, machetes, grenades, and all."

She looked disappointed, or at least she didn't put her arms down right away.

What the hell, I knew she didn't have her gun on her, it was in my back pocket. And I didn't need to pat her down to pinpoint her other lethal weapons...

Losers Live LONGER

by **Russell Atwood**

A HARD CASE · CRIME NOVEL

A HARD CASE CRIME BOOK
(HCC-059)
September 2009

Published by

Dorchester Publishing Co., Inc.
200 Madison Avenue
New York, NY 10016

in collaboration with Winterfall LLC

*This book is a work of fiction. Names, characters, places, and
incidents either are the products of the author's imagination or
are used fictitiously, and any resemblance to actual events or
persons, living or dead, is entirely coincidental.*

ISBN 0-8439-6121-X
ISBN-13 978-0-8439-6121-8

Cover design by Cooley Design Lab

Typeset by Swordsmith Productions

The name "Hard Case Crime" and the Hard Case Crime logo
are trademarks of Winterfall LLC. Hard Case Crime books are
selected and edited by Charles Ardai.

Printed in the United States of America

Visit us on the web at www.HardCaseCrime.com

DEDICATED TO
Bennett Coleman,
Tourette's Poet, Fire Animator, Damn Good Friend.

Acknowledgments

Supreme thanks to Charles Ardai, who refused to take "no thank you" for an answer;

Susan Wolfe, who has the dubious honor of being my best friend;

My parents, Russ and Mary Atwood, and my pals, Dori Poole and Jerry Schwartz, for never losing faith;

Rob Perry for his botanical information and sage advice;

Alan Santos-Busch for pathological suggestions;

S. J. Rozan for her tough-as-nails help at the finish line;

Christopher Rowell for putting up with assorted lunacies;

Hi-K for inspiring half the jokes;

Cathy for being an amusing mute-muse;

Debbie Suchman for standing by me when it counted most;

Rick Shrout, a fellow writer who knows the difficulties;

Joe and Bonnie, for giving me a job and their friendship;

Janet Hutchings of *Ellery Queen's Mystery Magazine*, Joe Blades, and Walt Taylor, early editors whose guidance was instrumental;

and Edward D. Hoch, whose untimely death shamed me into finally finishing this book. Sorry it took so long, Ed, we miss you.

"There are ideal series of events which run parallel with the real ones. They rarely coincide. Men and circumstances generally modify the ideal train of events, so that it seems imperfect, and its consequences are equally imperfect."

—MORAL ANSICHTEN,
BY NOVALIS (VON HARDENBURG),
TRANSLATED BY EDGAR ALLAN POE, 1842,
IN "THE MYSTERY OF MARIE ROGET"

"We're a nation of standup comics looking for an audience. One-liners, quick repartee, the zinger. A joke for every problem, a quip for every question. Maybe because we don't want to answer the questions, or even hear them."

—MINNESOTA STRIP,
BY MICHAEL COLLINS (DENNIS LYNDS), 1987

Chapter One
OWL'S CALL

The downstairs doorbuzzer buzzed.

I didn't answer it.

It was too early to be the mail lady, only half-past nine in the morning the first Thursday after Labor Day. Couldn't think who else'd be ringing my bell, not for a second it might be a client.

I never had walk-in trade before, and gone were the days when I lived in anticipation of any. Most of my work came from referrals, and all of it began with at least a phone call first. With no appointments on the calendar that morning, I was at my desk drinking coffee and smoking, fresh from the daybed, dressed only in t-shirt and jeans, and barefooted.

The buzzer I figured was just some drunk again, leaning against the doorframe buttons, getting back his bearings before another uncertain stagger forth.

Couple minutes later, the phone rang. I let the machine pick up.

And heard my voice from seven years ago give the outgoing message: "Hello, this is Sherwood Investigations. After the tone, please leave your name, number, and the time. I *will* return your call."

An outgoing outgoing message. My voice back then held in it a clear quality of confidence and conviction. I didn't dare record a new one.

After the beep, an old man's voice and a name I didn't recognize. "Hello, Payton. This is George Rowell." Out of breath and speaking over the radio-static sound of random street traffic. "We met some years ago, don't know if you'll remember the occasion—" The dry squeak of a truck axle. The roar of a revving Harley over the line. They sounded in stereo, coming in simultaneously through my open window. "—it was in Matt Chadinsky's office over at Metro. I'm calling to see if you're available today to hel—"

I picked up the phone. I was nothing if not available.

"Good morning, Mr. Rowell. Sorry, had my hands full," I said, a little embarrassed by how long it'd taken me to fill in his blank: Owl.

I'd only met him once before, over a decade ago, back when I was just starting out in the business, working at Metro Security, Inc. But I knew of him; everyone did. George Rowell was something of a legend in the trade: one of the most successful P.I.'s on the East Coast, he'd operated a one-man agency for over fifty years. People—well, other private investigators—swapped stories about him going back half a century and extending around the globe. He'd tracked down the Chelsea slasher in 1976. In 2000, he'd been instrumental in the rescue of an abducted American girl from a child pornography ring operating in the Ukraine. And when anyone talked about him, they only ever called him by his nickname, Owl. A drunken slurring of his last name that had stuck, I supposed. He didn't look owlish the time I met him; too tall and thin, he'd looked more like a hawk-nosed heron.

He'd been old then, had to be in his eighties now. I'd heard he retired to a small town in New Hampshire. Also a rumor that he'd gotten Alzheimer's and died. Sounded alive enough.

"Glad I caught you in, first wasn't sure..." He sought to catch his breath. "I rang your bell, but I guess I should've called first. I'm not...interrupting anything, am I?"

I looked around the office. A bare cement floor. A couch with a pillow and a rumpled quilt. Two leather-backed club chairs. My desk. All gathering dust, a dust partly made up of my dry, dead skin gradually shedding.

"No, not really."

"I was saying, I don't know if you, if you remember our meeting. It was some time ago that Matt introduced us."

"Of course, Mr. Rowell."

No surprise that I did. For me, shaking his hand had been like touching history. At the time, I thought my meeting him would prove a good omen.

He chuckled softly. "Please, call me Owl. How's Matt doing these days?"

"Fine," I said. Only Matt and I hadn't spoken to each other in over five years.

"I hear he's a father now."

About a year ago, I'd run into a mutual friend who told me Jeanne was pregnant, so I agreed.

"Boy or a girl?" he asked. He had me there.

"Probably," I said.

I heard metal clank, both over the receiver and through my window. I went over, looked out.

Owl said, "Boy, did you say? Sorry, this isn't a very good connection."

Across Second Avenue on the southeast corner of Twelfth, a delivery truck driver had just dropped his handtruck to the sidewalk. On the same corner, a pair of payphones, Janus-faced, with only one in use. A dome of sparse white hair and stooped shoulders in a light brown suit were all I saw of him.

"So, Owl, what can I do for you?"

"Matt gave me your card a while ago, said you'd opened your own office in the Village, and that you were the guy to call if ever I found myself in need here."

"That must've been some while ago," I said. Matt hadn't

referred any work to me in years and that loss stung as much as the loss of our friendship.

Maybe Owl detected it in my voice, because he asked, "Did Metro bring you in on that Law Addison business? That had an East Village connection."

The name rang a bell—something earlier in the year, May maybe. Then I had it: Lawrence Addison. "Law" to his friends, and to his victims/clients.

"Grand larceny case," I said, pulling it up from my memory. "Securities fraud. Independent money manager, ran an outfit called Isolde Enterprises, lot of high-profile clients. Turned out to be just a big Ponzi-go-round, only Addison didn't step off the ride soon enough."

Just showing I knew my onions, but no great feat; it'd been front-page news for a couple days this past spring before the next young starlet's D.W.I.

Owl said, "But he did manage to step off eventually. Addison was granted bail. And then he skipped. Ran off with the wife of one of his ex-clients. The bail bond agency hired Metro to track him down. I'd have thought Matt would've brought you in on that. Addison had a place in the Village."

"No."

"Huh. Probably why no one's tagged him yet, right? Ha." He chuckled softly, letting me know it was a joke. "Still, odd that—"

I decided to come clean, weary of the square dance. "Metro stopped dealing me in several years ago, Owl. It's a long time since I've talked to Matt about anything."

"Oh."

I listened to the city traffic over his end of the line. A young woman laughed broadly. An angry dog with a peanut-sized bark yapped itself hoarse. A bus surged by in a whoosh, its loose side panels and windows rattling like a haunted house on wheels.

"These things happen," Owl finally said.

"Yeh, well, I only bring it up so you know, any recommendation Matt gave you no longer stands up. I doubt he'd say the same today if you called and asked him."

"I don't think that'll be necessary," Owl said. "Cards on the table, I had heard something like that already, but wanted your side of it."

"No side," I said. "Just a professional disagreement."

"Over what?"

"Oh, my being a professional. Matt disagreed."

Owl snorted. "Guys like Matt, they don't understand freelancers like you and me, Payton. That's the trouble. He doesn't…doesn't get why we do it."

I cleared my throat. "Why do we do it?" I asked. I didn't even know myself. "But then again what I do, Mr. Rowell, and what you've achieved over your—"

"Oh fuck that," he said, and it shut me up, but to my credit I didn't sputter like my Aunt Fannie. "I mean going out on your own, Payton, starting your own business! Most people don't know what that means. It takes guts."

"Guts, yeh, but not brains," I said. "Like spelunking with my dick out."

He laughed.

"Something like that. But I made it. And it looks like you're making it, too."

"Maybe," I said. "I don't know how you managed it for fifty years, Owl."

"Tell you one trick. You don't think about the last fifty years. You don't think about the last year. You think about tomorrow, you move with the times. Y'know how old I am?"

"How old?" I said.

"Eighty-four last month. But I still stay current with all the new technology. Just to keep my hand in. Lotsa guys my age, all they do is bitch about young people always talking on their cell phones, and meanwhile they've all got one, too, only none of them knows how to use it. Me, I don't have a cell phone—but I've got a device that listens in on *other people's* cell phones from up to twenty yards away, and you better believe I know how to use it."

I heard a click on the line then, followed a moment later by the sound of a coin dropping into the phone's metal guts.

When his voice came back, he got right down to business. "Listen, Payton. The reason I called. I need your help to flush a tail out into the open. There's a meeting later today and one of the people leaving the meeting, I think, is going to be followed. I need to know who is doing the following. It's not much, just daywork, maybe into early evening. But you'll be covered for the whole day. What's your rate, Payton?"

I heard a sharp crack, like a distant rifle report or a wood plank slapping the ground, over the phone and out my window. I looked out, but didn't see what made it, then heard it again, just out of view directly below my window, sounding more clearly like a flat wooden board smacking pavement.

Something about Owl's call was bothering me, something *off*. My normal rate was $50-an-hour plus expenses, but I told him, "Hundred a day."

"Please, not your professional rate, Payton. What's your regular? C'mon, I'm retired, just a private citizen now, not a private eye."

"Doesn't sound like it."

"Oh, this? It's a personal matter. Client is someone I owe a favor to. Old time's sake. You live long enough, it's actually a pleasure to still be around to repay your debts."

Long as you don't chalk up more along the way, I thought. But didn't voice it.

"I should be comping you, Owl, professional courtesy.

If it gets around to the other agencies that I'm not, I'd never get another referral throughout the five boroughs."

That was it, the not-quite-right-something bugging me. George Rowell was connected, had friends in all the top agencies in Manhattan. Hell, he was tight with Moe Fedel. He only had to ring up Fedel Associates and have a half-dozen ops at his disposal, with probably a groovy spy-van thrown in, and all on the house. Even Matt Chadinsky—perennial tightwad—would have only billed him pro rate, and then torn up his check. Before he'd been recruited into the upper echelon at Metro, Matt had learned the ropes as Owl's apprentice.

So with all that at Owl's fingertips, why was he calling me? I'd be the first to say it: he could do better.

"Okay, a hundred," he said. "But I buy you dinner later."

I agreed. I'd never intended to comp him anyway. It was just bluff. I wouldn't even comp my own mom these days. But I couldn't just lap it up either. I asked him, "Why you bringing this to me, Owl? It can't be my mad skills."

Maybe the slang threw him, he didn't respond right away. If not for the background noises and my looking down at him, I would've thought he'd hung up.

Instead, he gave me a jolt. Turned and tilted his head up and looked right at me framed in my second-floor window. Knew I'd been watching him, *sensed* it; he was a canny old bird. He smiled, a big toothy grin. Tall and bony as he was, for a second he did resemble an owl, an old white owl like on the cigar boxes. He shrugged his stooped shoulders.

"It's short notice. And it's right here, just a couple blocks away. Thought about who could cover it and you came to mind."

"We talking hard cover? If it's muscle you nee—"

"Nah," Owl said. "Soft cover. Simple. Nothing rough. It's just legwork, but I haven't got the legs for it anymore. You do. And the Lower East Side is your neck of the woods. You've got the natural coloring."

I nodded my head, but wasn't completely convinced.

"And how's this job tied in with Law Addison?" I asked. "Don't tell me you've turned him up?"

Owl laughed, no mirth in it though.

"No, no…haven't found him. But I may have stumbled—"

Another click on the line. When no more coins dropped, an automated voice interrupted saying, "Please deposit twenty-five cents for the next three minutes."

I told Owl to save his quarter and come on over. He waved in agreement and hung up the phone. He put a slip of paper in his jacket pocket, then, squaring his shoulders, he walked to the corner. I got my first good look at him.

He was ancient and not too steady on his pins. Rickety. Yeh, he needed a legman, all right. Hell, he could've used a registered nurse; every day I saw geezers younger than him wheeled around the city by their vacant-eyed assistants.

What was a guy his age doing still mixing in the business? If that's what this was. That something-not-quite-right was still niggling at me. Possibly the rumor I'd heard that Owl had died from Alzheimer's, maybe a kernel of truth in it? Going off on tangents. Strong emotion in his voice a couple times, anger, agitation. Was I about to be enmeshed in some sad senior moment? Dementia might account for his approaching me rather than one of his old friends if they were already alert to such episodes of Owl imagining himself back in harness.

The light changed and he started across. He looked frail, but had sounded solid enough over the phone.

Well, solid enough for me because, fact or fantasy, I could use his hundred bucks, even if I only spent the rest of the day tramping after heffalumps and woozles.

Waiting for him to buzz, I tried to make myself and the office more presentable, but there wasn't much to work with. The floor was littered with debris, spent matches, scratched lottery tickets, splayed newspapers, and balled-up socks. I definitely didn't put on much of a front. Trouble was there wasn't much back of it either.

Two-thirds of the year gone by and I'd only had four paying clients, all small gigs lasting no longer than a week. In some ways, satisfying jobs. But I couldn't live on satisfaction.

It was demoralizing, doing the only thing I was ever good at and still I sucked. I wasn't bringing in enough business to pay my rent. I'd borrowed a grand from my folks last month and all of it went to pay overdue bills that had matured into final cut-off notices. The letter with my parents' check said for me to have a big dinner on them. I had to make up a hearty-sounding meal to describe before calling to thank them for the loan.

I was barely hanging on. The bulk of my possessions had been fenced on eBay. Most of my furniture sold off on Craigslist. Soon I'd be down to only a chair, the desk, and my gun tucked away in the floor safe. I was devolving, dissolving. I'd spent the last fifteen years forging a career for myself, and what did I have to show for it? A forgery.

Owl's words ricocheted in my mind, "Why we do it."

I shook my head. Some things we do are beyond our control, especially those things that take years to do, not just spur-of-the-moment lapses in judgment, but decisions we don't make as much as they make us.

My problem was I never found a niche, instead playing jack-of-all-trades. Should've specialized, trained to become an expert in some particular field: computer foren-

sics, document verification, corporate security, biological
detection, identity-theft protection, cellular counter-
surveillance, handwriting analysis, something specific,
anything instead of this master-of-none shit.

Knew a guy, little younger than me, who used to work
at Metro around the same time. A nerdy-looking guy—
thick glasses, pockmarked complexion, ink-stained pocket
protector, the works. Looked like a disguise, but he never
was an op, just the office's technical support, which when
I started there only meant clearing the copier's paper
jams and connecting fax machines. But the position blos-
somed. Suddenly he was in charge of finding the best
firewall for their computer network and establishing
their website, etc. The others at Metro—like at most
agencies, a collection of hard-ass ex-cops—treated him
brusquely, balking his attempts to join in on conversations. I sort of took him under my featherless wing, taking
pity on him, always thinking, "There but for the grace of
God go I."

Not long after I left Metro, he followed suit and formed
his own computer security and risk management company. Couple years later, he had expanded into nineteen
international markets. Last year, he was featured in a *Time*
magazine cover story, "Faces of the New Detective." I still
had the issue in my bathroom stack. Whenever I flipped
across it now, I still thought, "There but for the grace of
God go I."

I tidied the office, ditching the gunked-up ashtrays,
collecting empty soda cans, and hunting for shoes.
Managed to find a pair, but one was black, one was
brown, and both were lefts. I kept looking. I needed to
make a good impression on Owl.

His call couldn't have come at a better time. The
money was sweet, but so was the opportunity to learn
some secrets from an old master, maybe turn my life

around. And, if things went well—at least didn't go sour—possibly get some future work from the agencies where Owl had friends. I'd been waiting for this, for a break to fall my way. If only I didn't blow it.

I kept up the search for footwear. Minute later, still hadn't located a matching pair, but it was okay because the buzzer hadn't rung yet either. But that wasn't okay.

He couldn't have gotten lost, only a few dozen feet from the corner. I went to the intercom and pushed the button to unlatch the downstairs door and heard the latch buzz and clack.

I opened my office door and poked my head out, calling his name, but the only sound in the stairwell was my own voice.

Just furrowing my forehead over that when the morning's white-noise blackened to pitch with a sudden thick-sick meat-thud sound and a mangled-pig squeal of swerving tires. Brakes screeched and...then nothing. The city struck dumb.

Without even thinking about it, I was out of my office and going barefoot down the steps three at a time, not caring as my office door swung shut behind me, as if I knew in advance what it was, what I would see before I saw.

Nothing paranormal about it though, only me naturally imagining the worst that could happen. Because had it truly been a premonition, I would have at least known beforehand to grab my keys on the way, instead of locking myself out.

Chapter Two
FOOTWORK

I opened the street door and looked out. What I saw started me running to the corner of Twelfth Street and Second. I didn't even hear the door close behind me, because ahead in the gutter was a bundle of clothes with a man inside them.

Head cracked clean open from impact with the granite curb. Pale-pink, white-haired scalp ruptured, a skull shard sticking out and an emission of brain like a pupal discharge. Bits of gravel studded his forehead, cheeks, and chin. His eyes were open, but each pointed off in another direction like clocks of different time zones, Istanbul and L.A.

I didn't have to touch him to know he was dead.

That's not why I had to touch him.

I took a deep breath, like right before swimming to bottom, then sank to one knee and reached out for him. *Lifeless flesh and bone which could not do me ill.*

With my right hand, I went through the motions of seeking a pulse in his throat, while with my left I went through his jacket pockets.

I was quick and graceless. The first pocket I clawed for and dug in was empty, and when I pulled my hand back out, the lining came out along with it. The next pocket yielded folded papers, and within, something hard, flat and flexible like a credit card. I palmed them and, shielding my movements with my bent-over body, shoved it all down the front of my jeans. Then started standing up again, backing up, shaking my head in pantomime of no-he-ain't-going-to-make-it.

But I must've stood too fast or shook my head too solemnly, because suddenly I was a little sick at my stomach. A headrush of sparkles blotted out vision. I felt myself losing balance, losing sense of up and down. Not sure where I was, what I'd been doing or what I was going to do next. I sucked in deep breaths to keep it all together, to look normal, blend in.

I rode out the nausea, until my vision cleared again and I discovered I was still standing on my feet, but that was the only welcome news it brought me.

It was a clear, too-bright September morning, quarter to ten, at a busy Lower Manhattan intersection. I had a dead man at my feet and plenty of people—witnesses— all around.

Pedestrians, shopkeepers, deliverymen, and tourists, who'd been frozen in the shock of the sudden accident, but now were thawing out and beginning to creep closer.

I looked to see if anyone had seen what I'd done, but none of the naked looks of horror were directed at me.

The car, the one that must've struck him making its right turn onto Second, was pulled over to the curb thirty feet down the avenue. It was a livery cab, a black Lincoln towncar with a small dent now in its right front side panel as innocuous as a dimple in a bowler hat. The driver, a gray-bearded Sikh in a lavender turban, stood neck-high in the wedge of his open car door, his eyes unblinking, unbelieving.

Diagonally across the intersection was a traffic surveillance cam mounted far up on the wall of the corner building, the seven-story apartment building with the giant yellow pig painted on its blank side. The camera was a narrow box-like affair trained on the intersection. The spot where Owl lay would be just out of frame.

As more people converged, I eased into reverse. I had to go, I couldn't stay. No, I had to go.

Barefoot, no I.D., and I'd just rolled a dead guy. Not a reaction I could easily explain, not even to myself, let alone any authorities. I didn't know what I was thinking, maybe even calling it *thinking* was a stretch, trying to sanction the mob of forces that controlled me just then.

Bottom-line: I hadn't seen—only heard—the accident. There was nothing I could tell the cops that wasn't self-evident. An old man had stepped off the curb and been hit by a car still at the scene. Open and shut.

Except, that meant Owl had been going *away* from my door.

I shook it off, like a lingering effect of dizziness.

Maybe he'd had some sort of seizure, or gotten confused and wandered heedlessly into the road. No way to know for sure. Relating my share in the tragedy would only cloud the situation, and add to it more tragedy, my own.

Getting into the sights of the cops has never boded well for me. I'd done nothing recently, nor was I afraid they'd fit me up out of whole cloth. However, the police have a lot of open cases in their files and they're like seasoned off-the-rack salesmen, always measuring you with their eyes. "What are you, 34 medium? I got something looks like it was made for you. Sexual assault in NoHo—fit you like a glove. Here, try it on."

And why? Because they're corrupt, evil, or lazy? Nope, it's just every time they close a case, an angel gets its wings.

Frenzied sirens gibbered five, six blocks in the distance. One last look down at Owl. Would that be me someday? Dying in harness? Nah, I'd never last that long, not in this business at least, I was already on my way out. But not as out as Owl, he was well out of it. I still had lumps coming.

I made a hasty sign of the cross, turned to go, and—

There was this blond kid staring right at me.

Kid about fifteen with bangs the color of varnished oak hanging down over his eyes. He was dressed in baggy drab pants full of pockets down both legs and a white Mickey Mouse t-shirt, the mouse in his famous red shorts with big yellow buttons. Leaning against the corner building, balancing a skateboard on the toe of one sneaker, the kid kept staring right at me, or maybe just beyond, it was hard to tell because of his bangs.

I didn't try, I got going. And didn't stop at my building, but shuffled past. If that kid, or anyone else, had seen me going through Owl's pockets, the last thing I wanted was to be traced back to my building. Maybe if I'd had my keys on me I would've chanced it, but without them I'd have to buzz my upstairs neighbor and hope she was in. It wouldn't do to hang around waiting to find out.

A police cruiser pulled up to the curb and I continued putting distance behind me. Until things cooled down, it was best I had a little walk around. But that also presented a problem: nothing else for it, I needed shoes.

On the sidewalk were pulpy brown smears, broken beer-bottle glass, syrupy yellow puddles, Con Ed metal plates possibly live with stray voltage, rusty old screws. I had to watch my step; this was New York City and I was in trouble again.

Just like that. An odd mixture of emotions vied in me: exhilaration and repulsion, like when handfeeding a reptile.

I headed for the far end of the block.

The surge of traffic on Second Avenue registered as a steady throb against the soles of my feet, and when a flatbed truck ran over a pothole, the shudder traveled up my skeleton and rattled my back fillings.

I heard the EMS van arrive behind me—doors opening, radios squawking—but I didn't look back. At Eleventh I turned right round the corner and let myself breathe again when I was out of sight.

This stretch of East Eleventh was a residential side street, apartment buildings and three- and four-story brownstones with garbage barrels lined up in front.

I began lifting lids, looking for a pair of shoes roughly my size. I pick through garbage on a semi-professional basis, so I made short work of it, but without success.

Gingerly walking on down the block, I passed under a sidewalk tree, a ginkgo. Its pink cherry-size seed pods, fallen to the ground and mashed underfoot, stunk of vomit. Stepping on them felt like I was walking over open eyes.

I needed shoes. Comfort aside, if anyone had seen what I'd done and was now telling the cops, I didn't want to fit their A.P.B. description of "barefooted man seen leaving."

But not to worry, this was the East Village, there'd be shoes. Time was you couldn't turn a corner in this neighborhood without coming across a tossed-out pair of two-tone loafers, or snakeskin cowboy boots, or zebra-striped high-tops, or glittery platform pumps. Things couldn't have changed that much.

This is the East Village, I told myself, there'll be shoes.

Unless, of course, the neighborhood *had* changed that much, like the rest of the city around it, diluted and deluded, desecrated and desiccated, its character and flavor all but gone. If so, then I was lost here.

Your neck of the woods, Owl had said. Yeh, 'cept these weren't my woods anymore, and now there was only my neck.

I passed a walkdown basement entryway beneath a building's front stoop where years ago I'd been beaten up by three guys.

Maybe I'd never known the city all that well to begin with.

I cautiously rounded a shattered fluorescent tube.

Ahead of me, lined up along the curb for collection were a discarded computer monitor, a VCR, what looked like a scanner/printer or maybe it was a fax machine, even a miniature satellite dish. A decade before on this block, the danger would've been stepping on a junkie's discarded needle, not stubbing a toe on obsolete tech.

I lifted more battered lids, but the closest I got was finding a collection of old neckties all knotted in a jumble, like a hive of silk. There weren't any shoes.

A young goth couple with matching raccoon eyeshadow approached me and clomped by in black buckled combat boots which I watched pass near my toes with equal parts fear and envy.

And then I looked up and there they were, sitting atop the lid of the next garbage pail over. A pair of black leather men's dress shoes.

I pounced, snatching them up as if away from rival hands.

Size ten or eleven, with dusty tops and slightly curled toes. I turned them upside down, knocked the heels together, shook them, undid the laces, shook them some more, then peered inside. All clear, nothing creepy was living in them. Yet.

I leaned against a lamppost, getting a glimpse at the bottoms of my feet, already jet black.

I tried on the shoes. A loose fit, but better than too tight. I did up the laces, then took two steps. Their backs bit into my naked ankles like angry lobster claws, but their bottoms crunched nicely over a bit of broken glass.

I shined the dusty tops against the back of my pant-legs. A fine dust remained in the creases, highlighting spidery lines in the leather like wrinkles in an old man's face. Crow's feet. Owl's eyes.

I spit and tried shining them again against my pantleg, but the impression continued to linger like Marley's ghost.

With my head high, I crossed the street and walked to the spiked iron fence of St. Marks-in-the-Bouwerie church. The back gate was open and I entered the church-yard and found a flat surface to unload the papers I'd culled from Owl's pockets. It was a cracked marble slab, a vault stone with most of the lettering worn away by cen-turies. I could only make out part of a name: PHILIP HOAP—. I spread out the papers.

At first, it didn't look like much, except for a worn $20 bill, paper soft as felt. Which equaled 24 minutes of my time. Or 96 at the pro rate I'd quoted Owl.

The hard, flat, flexible thing wasn't a credit card but a magnetic card key for a hotel room, the Bowery Plaza at Third Avenue and St. Marks Place. It was four blocks above the Bowery and three degrees below a Plaza, but the receipt for the room quoted a reasonable rate and had the room number printed across the top and the date—9/2/08—when George Rowell had checked in.

The other papers were two leaflets—sale handbills, one for a men's discount clothing store and one for a Persian rug wholesaler, both in Chelsea on West 21st—a pink pasteboard receipt for a parking garage, and an empty chewing gum wrapper. Wintergreen. I turned them all over, but he hadn't jotted anything on the backs.

The only other thing was a business card, one of mine. The card stock was flimsy; I'd printed it up on my own computer. My first set of cards from the year I opened the office. So long ago, I hadn't begun to include my e-mail address or the 212 on my number. Back then there was no other Manhattan area code.

I'd given a stack to Matt and a few other operatives at Metro, to hand out if anything came within my line. For all the work it got me. Matt probably used most of them to pick gristle from his teeth, but he'd given one at least to Owl.

I refolded the papers and stuck them in my back pocket. The twenty I put in my front right pocket with the card key. I brushed off my knees and left the church-yard by the front gate, onto the cobblestoned triangle of Abe Lebewohl Park.

Across Second at the southeast corner of Tenth was where Abe's Second Avenue Deli used to be. Gone now, replaced by a glass- and neon-fronted bank, with rows of ATMs looking like exposed public urinals.

The deli had been at that location since the days of Yiddish Theater but couldn't survive there into the new century. Change is part of the city, its one constant— I accepted that—but the old businesses weren't being replaced by new ones starting a new tradition. Instead, commercial rents had bloated out of proportion, squeezing out longtime occupants; rents so high only banks and cell phone stores could afford the inflated leases.

The people who moved into the neighborhood now didn't even know the Second Avenue Deli had been there, didn't know what they were missing. Why did they move here now? Would I even want to move here now? I only stayed because…because…

I shelved the thought, a problem for another day. Today had its own problems. One was just rolling up behind me.

I heard a grinding sound like a ballpoint pen drawing endless circles on a glass tabletop.

He slid up alongside. The blond kid on his skateboard. He *had* been looking at me after all.

He rode parallel. Standing on his board, he came up to about my chin. Grinning ear-to-ear, he had angular, pointy features like a Bali devil-mask.

"Nice kicks, dude."

"Thanks," I said, not turning my head, giving him my profile like Lincoln on the penny.

He cackled, laughing so hard I thought he was going to fall off his board. See, it's all in the delivery.

Getting himself under control, he said, "You...you look ...like a clown."

I said nothing, wondering what his game was and if it was one I played. My sweaty feet made squishy noises in the alien shoes. He mimicked the sound with his mouth and it got him cackling all over again.

When we got to East Ninth Street I stopped. The light was against us. But the kid swept on like Mr. Magoo, sailing out into the middle of the road without looking either way.

A taxi cab racing through the intersection to beat a changing yellow slammed on its brakes in a screech of smoking rubber. Its front grille stopped barely a foot from the kid. The cabbie leaned on his horn, but since he had a fare in the back, drove on without making any more of it.

The kid waited placidly on the other side of the street for me.

None of my business if he wanted to play grab-ass with death, but I told him, "You almost got it, junior."

"Got what?" His blue eyes all bright innocence.

"Squashed."

He shook his head. "Never happen."

"Happens all the time, an old guy just got killed a couple of blocks back."

His eyes gleamed.

"What did you take off him?"

"How's that?"

"The old man, what chew get? I saw it. I saw you."

He had a put-on street accent and a knock-off attitude, which told me nothing about him except that he flipped through magazines and channel-surfed. His face was tanned, freckles clustered around his nose. Blue eyes flashed behind his veil of dirty-blond hair.

"Money, what? C'mon, tell me," he whined. "I could go back, y'know, and tell 'em what I saw."

I stopped.

"You saw it, the accident?"

He cackled.

"Accident? Right." His voice turned level and cold. "I saw what you did."

"Then that makes you a witness. You should go back and tell them."

He said, "I could say I saw more."

"Uh-huh? Like?"

"Like you shoved the old guy in front of that car. I could tell them I seen that."

That plank slap sound I'd heard beneath my window.

I said, "Were you practicing your ollies on the corner when it happened?"

"Ha, practicing? I got it down—I kill 'em every time."

He stopped briefly to demonstrate, making his board jump up by stepping hard on the back end. He had my interest now but not for his SK8R moves.

I kept pace with his smooth, even glide.

I asked, "So...what *did* you see?"

"I saw you...going through the old guy's pockets," he said, deliberately raising his voice, "so you better tell me what you got, or—"

One of the few upsides of having nothing left to lose was calling people's bluffs. I called his. I stopped in my tracks.

"All right, let's go back." I looked back toward Twelfth Street, lights of the EMS van and a cruiser's blue strobe still flashing.

The kid laughed harshly. "No way."

He spun on his back wheels and stopped beside a row of free-newspaper dispensers, clustered by the street corner like giant, multi-colored building blocks.

Used to be only one or two of these bins could be found on every other street corner, but over time more formed, sprouting up like mushrooms all over the city. Eight in this row: the *Voice*, the *New York Press*, *L* magazine, *Real Estate Market*, *The Villager*, *Our Town*, and the two free dailies, *AM NY* and *Metro*.

The blond kid reached into a Velcro-sealed pocket by his knee and pulled out a magic marker, an extra-large black Sharpie the size and shape of a store-bought hot dog. He uncapped it and shook hair out of his eyes.

"Like I'm goin' tell *cops*. For *free*? You're wacked. If I tell anyone, it'll be the TV news. And if I *don't* tell, cash only. I'm not wasting it. I'm going to be somebody. Be fucking famous one day, you'll see."

"Famous for what?"

He took instant offense, like it was a trick question people were always testing him with. He let his bangs settle back over his eyes.

"Famous!" he said, as if it was self-evident. "People

lining up to get my autograph. Girls, shit. You'll see. The whole world'll see."

Picking the newest newspaper bin—an unmarked bright yellow one—he began to scribble on it with his marker.

"Lot of kids with boards and Sharpies," I said. "That's not going to make you famous."

Tip of his tongue sticking out in concentration, he drew a long flowing stroke with the marker, adding a slash, then a dot.

"That's what you know, ha!"

"What, got yourself a sugar daddy?"

"Sugar mama, dude," he said to show me up, but his face went cross, like he'd said too much.

Something occurred to me and I asked him, "Why aren't you in school today, kid?"

"School? What for? Half the millionaires in America never finished high school."

"Where'd you hear that?"

"What, I bet you went to school, huh? And look at you, you're picking in the garbage for shoes. School's for fools. Shit, you're wasting my time, dude. Good luck with your dumpster-diving."

He re-capped his marker and put it back in its pocket. He mounted his skateboard, dipped down and shoved off with one foot, propelling himself west on Ninth Street.

I wasn't sure what that was all about, but was glad to see him go.

I read the tag he'd scrawled on the yellow bin. In big rounded letters like bloated black intestines: FL!P

A shout of "Hey!" made me turn round.

The kid had stopped only twenty feet away and was holding something out in front of him aimed at me. His cell phone.

"Say cheese," he shouted, snapping my picture. Pocketing the phone, he took off again on a glide.

I wondered had he snapped a shot of me digging into Owl's pockets? And what else?

I watched his retreat, an irrational urge in me to chase after him and smash his phone. Like an uncivilized native who'd just had his soul swiped.

But nothing worth chasing after for.

Not in these shoes.

Chapter Three
THE BRIEF CASE

Walking fast or slowly made no difference, the shoes still cut into me. After a while the pain dulled. Not much farther. Next street down was St. Marks. Owl's hotel was an avenue over.

At the corner, a white-haired guy with glasses, a tan Labrador lying beside him, was sitting cross-legged at the base of a lamppost cementing bits of broken china to its base. Jim the Mosaic Man retouching one of his pieces of art. I'd read an article the week before about the campaign to complete his mosaic trail through the East Village.

I nodded a hello as I turned right, but he was engrossed in his work. I walked down the block. On this stretch of St. Marks Place all the buildings were fronted with shops aimed at the tourist trade. T-shirts and souvenirs, used CDs & DVDs, sandwich shops, acupressure and shiatsu, leather goods, consignment clothing. At this hour most weren't open yet. Young Latin men in soiled kitchen whites scrubbed and hosed down the sidewalks in front of the eateries.

The Bowery Plaza's entrance was a single glass door on Third Avenue between a pizzeria on the corner and a hair salon. Easy to miss if you weren't looking for the hotel.

I hadn't been inside for years—last time tracking a runaway—and couldn't remember if hotel guests had to pass the front desk or not to get to the elevator or stairs.

Expense account item one: two cups of coffee bought out of Owl's twenty. At the corner, I grabbed one of the free dailies from a red bin. I went back to the Bowery Plaza and walked in.

The essence of disguise is to be easily classified. The goal isn't to be invisible, but to be seen and then disregarded.

I walked through the door of the hotel with Owl's card key in one hand and the two coffees balanced in the other. Walking on the balls of my feet to minimize the shoes' squishy sound.

The lobby was the size of a freight elevator and the elevator the size of a broom closet. The clerk, a salt-and-pepper-haired blur in a blue blazer behind the counter, didn't even look up as I cruised by.

I pushed three and ascended at a sluggish crawl, scanning the newspaper's headlines: GOP VP'S PREGNANT TEEN; FORMER SITCOM STAR, 19, DIES IN O.D.; FASHION WEEK PREVIEW. By the time I reached the third floor, I'd finished one of the coffees.

The anonymous corridor was as lively as a sun-shrunken condom. Crooked wall sconces with lampshades apparently made from recycled nicotine filters.

Outside the door marked 3-E, I stopped and listened before swiping the card key. Hoping for silence, but instead I heard a woman shouting, "No! Now!...I don't care."

I took a sip of overflow from the lid of the other cup, and waited. The voice wasn't from TV, none of the vacuous joviality, bright appeals, or musical bridges. Just the woman. And no other voice—her gaps in speech weren't answered, unless in whisper, but more likely she was on the phone.

I checked the receipt. The right room number. I inserted the card key and got the lock's green light.

Turned the knob, inched the door open a crack.

The woman continued to spew ire. A clear gravelly timbre to her voice.

"Listen you fucking shit, you owe me...I don't care, just get it...and *not* that same...what? No, now!"

I pushed the door open all the way. A single low-ceilinged room with a narrow bed, the bedspread ruffled but unslept-in. The woman was seated on it with her back to me, a cell phone to her ear, her legs crossed, one foot spastically tapping the air.

I walked in. The carpeting was the color of spaghetti sauce. The wallpaper was peeling, dog-eared in its high corners. To my left a dusty window with gauzy curtains. Two chairs, a TV—switched on, but mute—a nightstand with a lamp, a digital clock, a full ashtray, a scratchpad, pen, and the telephone. To my right, a mirrored dresser with a closed brown-leather briefcase on top, and beyond that the bathroom, its door partly shut.

"No, I don't have to listen—you do. In half an—"

Must've caught my motion, because she whipped round.

"Call you back." She closed her phone and stood up.

She was a tanless white with straight short hair dyed the purplish-red of beets. In her late twenties, five-eight and too thin. Eyes with that sunken-skull look associated with eating disorders and substance abuse.

But what eyes. A strange sparkling color, neither green nor grey, but like emeralds with an embedded diamond swirl. She had a too-wide mouth and long nose, but it didn't matter, not with those eyes. She was dressed in a clinging green silk blouse and black knit skirt revealing shapely legs.

"Who the fuck are you?"

"Morning to you, too, bright eyes."

I'd left the door wide open on my way in, for a clear exit. She shoved past me and slammed it shut.

I crossed to one of the chairs and sat down, my tortured feet singing hallelujah.

A wastebasket beside me. Empty pack of cigarettes and crumpled tissues at the bottom along with something else. A plastic wristband like the kind you get when admitted to a hospital. I dropped my empty cup on it.

The woman came back from the door.

She held her cell phone in a tight fist. There was a ring on her left hand's fourth finger, a diamond-shaped diamond.

"Who are you, what do you want?" she asked.

Even with her voice pitched low, it still had that gravelly quality, like she'd spent her youth shrieking to be heard above house music.

"Did the old man send you?" she asked.

"Yeh. Owl sent me."

"Who?"

Sounded like a joke, but neither of us laughed.

"The old man," I coughed up. "George Rowell."

"Well?"

"He had an accident, can't make the meeting."

"Fuck! What'm I supposed to—fuck! He dumps me here and tells me—FUCK!"

She opened up her cell phone and stared at the screen. Maybe checking text messages, maybe considering her options.

I considered my own. Owl had said he was returning a favor for a friend. But this woman had no reaction to his name or concern for his well-being. So if not the client, who was she?

For a brief instant, I wondered if she might be a hooker. But Owl had been in his eighties... Maybe that was the secret to his longevity?

But no, she was no hooker, not if that rock on her finger was real, and it looked just gaudy enough to be genuine.

"What did he tell you?" I asked.

She stared at me with those eerie sparkling green eyes, drilling into mine, like they were unearthing something. As they narrowed on me, the skin around them showed etched lines like dry papercuts. "What is this? Who are you?"

"Question of the day."

I finished my other coffee and dropped the cup in the wastebasket, then stood up. I absently tossed the free newspaper I'd brought with me on the bed as I walked across the room. A small room, but she didn't move an inch as I passed; her head was turned away, looking down at the bed.

Passing by the dresser, I looked over at the briefcase on top. Old scuffed leather with reinforced brass corners. Initials G.R. engraved in gold below the handle. One of the latches was up.

I continued on to the bathroom door, opened it, and peered in at a slant. It was empty. Toilet seat down. A lipstick-stained washcloth in the sink. No toothbrush.

I turned back.

She was fast, I was slow. The first I heard of her was from the shifting of contents in the briefcase she lifted up over her head.

And brought crashing down on mine.

It landed like a red-hot charcoal briquette. One corner hit my left temple and down I went, more from the blast of pain than the force behind her blow.

And perfect pinball that I was, the other side of my head connected with the dresser's edge on my way down, and that's all I knew for a while.

Time for a commercial break.

Less a dream than a rerun from a long-ago Saturday morning TV fest flitted through my reeling skull. A pencil-drawn cartoon of a shaggy-haired boy approaching the tree where an owl wearing a professor's mortarboard is perched. The boy poses the eternal enigma, "Oh wise Mr. Owl, you know everything. How many licks does it take to get to the Tootsie Roll center of a Tootsie Pop?"

Mr. Owl grabs the lollipop in a talon more used to snatching voles in mid-flight, deftly unwraps it, and says, "Let's see." Lick. "Uh-one." Lick. "Uh-two." Lick. "Uh-three." Crunch!

I woke staring at the carpet. The nap of the tomato paste rug. A single loose fiber broken free from the ranks rode above the fray, no longer part of the carpeting, now something that had to be vacuumed up in order for the rest to look clean and orderly. I felt sorry for that lost little fiber, little curly-cutie.

I raised my head and pain like a jagged wire suture joined my temple, left eye, and chin. Hit on head no good. Payton no like. Make go way pain.

I crawled over to the bed and climbed up onto it.

By the time I was on my feet again the woman was long gone.

The briefcase was where she'd dropped it after dropping me. Open now, some of the contents spilled out.

I walked around it to get a damp washcloth from the bathroom. I bathed my temple and drank water from the faucet. Took a piss while I was at it and noticed my front pockets were turned out. Both back pockets empty, too.

Tsk, imagine going through someone's pockets...

I went back into the room and found most of my stuff scattered on the floor by the open briefcase. Something missing though. My head hurt too much to sort it out. Later. I pocketed what was left.

I let out a low whistle and, with the washcloth pressed to my head, gave the room a quick once-over. Scratch pad by the phone was blank. I tilted it under the light, but no embedded impressions were revealed.

Dresser drawers empty, Owl hadn't unpacked. I found his suitcase on the floor by the far side of the bed.

Inside were a couple days' worth of clothing, neatly packed: three white dress shirts, one yellow sports shirt, a pair of tan khaki pants, four pairs of boxer shorts, and five pairs of socks. Only other thing, a zippered toilet bag with a denture brush in it, tooth polish, an old fashioned razor, and a can of shaving cream.

I helped myself to a pair of brown argyles before shutting it up again. Then sat on the bed, unlaced the shoes, and slid them off. The bottoms of my feet were streaked black like I'd been kicking Alice Cooper in the face. I wiped them on the bedspread before putting on the socks. My ankles were bleeding.

I put the shoes back on. It was an improvement.

I went over to the wastebasket and picked out that plastic wristband. It had been stretched apart, not cut. I turned it over looking for outpatient info, but both sides were blank. I pocketed it, I was a magpie for clues.

Back to the bathroom to splash water on my face.

I left the briefcase for last because I already saw what it contained. The contents were like the bottom left drawer of my own desk, full of red wires, black wires, white wires, and gray wires bound with rubberbands. None longer than three feet and each with a different end attachment, a phone jack, a microphone plug, an alligator clip, a suction-cup device, a USB connector—whatever a P.I. needed in the course of his work. A wafer-thin digital recorder. I switched it on, but it was blank.

I sifted through the rest: stopwatch, pocket binoculars, magnifying glass with light attachment, brown work gloves, assorted batteries, a pack of blue Bic ballpoint pens, large and small paper clasps and paperclips, a disposable camera with 24 exposures (none of them used), an old mercury oral thermometer, a clear plastic ruler, a compass, and a black plastic box for a .32 automatic with an extra full clip inside and a rag and brush for cleaning, but no gun. Great. A simple matter, he said. Soft work, he said. Nothing rough.

Sticking out of a pocket sleeve under the lid was a bus ticket folder. Inside was a round-trip ticket, New Hampshire to New York City. He'd expected to go back Sunday morning.

It was nothing I could use, though. What was I missing?

I thought back to the indisputable techniques of investigation my old boss at Metro, Matt Chadinsky, tried to drum into me during some of his loftier harangues. Most of it bullshit on how no one ever rewarded you for doing the job better, that doing the job better *was* the reward. But one of his more useful axioms had been, "Never look just with your eyes." Poke into every hollow, he'd say. Get dirty. People lose things all the time that drop into tight spots and corners, dirty places they don't want to reach into.

I slid my hand down into the pocket sleeve, dug to the bottom. It wasn't dirty inside, it was smooth. At first I thought nothing was in it, until my fingertips snagged on a corner and I pulled out a color photograph.

A 4x6 snapshot of Owl standing with a thin young girl about twelve years old with shoulder-length dirty-blonde hair, a flattish nose, and big ears. He was crouched so their heads were at the same level. Both mugged for the camera, teeth bared in fierce smiles. The girl's nose was wrinkled-up in a snarl. The flash camera colored both of their eyes hellhound red.

They were casually dressed, the girl in a pink t-shirt and blue jeans with swirly embroidered rhinestone designs. Owl wore a plaid sport coat, open-collar shirt, and gray slacks. Behind them was a large potted rubber-tree plant and a pale-blue wall with a partly visible sign, the word GATE in black letters.

I turned the photo over. No date written on the back, only one word in blue block letters: ELENA. I pocketed it.

Still hadn't found what I was looking for, what I needed. A scrap of paper or anything with a local phone number or address that would lead me to Owl's friend, the client he owed a favor, connecting me to the job he'd hired me for. But nothing.

My force of purpose going down the drain, nothing left behind but the gurgle. No job, never was really hired anyway.

I didn't know what I'd been thinking, maybe couldn't know. Do dogs think when chasing a squirrel? It's just part of them, an impulse that defines what they are. Problem was, some chased their tails with equal enthusiasm.

Practical matters came back into sharper focus. I had to get back into my office and only two people in the metro area had a spare set of my keys, and one of them I hadn't spoken to in over five years.

I reached for the bedside phone, read the instructions for an outside line, dialed out, and then the number. It rang only twice before she picked up. Gone were the days when my upstairs neighbor slept until noon, Tigger had a bambina now who got mommy up early.

I simply told her I'd locked myself out, not wanting to get into it over the phone. Would she buzz me in?

"Good thing you did it this month, Payton, and not next."

At the end of the month, Tigger and Company were moving out—not just out of the building, but the city. I refused to think about it, I didn't even answer her, I was in locked-down denial. It was like facing an upcoming operation, a scheduled amputation. With any luck, I'd get struck by lightning first and never have to face up to it.

I told her I'd be there in a few minutes.

I stared at the cigarette butts in the ashtray. A pack and a half worth of Marlboro Lights.

I had another call to make, but put it off until later. Not a conversation I was looking forward to.

About to get up, I noticed the tiny red message bulb on the phone was lit. I followed the instructions for retrieving the message and heard a woman's slightly accented voice say: "All set for 11:30, Yaffa Cafe."

I checked the nightstand clock. Quarter to eleven.

I closed Owl's briefcase and took it with me.

At the hotel room door, I stopped for one last look around, feeling like I was forgetting something. My eyes went to the rumpled bedspread. Nothing was on it.

The newspaper I'd tossed there was gone. She must've taken it with her. Not that that had to mean anything. If she'd taken the gun, she would've needed something to carry it out in.

I was just puzzling over it when the bedside phone rang and I nearly jumped out of my borrowed socks.

I went over, picked up, said hello.

"Michael?" A woman's voice.

"Yes."

"May we speak to her?"

We? Her?

I said, "Ah, she just stepped out."

"We have that number for her." She sounded official.

"Oh, I can take it."

"No. Have her come by or call us here at the pier office."

"Sure, but—"

She hung up on me, not so much as a have a nice day.

Who the hell was Michael?

I shrugged and filed it away. I left the room with Owl's briefcase grasped in my hand. I felt like an upright citizen off to do an honest day's work, which in a way I was.

I now had a time and a place. I had direction.

Somewhere out there in the city was a billable client. And I was going to find him.

Chapter Four
HOMEWORK

Leaving the lobby of the hotel, I almost collided with someone coming in. A stubby old man with bulbous features but no chin, black hornrim glasses, and a stiff gray pompadour. He was dressed in a white short-sleeve shirt and black trousers.

We danced a few steps of the back-n-forth polka attempting to get out of each other's way. My head couldn't take the jostling. I turned sideways and let him pass. I grinned, but he didn't make eye contact.

Outside, I turned right and headed up Third, cut down the diagonal slice of Stuyvesant Street, back over to Second Avenue and Tenth.

A passenger airliner shrieked and moaned overhead. I looked up to see a peerless blue sky, not a single shred of cloud in any direction, absolutely clear.

It made me uneasy.

The gleaming white airplane seemed kind of low. It must've been in a holding pattern for JFK. I watched it slowly creep across the narrow column of airspace above me. I was the only one around who seemed to take any notice. I was like a housebroken dog forever shy of rolled-up newspapers.

When the plane finally passed out of sight beyond the edge of a roof, I moved again, breathing evenly.

The briefcase barked against my left knee twice. I switched hands and it barked against my right knee.

I couldn't get the hang of it, just wasn't executive material, I guess.

I stopped on the corner a block from my building, by the end of the churchyard gate where for at least a dozen years the little black lady, Evelyn, used to station herself, bouncing change in her paper cup and exchanging friendly words with anyone who passed. She had died that January.

I rattled my pockets for coins, none. Fished in my watchpocket and came up with a quarter, Oregon back. I left it right where she used to sit.

Ahead, at the corner of East Twelfth, the commotion had died down, everything back to normal. People crossing the street, cars repeating that same sharp right onto Second, over and over where Owl's body had been. As if nothing had happened.

I walked to my building and pushed the buzzer for T. Fitchet, Penthouse.

The intercom speaker clicked.

"Who is it?"

"It's the plumber, I've come to fix the sink."

Speaker click.

"Who is it?"

"It's the plumber! I've come to fix the sink!"

Click.

"Who is it?"

I hollered, "IT'S THE PLUMBER, I'VE COME TO FIX—"

The door buzzed and I pushed it open.

At the first landing, I stopped at my office door, tried the knob—yep, locked—and set down Owl's briefcase, then went up the next flight to get my spare keys from Tigger.

Her door was open and I walked in.

She wasn't in the front hallway. She wasn't in the living room, either. Her array of computer monitors unmanned looked like an abandoned UFO console, hard copies of design projects draped over lamps and chairs like hastily discarded alien star charts. I went further in, calling out, "If you're naked, I warn you—I brought my pastels."

I turned the corner into the kitchen nook and Tigger was seated at the table with two men with shiny black hair dressed in shiny blue suits, a sheaf of legal documents spread out before them.

She stood up—a short trip, she's only five-two—dressed in a belted blue-striped cotton dress and black regulation-issue army boots. She swept out her right arm, flashing her four-aces wristband tattoo.

"Payton, this is my realtor Mr. Ecuador—"

"It's Acquidar, actual—" Mr. Ecuador tried to assert.

"—and my accountant, Midge," Tigger swept on.

"How'ya doin'," Midge said.

"Hi."

"My downstairs neighbor, Payton Sherwood. A noted investigator, no doubt in disguise at the moment. We're finalizing details on the closing. I'll get your keys." Her grin was so wide and cunning, her silver and turquoise septum-pierced nose-ring tapped her two front teeth.

She got me the keys and walked me to her door. I asked where the little bambina was. Her 18-month-old, Rue, was off with her father; Retz's visiting parents—Rue's grandparents—were off "taking in" the Museum of Modern Art.

"I told them she's too young for it. Better off planting her under a tree in the park for an hour."

"She'd like the mobiles."

Tigger grunted, non-committal.

"What's with the Charlie Chaplin shoes?" she asked.

"You're the second person today to tell me I look like a clown."

She raised a pedantic finger and corrected.

"So far. I'm the second person today *so far*—it's not even noon yet. So what's with the shoes?"

I told her how I found the shoes after locking myself out, but nothing about the accident, Owl's death, or what I'd done after. Partly because it would take too long, mostly because I didn't trust her reaction. The thing with Tigger Fitchet was: never did know which way that tree was going to fall. More often than not, right smack on top of you.

I said thanks for the keys, I'd bring them back.

She said, "Well…maybe you should…you know…"

"What?" She gave me a look and I gave it right back to her.

"Nothing," she said. "Bring them back."

I turned to go, but stopped and said as naively as I could, "Okay, who are those two guys *really*?"

Her fuzzy caterpillar eyebrows sank in a frown.

"Payton. It's really happening."

"O.K., don't tell me. Be that way."

I tried a hasty retreat, but she put the Vulcan neck-pinch on me before I took a step.

"What've you been up to? You look…different."

My subtle lycanthropy showing. It'd begun.

"Nothing, let go. Release release." She unclamped her hold on me. "Ow. I've gotta shrug these shoulders, you know. I'll call you later." I went downstairs, but didn't hear her door shut until I was at mine.

Yeh, see what you'll be missin' out on, missy? The exotic air of mystery—won't get that when you move out to Melonville.

I opened my door, nudged Owl's briefcase in with my foot.

As soon as I sat down behind my desk, I found my sneakers I hadn't been able to find before, right where I'd kicked them off. Some detective.

I undid the laces on the black shoes, removed them and the socks. I washed my feet in the bathroom, toweled them, then put on a pair of clean white socks, sat back at my desk and put on my sneakers.

Two messages flashing on the machine. I played them.

But only one of them was new, the first message was Owl's call. I listened while pouring loose tobacco into a cigarette paper, rolling it, licking it, letting it dry a second before setting it on fire. I lit up, so eager I even took in the match sulfur. I drew deeply and held it. The smoke tasted delicious and foul streaming out my nose and falling from my lips.

"…at Metro. I'm calling to see if you're available today to hel—" End of Owl's message, cut off where I'd picked up.

The new message was from my mom, received at noon, calling to ask if that was near me where that young actor who played that doctor on that comedy series set in the hospital died—they say he shot up drugs? You know who I mean, the one on that series that used to be on, who played the doctor? Where is the Meat Packing District? Is that near you? How close— Time expired.

I picked up the phone, but not to call my mom.

No use putting it off any longer. I dialed the number of Metro Security, got the switchboard, and asked for Matt Chadinsky, giving my name.

He didn't keep me waiting, but his first words were, "What is it? I'm busy here."

"Owl's dead."

"What?"

"George Rowell, he's dead."

"Bullshit, who told you that bullshit?"

"No one told me. I'm telling you. He died this morning, here in the city. Hit by a car on the corner outside my building."

"Are you shitting me? What was he doing there?"

"Coming to see me?"

"What for?"

"To hire me."

"You're shitting me. You sure it was—"

"I'm sure. I've got his toolcase here in my office."

"He left it there?"

"No, it's…I took charge of it," I bobbed.

"What did the blues say?"

"What do they always say?" I weaved.

"Was it a hit and run?"

"No. Driver remained at the scene. Livery cab. Looks like an accident."

"Where'd they fucking take him?"

"I didn't, uh…"

"No shit, I can imagine." He coughed and spat in my ear, I was glad it was over the phone. He sighed a powerful gust of disgust. "Hohhh, I've got calls to make. Stay put!"

He hung up.

I switched on the radio and tuned in local news. Nothing about Owl's death, but I hardly expected it. An advertisement came on for an institute specializing in wounds that won't heal located in Sleepy Hollow. I switched off thinking of that poor Headless Horseman and his wound that never healed properly.

I went over and turned on the TV. Didn't have a cable box, but I'd attached the old line directly to the back of the set and still picked up the feed for NY1, New York City's 24-hour cable news channel. I also got a few other stations and listened to the audio of scrambled signals whenever a movie channel aired *Murder, My Sweet* or *The Big Sleep*. I've seen them so many times, I didn't even need the pictures to watch 'em anymore

Nothing about an old man's death in a traffic incident

on NY1. Their top local story was the ex-sitcom star that'd
died the night before of a heroin overdose. It was a big
story, had to be if my mom saw it aired nationally.

Craig Wales had overdosed in a back room at the club
hosting the after-party for a premiere of his first feature
film. What made it even more sensational was that, on
behalf of a fan website devoted to the TV show he used to
star on when he was still in his early teens, *Healthy
Assets*, he'd been blogging the entire event via text message, right up until the hour he died.

The TV screen was flashing excerpts alongside an old
photo of him wearing a doctor's white lab coat. His last
blog entry began, OFF 2 °^° w/ MC!!!

I tried to suss it out. OFF 2 °^°. Well, but of course, it
was so simple a five-year-old could make it out. Quick,
run and get me a five-year-old. It made me wonder what
direction our language was headed in. Rebuses and cha-
rades, grunting and pointing?

At the left-hand corner of the TV screen was the current time and temperature. 11:11 and 81 degrees.

I emptied my pockets on the desk. The photograph of
Owl and the girl, Elena; the pink parking garage ticket;
the three handbills, Owl's hotel receipt, my business
card...what else had there been? The money. She had
taken that, but anything besides? Couldn't put my finger
on it. I looked at the wristband I'd found in the hotel
wastebasket. Nothing new came to me.

Everything but the photo, I sealed in an envelope. The
photo I folded into my wallet.

I took off my shirt and put on two new ones, one a
bright lime-green t-shirt with a white collar, and, over
that, a button-down long-sleeve blue dress shirt, which I
buttoned all the way, except for the collar. It wasn't a
fashion statement, these were my work clothes. In case I

was spotted, I could shed the dress shirt and, at least superficially, become another person.

From a desk drawer, I got a folded paper painter's hat and stuck it in my back pocket for the same reason.

Finally, I slipped on my battered old camper's watch. Checked the time against NY1 before switching it off, just as the handsome young face of Craig Wales flashed once more on the screen. The news loop reporting his O.D. was coming round the bend again, round and round all day long, same on every network, until it was no longer sensational or shocking, merely predictable, monotonous as a carnival wheel's odyssey.

I left the office with keys in hand and someplace to go.

Chapter Five
LEGWORK

It was a short walk to the Yaffa, back to St. Marks Place and a block east, and with my sneakers on almost a pleasure.

Yaffa Cafe was a holdout from the old East Village, an enduring landmark still standing and in operation. It had survived the wave of upscaling gentrification that had swept through the neighborhood because it was a favorite with the yuppie crowd and tourists. Probably half the place's income came on the weekends from late-night snackers and afternoon brunchers.

It was still early for the lunch crowd, but the sidewalk tables were almost full. I didn't go in, just took up position on the opposite side of the street and watched, pretending I was carrying on a cell phone conversation. My empty left hand held to the side of my face, I rattled off inane drivel.

It dates me, but I recall a time when a person couldn't stand around doing nothing without someone wondering what he was up to, maybe even approaching and asking outright, "What are you up to?" To stand around without attracting attention, a guy had to be smoking a cigarette or reading the paper. But that all changed when 90% of the population began walking around with cell phones attached to their heads.

I repeated my location in a too-loud voice, then said, "Ah, yeh…hmm what…uh-huh…right, yes…eleven…

before, uh-huh…" And on and on in a constant spiral, like a toilet that won't quit flushing.

To nail the cell phone disguise, you have to be completely unaware of and unresponsive to your immediate surroundings. Having a real phone isn't even necessary; they're so compact nowadays, just holding a cupped hand to the ear does the trick.

I've picked out undercover cops trawling for drug dealers around the neighborhood using the method with real phones and, no doubt, actually conversing with someone at the other end, but they blow it by noticing me when I clock them. A true cell phone zombie you can stare at for hours and they're unaware of your inspection. Off in another dimension, a connecting anteroom between themselves and whoever they're talking to, half-between here and there, but nowhere.

I said my location a couple times and paced ten feet one direction, ten feet the other direction, keeping my vision wide, attention on Yaffa.

Most of the people at the sidewalk tables were finishing late breakfasts, so by half-past eleven half of them had gone. But they weren't my primary interest. I only watched the people who left to determine whether they were followed or not. It wasn't foolproof. If the person doing the following were halfway decent I might not even tag him or her, and all of this would be for nothing.

But luck was on my side, because he sucked. I pegged him as my squirrel before he even got underway. He loitered on the same side of the street as me, but he stood directly opposite the cafe while I was positioned about thirty feet farther east, watching from an angle.

He was a rail-thin twentysomething with a shaved head darkened by a bluish five o'clock shadow. Eyes squinted in Internet slits, from too long gazing in dim light. He had the complexion of a trout's belly. He wore tan corduroys and a gray work shirt with a name stitched over the pocket: Jeff.

While everyone around him—young men and women in tailored suits hurrying west in the direction of NYU or the subway, younger men and women in soiled black jeans and skeleton-and-skull t-shirts slouching toward Tompkins Square Park to sleep, old women pushing wire carriages off to the grocery store—was going someplace, leaving someplace, all in varying degrees of hurry, his sole movement was to lean on one foot, then the other, and back again, like a top-heavy metronome.

I guess whenever you see an amateur doing something you do professionally, you feel a certain pique. I almost wanted to shout at him, "Stop looking directly at your subject, dummy!"

His lips were tightly compressed and his eyes straining, white-rinded, glued on the Yaffa.

I followed his gaze to the sidewalk tables. Which of the remaining patrons was his study? I knew who I'd be watching, the striking young woman with the Degas-bronze profile and long brown hair that fanned around her face whenever she leaned forward to sip cappuccino or look up and down the street. I could barely take my eyes off her myself.

She was waiting for someone, checking the watch on her slender wrist inside the sleeve of an ochre yellow silk blouse.

At another table, a gray-haired couple in matching checkered-flag outfits who'd been consulting a fold-out map refolded it, paid their bill, left. I turned to my squirrel, but their departure meant nothing to him.

I went back to studying the lanky brunette, all the while keeping up my cell phone act, repeating my location, what time it was, what time it was going to be, my location, what time it was, etc. There was something irresistible about this woman, something that made you think of Pavlov and dogs and bells, or maybe moths and flames.

Twenty minutes went by. People left, a few more arrived, but my squirrel still watched and waited, and the brunette remained alone. She'd been stood up. It was a crime.

A nearby churchbell rang in the noon hour.

The woman signaled the waiter to bring her check.

My squirrel stopped his swaying and stood still and flexed his hands. Gentlemen, start your engines.

The check came and she dug into a suede shoulder bag as she went inside to pay. She came out again, left her tip, and we were on our way.

She looked west to First Avenue, waiting just that little bit longer before she started walking east in the direction of Avenue A. Long legs in black pants like sheer silk pajama bottoms.

My squirrel started right off. He took the job of shadow literally, matching her step-for-step on the opposite side of the street. I sized him up, wondering what he was capable of. Hundred twenty pounds tops, but plenty of bunched-up nervous energy.

I waited. Thirty feet. In my too-loud outside voice I said my location one last time, then goodbye, call you later, and pocketed my imaginary phone. Forty feet. I turned and looked in the shop window of the artist De La Vega's store. Some wild stuff on display as well as handmade books of his artwork and collections of his writing. I'd have to come by again when he was open. Fifty feet. I started after them.

At Avenue A, she stopped for the light to change, so I caught them up a little. He matched her on the opposite corner, but at least he didn't stare right at her. She crossed the street and entered Tompkins Square Park. He followed at a slackened pace.

She led us through the park, passed stone chess tables occupied by men playing cards, snaking by the sprawling green lawns where people lay bathing in the sun, many of them drably dressed street kids sleeping off the previous night's debauch. We went by where the bandshell used to be before the 1998 riots and the destruction of the shanty-town. Now there were jungle gyms. We threaded our way southeast along the narrow leafy paths, finally exiting at Avenue B and East Seventh Street.

Our parade continued south along Avenue B, through an Alphabet City unrecognizable to anyone who hadn't arrived in the last fifteen minutes. Most of the older businesses—dive bars and dodgy bodegas—had been consumed, replaced by upscale boutiques, curtained lounges, French crepe shoppes; new money remaking the neighborhood in its own image. There stood a hair & nail salon where once had slouched a beer-drenched saloon.

But down these gentrified streets a man must go...

Was a time, I wouldn't've walked in this neighborhood except under extreme duress or a high cash retainer (often one and the same), but times had changed.

Or so we'd been told. Statistically, crime was down to a record low in the city. But statistics only measure what they're designed to: crimes reported and arrests made. When crime goes underground, out of sight, and the crooks become more sophisticated in avoiding detection, then the stats are useless to judge by and it's time for a new means of measuring.

The numbers people saw reported supported the hyped image of a new New York City, crime-free and user-friendly. "Come one, come all, you'll be safe as houses. Bring the kids. This isn't your grandpa's NYC." Only when they get here, they discover it's a lot less like *Sex and the City* and a lot more like *Law & Order*.

The truth is the city isn't an animal you can domesticate. Those who imagine it is make the same mistake as people who try keeping grizzly bear cubs as pets: sooner or later, they get their faces clawed off.

We passed by a grade school and the Sixth Street Community Garden. At East Fourth Street, the woman crossed the avenue and continued east, halfway down this darker, less-tenanted, tree-lined street, coming to a stop at a waist-high black wrought-iron gate in front of a trim three-story townhouse. This building hadn't even existed the last time I'd been here. The stark newness was offset by its neighbor, a six-story pre-war brownstone, painted white, with the black trails of rusted porticos running down its facade like tear-streaked mascara.

The young man was directly across the street as she went in.

I tightened up on him, closing within twenty feet. Too close really, but I wasn't sure what he was liable to do.

The front gate swung shut behind her as she mounted the white cement steps to the door. She stirred the contents of her suede bag until she brought up keys, then opened the door and went in.

He watched. I watched. We watched. After she'd gone, he crossed the street to the gate and looked up at the door. A brass plate was mounted to its right. I supposed he read it. Too far for me to make it out.

The first floor windows had inside shutters of light-colored wood and they were closed. The second floor windows had dark, gypsy-shawl patterned curtains which were drawn shut.

The top-floor windows had the same curtains. One of them twitched as my eyes rested upon it.

My squirrel, "Jeff," had his hand on the front gate, but he didn't take it further. He turned left and walked away. I

followed with my eyes, not losing sight of him as I crossed
the street to the gate. I noted the address and the name
engraved on the townhouse's brass plate.

Rauth Reality.

I read it again. Rauth Realty.

My squirrel was thirty feet away. Enough of a head
start. I followed.

He led me to the next corner where he turned right on
Avenue C/Avenida Loisaida and headed south into the
barrio. The cover of trees thinned out to stark empty
sidewalks crumbling in spots. Fewer people around and
more CLOSED signs on businesses yet to be revitalized.
Fantasy-art murals on the side street brick walls.

I kept him on a long leash, but the precaution was un-
necessary: leading me down C, past East Second and a
half-block further to a five-story apartment house, he
never once looked behind him.

I thought it funny, a guy follows someone but never
looks behind himself to see if *he's* being followed.

Yeh, hilarious. Same was true of me.

A familiar grinding sound turned my head, but I saw
no one behind me. And then didn't hear the sound again.

The building was #27 Avenue C, a dilapidated tene-
ment, one of the older buildings still remaining on the
block, decades of touch-up paint, olive and gray, peeling
from the bricks like scabby flesh.

Its entrance was between a TV repair shop with a
CLOSED sign in its dusty window and a scaffolded four-
story building covered in wind-torn blue tarp. No construction workers on the scene. A project that had begun
with great fervor but stalled in the economic slump. The
wave of gentrification stuttering, falling behind.

As my squirrel inserted his key in the street door, I
broke into a jog, spanning the short distance between us.
I was a few feet away when the door shut.

It was a battered metal door covered with wild tagger scrawls, which looked like the miscellaneous symbols that appear above a cartoon character's head when conked.

The clouded view into the vestibule was a small square window of chicken wire-reinforced glass, grimy-yellow and etched by battery-acid graffitists.

I strolled up and peered in, hoping just to catch a glimpse of him maybe going up the stairs. But when I looked, he was still in the entryway, removing a key from the door of one of the mailboxes, top row, third from the left. No mail though, his hands were empty.

A car sped up the avenue, music on mondo, a thudding Latin beat and sugary rhythm that sustained in the air long after it passed, like the echo of a discharged cannon.

I hung back from the door, casually studying my watch. 12:18. Inside, the squirrel opened a second door and entered the building's hallway. He went toward the stairs but passed by them, on to a rear left ground-floor apartment. Bit of luck.

He stopped with the key in his hand and knocked on the door twice. He said something, then opened the door himself and went in.

The squirrel was in his nest.

I turned my gaze back to the mailboxes. A name on the one he'd opened. I tried to read it, shifting my head around, standing on my toes, looking for a less clouded section of glass. First initial: L. Last name: A-N-D—was that an R?

"What you want?"

He was a thick-featured Latin about 60 years old, dressed in pine-green overalls and a pine-green visored cap, carrying a bucket full of black water and a mop the color of storm clouds. He had a keyring crammed with about 30 assorted keys clipped to his belt. The building's super. From the corner of his mouth hung a small smoldering cigar like a soggy stuffed grapeleaf.

I smiled. "Afternoon. Was looking to see if a friend of mine still lives here."

"Who's your friend?"

I took a chance on the name.

"Andrews."

His face softened, his mug looked like a flabby kneecap. He had bushy gray eyebrows below which his black eyes were bright but deep-set like two coins out of reach under a grate.

He asked cautiously, "You a friend of Mr. Andrew?"

"Yes. Is he still living here?"

He shook his head sadly. "Mr. Andrew went away. The people who stay in his place are no good. Very bad."

A vapor of alcohol traveled on his words.

"Really? Well, that's not right."

"But I don't know how to call Mr. Andrew," he insisted, grieved nearly to tears. "I would tell him of how bad these people are."

"Well, maybe I could get a message to him for you."

"You call Mr. Andrew?" His dark eyes sparkled. "Yes? You talk to him, you tell him to call me, Luis, right away. He has my number, but I give to you."

From his back pocket, he pulled a stubby pencil and a brown paper bag with a pint bottle still in it. He wrote something on a corner and tore it off and handed it to me.

"You tell him about this man and this woman? Specially the woman. She's…" He searched for the word in English, but couldn't find it and shrugged ashamedly.

"Bad?" I offered.

"*Loco*," he said, and he said it darkly. "When I tell them not to leave garbage always in the hall outside their door, she punch a hole in the wall by my head. I call police, when they come she tell them I was drunk. She lies and says *I* punch the wall. They almost arrest me. I call the police and almost they arrest me. Ha! But other building people come out, come down to the sidewalk, and tell police who I am. Good building people, nothing like them." He spat on the sidewalk.

I thought of the woman at the hotel who'd bashed me over the head. I asked him, "Red hair? *Rojo*? This woman?"

He shook his head. "No, blonde. Like an angel." His lips contorted with the irony and made a wet-fart noise. "But she's a *diabla*. You know? If devil were a woman. You know?"

I described Jeff to him and he nodded his head. "Yes, him. I see him at the garage, the one on Tenth, across from near the pool. He's not so bad, but she is…she is…"

"Bad?" I tried again.

He nodded. "Bad. You tell Mr. Andrew, he come back, see what these people do. I know Mr. Andrew, he will not like what they do. But I don't know how to call. You call?"

I nodded my head, assured him I'd make the call.

He smiled broadly. Several bottom front teeth were missing, the rest slanted into a craggy yellow W.

He landed a meaty, callused hand on my shoulder.

"You tell?" he asked again, now with a smile.

"I will."

He gripped my shoulder and squeezed hard in appreciation. Don't think it could've hurt more if he'd meant it to.

He pulled out the paper bag from his back pocket again, but not to jot down a number this time. He unscrewed the cap and offered the open bottle to me.

I asked what it was. He told me, but it didn't sound like anything I'd ever heard of, maybe he said it in his native tongue.

What the hell, I thought, it had to be nine A.M. some-place. I took the bottle and had a gulp from it.

His grin broadened and that should've warned me, but on I glug-glugged and swallowed.

Heavy duty tequila. Tears streamed from my eyes. I whooped and cast out a demon. The warmth in my chest was active and alive, but at least not rebellious.

He took the bottle and had a small dainty sip before replacing its cap. He shook his head, chuckling.

He reached for the jumble of keys on his belt and deftly selected the one he wanted, opened the building's street door. He propped it open with his bucket.

"You call, you tell Mr. Andrew," he said and turned his back on me, getting back to his work.

He sank his mop into the bucket's murky black water and swirled it around.

I walked away, essentially off to do the same myself.

Chapter Six
THE RIGHT CLIENT

I walked, steady enough, retracing the route back to the townhouse the woman had entered. I stopped, again steady enough, but no mistake, I was feeling fine. That good was tequila was good, that tequila was.

I opened the gate and mounted the steps lightly, Vesuvius milk swishing and swaying behind my belt and spreading all through me a warm, cascading buzz. I pressed the bruise on my temple and it hardly hurt.

On impulse, I pushed the single intercom button, no idea what I was going to say when someone answered.

I guess, if not for the shot of tequila, I might've handled it differently. First gone back to my office and thought about it, maybe done something else.

But I can't entirely fault the liquor. She shared in the blame. And was the more intoxicating from the very first sip.

It's not that I believed in love at first sight, just that as I saw her for the first time up close, I believed in nothing else.

She came outside to see me rather than speak over the intercom. Hot, smooth, and languid as honeyed liquid, she slipped out and closed the door behind her. Softly, she leaned her back against it.

"Yes? Can I help you?"

Her frank eyes were almond-shaped and black as a bird's. Eurasian? A dark complexion, deeper than tan. Maybe the gypsy curtains were more than mere decoration. A small flattish nose over thin lips, the ends of which curled into an arousing smirk. A wicked, impish chin and a slender downy neck with deer-taut tendons and a lively, animated throat.

"Yes," I said. "Yes yes yes."

Some wise old freak once said, you can have anything you want in the world, all you've got to do is want it so badly it means more than anything else. Lot of people you talk to have no idea what that means. If you've never been hungry ever in life and you want a sandwich, you don't really *want* that sandwich. But when you've been hungry for weeks, starving, no relief in sight—and you come across a sandwich, a stacked, lightly toasted club sandwich, so fresh there's beads of dew on the pert overhang of lettuce? You want that sandwich.

That kind of want. But fuck the sandwich.

I wanted her.

On top of the way she looked, I sensed something I never could resist. She was and/or was in trouble. And I could see from the look on her face she was trying to figure out just what I was. Would I be her knight in shining armor or another dragon?

A low sound in her throat, not a laugh, more like a confused cough. I couldn't stop staring at her and she wouldn't break eye contact with me. Like when someone's got a grip on a high-voltage wire and can't release it, and the people around watching him, his brains frying, sparks shooting out his ears, are all thinking to themselves, Why doesn't he just let go?

She blinked and broke the spell, or at least suspended it.

"Who are you looking for?"

"You. Well, not exactly."

What had I been thinking? She wasn't all that pretty. Her features heavy, her nose a lump. Really kind of ugly, or else that was all just from the ponderous frown she leveled at me.

"Not exactly," she repeated. She had some trace of accent I couldn't place, but not American, more guttural, her words spoken under her breath. "Could you be exact?"

"Possibly. Given time."

"I do not have time, I'm about to go out."

"But you just got back in."

She cocked her eyebrow, but ignored the deliberate provocation. "And now I go back out again." She pushed the intercom button and, when she heard a crackle from the speaker, said, "The door." The latch clacked and she pushed the door open behind her and took a backward step.

"That's in," I said, feeling playful.

"What?"

"You're going in. You said you were going back out again, but that's *in* you're going. I learned all about it. From this guy, Grover. Shaggy blue hair, red nose, thin dangly arms? No? He also taught me about near and far. If you like I could teach you sometime."

"Yes. Let us begin with far." She started to swing the door closed.

"I have information."

Her eyes narrowed. She stepped out again, keeping one hand behind her back. I heard the door shut.

"Who are you?"

I reached into my back pocket and she stiffened, her shoulders tensing, until my hand came forward with my wallet. Her reaction made me uneasy—what had she expected, what sort of thing was she used to?

I opened my wallet, keeping my thumb on the snap-shot of Owl, while I extracted one of my business cards, one of a batch I had printed last year. Nicer than the old ones. Heavy cardstock, raised lettering. Nine boxes of them left. Hardly ever gave them out to strangers, even felt a little odd handing one over to her now, like an indecent exposure.

My head started to ache again, the tequila buzz was wearing off.

She read my card, her fingernail flicking its edge.

"Private...investigator." She said it like she was tasting the sound, as if she never had the opportunity to say the two words together aloud before. But she didn't repeat it, the novelty already stale on her lips.

"And you are?" I asked.

"My name is Sayre Rauth." Oddly formal, like a ritual recital. "You said you have information for me?"

From over her shoulder, the intercom speaker crackled a little. But it didn't have to mean anything, could've been stray radio-dispatch noise from a passing taxicab.

"I have information. Maybe it's for you. Do you know this man?"

If she had glimpsed Owl's picture inside my wallet before, she hadn't reacted. Now I handed her the photo, made her look at it.

"Who is he?" she asked.

Strike one.

"George Rowell. His friends call him Owl."

She looked up at me sharply, as if I were trying to confuse her again, then back down at the photo. She unfolded it so the young girl was in the photo, too.

"He's another private investigator," I told her. "Do you know him?"

She shook her head, not lifting her eyes. But I saw a reaction, a tiny tightening of the muscles around her lovely, lovely jaw.

"Are you sure?" I leaned in.

She looked up. "Yes."

Strike two and strike three, caught looking, I was out. I sighed.

"You don't know me," I said, "so I understand if you're cautious and holding back. That's only natural. But you can trust me."

She laughed, no confusion in the sound this time.

"You are trying to find this man?" she asked.

"No, I'm not." I didn't want her to get the wrong idea that I was after George Rowell. If she was keeping her association with Owl a secret, she'd deny anything about him. "Do you know him?"

She shook her head, still looking down at the picture. I had to ask her to hand it back in order to make her look up again.

"Is that all you wanted? To ask me if I know this man?"

"No, there's more. I wanted…I came to tell you about a man who followed you back here from the cafe this morning."

She said nothing.

I tried again. "He was watching you from across the street. He waited for you to leave. Then he followed you all the way back here."

Calmly, she asked, "How do you know this?"

"I was watching him. I followed him."

"So…where is he now, where's my stalker?" She leaned forward. I watched the fine, taut and tender line of her neck. A fresh flowery scent wafted by me and I inhaled deeply.

She looked to the right, she looked to the left, her dark eyes settled back on me. I liked having them there. "I don't see anyone. The only man I see who followed me is you."

I winced. She had a point there.

"So you don't want my information about this guy?"

She narrowed her eyes. "Is this really what you do, follow people who follow people and then ring their doorbells looking for work?"

"Yeh," I said sourly, "that and chase parked cars."

"I don't understand. The photograph of the old man, who is he? Why are you looking for him?"

"I told you, I'm not." I met her eyes and held them, then dropped the D-bomb. "He's dead."

It was a cheap maneuver, not designed to get me any-thing worth having, even if it hit its mark, like swinging away at a pitch after already being called out. And missing again. Strike four.

She had no reaction. Unless she was the world's greatest actress, had incredible control. Or else didn't believe a word I said so it didn't matter. Or…

Or she was simply telling the truth, she didn't know Owl, he was a complete stranger to her, she wasn't his client, it was all just my wishful thinking, and I'd somehow gotten it completely wrong.

The extent of just how wrong began to dawn on me, though dawns are seldom so bleak: what if I'd followed the wrong ones from the cafe? The people I was meant to tail long gone now, along with the only link to Owl's client.

The woman's voice softened. "I'm sorry."

"Sorry?"

"You look so…I didn't realize. He was close to you?"

"I hardly knew him. He hired me only this morning to follow this guy and report where he went to ground. Except now, I've got no one to report to, he's dead. Unless I can find whoever hired him."

She nodded her head, pursed her lips. "I see. And you thought I was this person?" She said it like she was diagnosing my particular mental disorder.

"I thought you might be. But that doesn't matter.

There's this guy following you, see? I thought you'd like to know."

She appraised me with a tolerant air, her smile kinked at one end.

"Let me ask you, do you think it's the first time men have followed me?"

I took her question seriously, looking her up and down. That body hadn't been overnighted to her, she'd grown up with it, grown up in it. No answer required.

I heard a sound I recognized and looked to the sidewalk in time to see the blond kid again, gliding by on his skateboard and yakking on his cell phone, not even looking over at me. It could've been a coincidence, I suppose. Yeh, a coincidence, like when it rains you get wet. He must've been tailing me.

She called my attention back. "What does he look like, this man you say is following me?"

I described him without using specifics, only color, weight, and build, but she seized on my sketchy phantom.

"I know this man, he is a friend of mine."

"Why was he following you then?"

Her lips sought the taste of an explanation, something with the flavor of truth in it. I watched her tongue's pink nib.

"He is not quite right. But harmless."

"My description fits a lot of people, how do you know it's the same guy?"

"Well, where did he go? I'll tell you if that's where my friend lives."

Our eyes met and I felt something stirring in my chest, something strong and horrible. Maybe prelude to a heart attack, but my left arm wasn't the appendage that was tingling.

I gave her the address where my squirrel had nested. "Number twenty-seven Avenue C."

And, just like that, my assignment was over.

She nodded several times. "There, see, that is the same man, I told you. That's where he lives."

"Oh. Then I must've got it all wrong."

She nodded.

"And I'm just wasting your time here."

She nodded again.

"Then I will get out of your way."

"Wait…"

I stopped my descent and looked back.

"You…interest me."

I grinned.

She frowned.

"Not you, exactly. Your job."

I kept on grinning, unaware of any difference.

I noticed rat-furtive movement from the building's top story and looked up in time to see a curtain falling back into place behind a closed casement window.

She said, "Maybe I could…use you. How much do you charge?"

"Fifty dollars an hour."

"You joke?"

"I get a lotta work from lawyers. I have to charge that much or they'd think I wasn't working. Half 'm wouldn't roll over in bed for less than $100 an hour, let alone get out of it."

She gazed at me as if fascinated.

I pointed to the polished brass plate beside the door. "Rauth Realty. Is this your family's business?"

"My family? No, it's my business."

"You're kinda young to be running your own real estate agency."

"Thank you. I've been very fortunate with…investments."

Behind me, a car pulled up at the curb and came to a

skidding stop. I gave it just a brief over-the-shoulder glance—a gold Grand Cherokee four-door, tinted windows and whitewall tires—before I turned back to her.

I heard the car doors open, but none shut.

Two or three pairs of hard-soled shoes suddenly slapped the sidewalk like a spontaneous round of applause.

The gate didn't make a sound opening, well-oiled. The hard shoes came up the steps in quick snappy hops.

A hand landed on my shoulder, that or a brick.

A hand. It spun me around. Bricks don't do that.

Stocky, thick-necked, cold-eyed, his mouth concealed behind a black mustache the shape and size of a satchel handle. His auger-edged voice barked, "Tell me where is Michael Cassidy?"

"Who?" I answered stupidly. "I don't—"

English was not his first language, nor his second. His thick base accent was Russian, presumably his native tongue. But he was also fluent in violence. He seized my throat and squeezed, shutting off all air. Not a squeak.

"Where is she?"

My eyes swelled. Don't panic. *You need air to breathe.* I know, I know. Don't panic, you have time—always that false premise. She? Deafening pulse pounding in my ears. He released me. Air again.

"Tell," he barked. "Where is she? Or I mess up your pretty face."

I swallowed and stammered, "You...you think I'm pretty?"

He walloped the back of my head with his open palm, a fat gold ring on his middle finger ringing my chimes.

Behind me, the woman shouted something and he stopped dead.

Her use of his language seemed to surprise him more than the sudden appearance in her hand of the silver-

plated .22 automatic. It was squarish and the size of a
cocktail lounge's ashtray (if cocktail lounges had ashtrays
anymore, which they didn't—thanks to Mayor Droopy
Dog banning smoking in all our fine city's restaurants
and bars).

I hated the gun on sight, like she'd reached behind her
and pulled out a bloody fanged stump blindly chomping.

She wasn't pointing the gun at me but it was still
pointed at me, at anyone in front of her, anyone in
her way.

Black mustache said something in Russian that I
thought sounded innocent like maybe, What village
you from?

She answered with a more universal turn of phrase.
She cocked the pistol's hammer. No translation required.

He thought it over. Would she shoot, wouldn't she
shoot, was it worth finding out? He seemed to make up
his mind. What he wanted from me could wait. He said
something to the two behind him, and they all retreated
down the steps. Got in their car and drove off.

When I turned back to her, the gun was out of sight
again. Some kind of holster concealed at the small of
her back.

I asked, "Are you Russian?"

"No, but they are."

"You didn't have to do that," I told her, trying to keep
my voice level. "I could've handled them."

"You don't handle them. They handle you." She smiled.
"You blushing?"

I wasn't blushing, but no doubt my face was red. I guess
I should've been grateful, but I wasn't. I didn't know
exactly why, unless it was the emasculation of being saved
by a woman.

"This isn't the wild west," I told her. "You can't just

pull a gun out in the middle of the street. Pull that again and I'll take it away from you."

She gave me a dark look, like she wanted to pull it right now and use it, too.

Instead she reached for the intercom again and pushed the button. Without her having to say anything this time, the door latch clacked behind her and she opened the door and shut it between us with a slap.

So much for that. I wouldn't be getting any work from that direction. Ms. Rauth didn't need my help, Ms. Rauth clearly could take care of herself.

Whatever spell she'd had over me was broken. I felt glad. Like I'd just dodged a bullet.

Chapter Seven
THE WRONG CLIENT

I stopped at the first mini-mart I came to on Avenue B. Bought a small bottled water and stripped off my dress shirt as I paid, telling the clerk, "It sure turned warm." He was a stocky, middle-aged Middle Easterner with a puckered scar on his left cheek and gold in his smile. He nodded and grinned full agreement like he didn't understand a word I said.

On the way out, I untucked the green t-shirt I'd worn underneath and put the paper painter's hat on my head, tucking up my loose hair. Altering my appearance in case those goons in the gold Grand Cherokee were circling the block for me. I traveled back facing the oncoming traffic along one-way side streets.

I re-entered Tompkins Square Park at the Ninth Street entrance by the handball courts and the dog run. Stopped and leaned against the fence to check out the dogs and their owners and see if anyone I knew was around, but all I saw were the faces of young strangers.

At the base of a high wooden chainsaw-sculpture of a femur bone, a black Yorkie was digging furiously into the cedar woodchips exposing dark soil beneath.

A tawny Great Dane loped up behind it and sniffed the little dog's ass. Then, like a man on stilts bending down to tie his shoes, the Dane squatted low on his bunched-up hind legs to mount the Yorkie with amorous intent. But before even the first thrust, the little black dog scampered away from him and darted off across the dog run, leaving the Dane, awkwardly over-balanced, dry-humping the empty air.

I turned away. I knew how he felt.

Exiting the park at the St. Marks Place entrance, I returned to the Yaffa Cafe. This time, I went inside and ran the name of George Rowell past the hostess, asking her if he'd made a reservation or if anyone had asked for him. She was a dumpy woman in her early twenties and had copper-orange hair and harlequin eyeglasses with sea-shells and tiny starfish glued around the edges. She shook her head no.

I ordered a take-out cappuccino. The purchase left my wallet with two fives and three singles. Lucky me.

I walked up First Avenue to Twelfth Street and turned left, passed the fenced-in blacktop behind Asher Levy Elementary School where kids were filing in from recess, their cumulative voices a high-pitched roar.

At Second Avenue, I stood on the same corner Owl had three hours ago. In the road the tar and pavement was partly worn away, torn up by snowplows and the patches never setting, so the cobblestones beneath peeked out like bare ribs through a tattered shroud.

I waited for the light to change. It only took a minute, and I wondered again what had taken him so long to make it from the phone to my door. What could account for that two or three minute lapse before the accident? Again the only answer I came up with was a sudden attack of disorientation. But could it have been another sort of attack?

I didn't wonder about it long because at the front door of my building a tall, well-dressed man with curly blond hair was jabbing one of the buzzers, and as I got closer, I saw it was mine.

I thought maybe it was one of Tigger's team of financial advisors pushing the wrong button. He had a long, lean, handsome face. Ten years younger than me and four inches taller, wearing clothes that would've covered my rent.

Five hundred dollar suit, three hundred dollar shoes, hundred dollar hair grooming, a fifty dollar tan, and twenty dollar aftershave, of which, as the breeze changed, I figured he wore ten bucks' worth.

I approached, consulting my empty cupped hand like it held a piece of paper, and rang my own buzzer.

He turned, looked at me, and said, "Mr. Sherwood?"

So much for playing it cagey. He knew me by sight, but I'd never seen him before in my life.

He said, "I've been trying your bell for the last five minutes."

"Oh. How do you like it?"

"What?"

"Skip it." I put my key in the door and opened it. "What can I do for you?"

"My name is Paul Windmann. Two N's, M-A-N-N. I need to hire a—" he lowered his voice "—a detective."

I stepped into the entryway. He followed on my heels. In the closed space, his cologne reeked like concentrated formaldehyde. My nostrils revolted against it. I breathed in through my teeth.

"Well, then you better come up, Mr. Windmann."

"Please call me Paul, Mr. Sherwood. But before we go further, I need to know, are you free today?"

"No. But I'm reasonable."

He forced a chuckle. "Bad choice of words. What I meant is, are you available to help me?"

"That depends on what kind of help."

He waved that away. "I mean, will you be able to act immediately? Give it your full attention? You aren't, by chance, working on anything else that would...conflict?"

I shook my head.

"Nothing but a recovery."

"A recovery?"

"My own."

"You're joking."

"Good on you to spot it. Most don't."

"Well, it's funny you should say that, because the help I need involves a recovery. But, you're sure you aren't engaged? It needs your undivided attention."

I was getting a bad feeling about this guy. I said blandly, "I'll worship it as a deity."

"Please, there's no need for sarcasm."

"Isn't there?"

"I merely stress the point because I don't want to waste time—yours or mine—discussing it with you if it happens you're busy working on…something else."

"How did you come to choose me?"

He blinked, one two three.

"You were recommended."

"By whom?"

"One of your satisfied customers, of course."

If only he knew what a short list that was.

"And who would that be?"

Blink, blink, blink.

"I'd rather not say. Privacy, you understand. But does it matter? Maybe I should've said I picked you out of the phonebook. Do you check references on all your clients? I thought it worked the other way round."

He was getting exasperated with me and I was getting sick of the smell of his cologne. I was going to have to light a match soon.

I bowed my head. "You got me. Come on up."

Once inside, he gave my office a sweeping glance. Something about its barrenness made him smile.

"Take a seat," I said, indicating the club chairs as I went behind my desk and sat down. The light on my answering machine was flashing four new messages, but I didn't play them now.

Windmann looked at the answering machine, too, inclining his head slightly as if to say, "Go ahead, don't mind me." But I did mind him.

I picked up the pouch of loose tobacco and started to roll a cigarette.

Windmann smiled wryly, reached into a breast pocket, removed a thin silver case, and pushed a button which flipped open the *P.W.*-engraved lid.

"Have one of mine?"

Dunhill Blue. I selected one from the side near his thumb and lit up. I drew deep. After my harsh diet of roll-your-owns, the filtered cigarette was like smoking morning mist.

"How can I help you, er…Paul?"

He told me. And within thirty seconds, I pegged him as a wrong client. I recognized the signs because I've had a few over the years. Evasive, reluctant to give details, curious about what method will be used, restrictions on what they want done, and, above all, no police involved.

The most typical wrong clients a P.I.—especially a one-man operation—has to contend with are stalkers. They want to hire you to do one specific job, either get an unlisted phone number or find the new address where someone has moved to, and they're willing to pay for it; money is no object (as long as you tell them how you do it, so next time they can do it for themselves).

All of which you sometimes get with a right client as well. But the decider is the story. A wrong client always has a story prepared.

A right client, half the time, doesn't know what he wants done. He has a problem, and by coming to you shows he's run out of ideas on how to solve it. Getting his story is like removing shrapnel from a fleshy buttcheek with tweezers. Grab a bit here and drop it in the dish—kaplang—grab another bit there—kaplang—and probe deeper into the meat for a missing piece that might connect the two. Sometimes it requires more skill and finesse than the actual job itself.

But a wrong client'll always tell you a tale.

I leaned back, smoking, and listened to Paul Windmann's.

"Two nights ago," he said, "I was robbed. I went for a drink with a business associate at this place that just opened on Rivington Street called The Parallel Bar. We had a couple of drinks and then my associate left around ten P.M. I stayed for another and while I was drinking it, this blonde woman came over and started talking to me. A real hottie. Sounded foreign, sort of a thick accent, but she didn't say where she was from. I bought her a drink and we seemed to connect, so we had a few more. By midnight, we were both a little drunk. I had an early appointment the next day, so I decided to call it a night. I asked for her number so we could hook up over the weekend.

"But she made it—how shall I say—very obvious she didn't want our evening to end. She suggested we go back to my place. Now, that's important, because it was her idea, not mine. Not that I didn't immediately concur, but generally I like to get to know someone first. When a woman is that eager, it usually means she does that sort of thing a lot, and I've no interest in catching an STD. But as I said, I was under the influence and she was very attractive and very willing, and well...I relaxed my caution. We took a cab back to my place."

"And where's that?"

"I live at the Crystalview. Do you know it? Well, it's a relatively new condominium on the west side, just below Canal."

He gave me the exact address and I jotted it down.

"Well, on the way, she practically raped me in the cab.
I had to peel her off me in order to pay the fare. By the
time we got up to my apartment, I was more than ready.

"But as soon as we walked through the door, she
cooled off, didn't act nearly as drunk as she had been—or
as I felt. She wanted to talk, listen to some music, have
another drink. She said she had this special drink she
wanted to make for me."

I arched an eyebrow.

Windmann said, "You can see where this is going.
She made up these drinks that looked like Cosmos. She
downed hers in two gulps and I followed suit. Suddenly
she had her dress off and was taking my clothes off, and
we were both naked on my couch. I tried leading her to
my bedroom, but I couldn't keep my legs straight under
me, and she was laughing and laughing. That's all I
remember clearly until about dawn.

"I woke up naked on the floor. She wasn't anywhere to
be seen. I only realized when I was about to call out to
her that she'd never told me her name. And I felt sick,
sicker than any hangover I ever had. She must've drugged
me with some sort of date-rape drug."

"A roofie." Rohypnol, one of the benzodiazepines.
Better living through chemistry.

"Whatever, only she didn't rape me, she ripped me off.
All my money was gone, credit cards, two wristwatches,
and my iPod. All gone. The little bitch."

I sat forward and planted my elbows on the desk.

"Did you report it to the police?"

"No."

"Why not?"

"Well…to be honest, I'm afraid to."

"Afraid of what?"

He smiled sheepishly. He had even white teeth. "Well, in retrospect, I'm not a hundred percent sure whether she was eighteen or not."

"You're saying she may have been underage?"

"I'm not sure. They were serving her at the bar, so I figured she was old enough. But if not, well, I might end up getting arrested myself."

I nodded. That made sense even if nothing else did. I reached for my pouch of tobacco to roll a cigarette, but Windmann got his engraved silver cigarette case out again and offered me another of his. I took one, but not because I really needed a cigarette. I wanted to see his case again. Looked like real silver to me. But if he'd been robbed, why hadn't it been taken too? *If* he'd been robbed...

I lit up and smoked. It felt strange not to be constantly picking shreds of tobacco off my tongue.

I asked him, "You've cancelled your credit cards?"

"Naturally."

"So, what you want me to do," I said, anticipating the payoff, "is find the woman."

But he surprised me.

"What? No. No. I never want to see her again. I just want my...things back."

"Still means I'll have to find this woman."

"Does it really? I hoped you might have...other ideas."

"I always have other ideas. Have you got a list of everything that's missing?"

He blinked one, two, three.

"No...I mean, well, most of it I don't care about. Actually, all I really would like returned is my iPod. You see, my entire music collection is on it. I've been assembling it for years. And like an idiot, I never backed any of it up on my computer."

"What about the wristwatches?"

He waved it away. "They're both old, and one doesn't even work anymore."

I nodded. I thought it over.

A private investigator confronted with a wrong client typically should respond by showing him the door and telling him never to come back. That's if the P.I. wants to safeguard his bond and keep his license. Okay, so maybe this guy wasn't a stalker, but he was something, something wrong, possibly even dangerous.

I told him, "I'm sorry, Mr. Windmann—"

"Paul."

"Yeh, Paul, but I don't see how I can help you, given that you don't want me to do anything."

Windmann crossed his legs, straightened his pantleg, uncrossed his legs again, then leaned forward.

"May I speak frankly to you, Mr. Sherwood?"

"I wish you would."

"I...this morning, I got a phone call. It was from a man who knew about my being robbed the other night. He said he had nothing to do with it, but that he might be able to arrange for the return of my things."

"For a price?"

"Naturally."

"How much?"

He waved that away, too. "The point is that I don't trust myself to remain calm in the situation. I'd like to retain you to be available to retrieve my things if and when this person does call me back."

I started to mumble a protest, but let it peter out as Windmann reached into his jacket pocket for his billfold. He extracted four bills, laying them down one at a time on my desk.

The whole set-up stunk, but I put my olfactory objections on hold as soon as I saw the color of his money. It was orange. Euros in the denomination of fifty. I'd never been bought in Euros before, it was a novelty. Times had certainly changed. The U.S. dollar was no longer the currency of coercion.

"It's all I have at the moment," he said. "Is it sufficient? To start with?"

I held one of them up to the window to see its watermark. Peek-a-boo. As far as I could tell, the bills were genuine.

I said, "Consider me retained. Paul."

He smiled winningly.

"Thank you, thank you so much. I feel better already."

Well, that made one of us. I opened my center desk drawer, swept in the bills and took out my carboned receipt pad. I started to write.

"I really don't need a receipt," he said.

I kept writing. "Yeh, well, I do."

I had him sign it—his signature looked like a broken kite string—then handed him the copy and kept the original.

He stood and we shook hands.

He said, "I'll call you as soon as I hear anything."

He started toward my office door.

I called to him, "By the way, Paul, what kind of business are you in?"

"I don't see how that—"

"Would it be real estate by any chance?" I was thinking back to that curtain-twitcher at Rauth Realty.

He triple-blinked and his lips curled into a half-smile lazily like worms awakened from dark soil. He said, "I've got my fingers in a lot of different pies, Mr. Sherwood."

"Sounds messy."

The smile went away. He said, "I'll be in touch."

After he left I changed clothes, into a pair of khakis and a dark blue Polo sport shirt. I got my last can of Coke out of the mini-fridge and sat back at my desk. I played the four new messages on my answering machine.

The first two were from Matt Chadinsky, both long messages, richly embroidered with expletives, which ate up the allotted times. Omitting all the swear words, the messages only amounted to, "Where are you? I told you to stay put."

Yeh, easier said than done.

The third and fourth messages were both from women. None from Paul Windmann, which meant he came by and rang my bell without even calling first. His wrongness was growing by steady increments, but I was past being surprised.

But life still offered some surprises: the third message was someone who wanted to hire me.

"Good afternoon. This is Mrs. Dough. D-O-U-G-H, like bread." She had a clear, young voice with just a twist of New England twang to it. "My husband John and I would like to discuss the possibility of hiring you. Your Yellow Pages ad says you perform background checks on potential employees. We're new to the neighborhood and are in the process of hiring a nanny for our two-year-old daughter. We'd like to stop by this afternoon, say about three o'clock, if that's okay. We don't have a landline yet, but my cell phone number is…" She read off a 917 number and I wrote it down on the same sheet I'd jotted Windmann's address on. I paused the message and called her back, got her voicemail and told Mrs. Dough three o'clock was convenient for me.

Then I played the final message.

"Hello, I am trying to connect…to contact George Rowl. I don't…he told me he was to be seeing you this morning, but I do not heard from him since…is maybe I misunderstood. I am sorry, I will call you again." Click.

Since it was the last message I'd received, I picked up

my phone and dialed *69, but it was a number with a
masked I.D. I listened to it again, a distinct accent in the
woman's voice. Sayre Rauth? No, her accent was barely
noticeable. This woman's was thick, nearly as thick as that
mustached goon's had been—or the woman Paul Windmann described to me as the one who robbed him.

But I wasn't any linguist, it could've been anything
from Croatian to Ukrainian to Turkish, for all I knew.
That was the problem, what I didn't know outweighed
what I knew ten to one.

Time to remedy that and get the odds on my side.

Just for a change.

Chapter Eight
KNUCKLING DOWN

I powered up my laptop computer, unplugged my phone, and switched the line over to my modem. I logged onto the Internet and brought up a search engine.

I started by searching on some of the names I'd come across so far. I began with Sayre Rauth.

Nothing.

I next tried Rauth Realty in Manhattan.

Again nothing.

I tried words at random, typing in "spinach manifold," and got six hits. So the search engines were working, if not properly, at least to form.

Next I typed in, "Paul Windmann." I got several results, but none that were relevant. Most of them pertained to a Water Board commissioner in Melbourne, Australia. There was even a picture of the guy, a dark-complexioned man in his late fifties.

I was beginning to feel like I was wasting my time, so I typed in a name I knew would at least get me some direct results. Law Addison.

This time I got thousands of hits, which presented the new problem of too much information—*Forbes* and *Vanity Fair* magazine articles before his arrest, newspaper articles after, Lincoln Center patrons lists, SEC filings, miscellaneous blogs—forcing me to skim and put my *Evelyn Wood Reading Dynamics* to work.

Lawrence Addison, age 39...born in Taunton, Massachusetts...attended Boston University...worked in now-defunct Boston-based brokerage firm as a financial analyst before starting Isolde Enterprises, a financial management firm based in Manhattan…a roster of A-list celebrities as clients, supporting his intoxicating international lifestyle…"Stockbrokerage is as much an art as painting a picture or writing a sonnet," said Addison in a recent… adhering to a conservative investment strategy…$100,000 on corporate credit cards for airline tickets…trips to Rome, Switzerland, Bahamas…$80,000 sky-blue Mercedes-Benz…avid opera buff…$20,000 donation to Lincoln Center Performing Arts…web of fraud…over 100 wrongfully endorsed checks from client accounts…unapproved transfers…deposited funds in Isolde's corporate bank accounts…mingling personal expenses and the firm's operating costs…managed 250 portfolios…assets with a market value of over $2 billion…among those who trusted Addison with millions…star-studded clientele included Oscar winners, rock musicians…allegedly paid complaining clients with funds siphoned from other clients' accounts…were said to be held in escrow, trust, or sub accounts, but Isolde had no escrow, trust, or sub accounts…Ponzi-type scheme…Manhattan federal grand jury indictment…separate civil action brought by the Securities and Exchange Commission…forensic accounting probe revealed…MONEY GURU TO THE STARS ARRESTED…faces up to 20 years in prison on three federal counts stemming from his alleged…prosecutor argues flight risk…Addison released on a $2 million bond …CELEBRITY BROKER SKIPS BAIL, MAY 11…fugitive thought to be in the company of the wife of one of his former clients…

All of it seemed useless until one name sprang out at me.

Michael Cassidy.

I scrolled back. Estranged wife of one of Isolde's former

clients, Oscar-nominated screenwriter Ethan Ore, Ms.
Michael Cassidy was Law Addison's live-in lover at the
time of his disappearance and was thought to have fled
with him.

Ms. Michael Cassidy.

I started a new search, typing in "Michael Cassidy."
Again, there were thousands of results. Some were for a
male actor by that name, but more for the woman. She
was famous, apparently. Hundreds of jpeg images of her,
and though the hairstyle and coloring were different, I
recognized her from the first shot. Those crazy green
eyes were unmistakable. She was the woman from Owl's
hotel room.

I clicked on her bio. Her father was Kimble Cassidy,
lead singer of the '70s rock band Leavenworth. She was
the child of his third marriage, this one to a back-up singer
he met on the band's fourth reunion tour. He died of a
brain aneurysm when she was eleven.

In the mid-1990s, she'd risen to what passes for fame
nowadays as part of a reality TV show featuring children
of dead celebrities, and gained notoriety from two drug
busts on heroin possession, which got her booted from
the program.

Shortly thereafter, Michael Cassidy met and married a
young actor and wannabe Orson Welles by the name of
Ethan Ore. Ore subsequently rose to fame of his own for
writing and directing an independent film called *Dazey
Miller*.

I checked the IMDB listing and read the synopsis:
"Daughter of has-been rock star gets turned onto drugs
by members of her father's band and becomes a call-girl
in Milwaukee until a Rwandan cab driver helps her get
clean."

The film was nominated for an Academy Award for
best original screenplay that year, but it didn't win. Maybe

because Ore's screenplay, far from original, had mirrored his wife's true story. The week before the Oscars, Michael Cassidy had been busted again buying heroin from an undercover cop in L.A. The couple separated shortly after, but there was no record of their divorce being finalized.

I started a new search, this one on Ethan Ore. Fewer hits this time, but the very first one surprised me with another unexpected connection. Ore's new film, *Reneg*, was being screened this week at the same West Side Film Festival that had premiered the unfortunate Craig Wales' new star vehicle. In fact, Ore's film had been rescheduled at the last minute to provide a more prominent time slot for Wales' movie. It was after that screening that Craig Wales had overdosed.

Law Addison, Michael Cassidy, heroin, Craig Wales, Ethan Ore, and Owl. I was trying to wrap my mind around it, wondering what it all meant, wondering if it meant anything at all. It didn't have to. Nothing had to mean anything. After all, this was New York City and there was the random element to take into account, the six-degrees effect; always layer upon layer of non sequiturs to wade through. I should've known that by now, but I persisted in seeking out connections.

I was still turning all of it over in my head, like a wire cage of bingo numbers, when my downstairs doorbuzzer buzzed.

I got up, went over to the intercom, pushed the SPEAK button, and asked who it was. But I got no answer. I shrugged and went back to my desk.

I was just clicking on a browser link to the West Side Film Festival when I heard a key turning in my lock.

I looked up as my office door swung open.

"What the hell? Come right in, why don't you?"

No point in my saying it, he was already inside.

My old boss, Matt Chadinsky, had lost weight, but he

was still built like a concrete traffic divider, with a hard expression on his face I wanted to veer away from.

"I called," he said. "Your fucking phone's been busy."

"I was on the Internet."

"What, you still using dial-up? Shit, Payton, churn your own fucking butter, too?"

I ignored it. I logged off the Internet and folded down the lid of my laptop without turning it off. I said, "You've lost weight, Matt. And shaved off your mustache."

Matt touched his bare upper lip like someone checking his wallet on a crowded subway.

"Yeh, over a year ago."

He sat on my couchbed, planting his ass down on my pillow. Where I put my head at night. Not the stuff dreams are made of.

I asked, "How'd you get in?"

He held up his hand, my other spare set of keys dangling from his forefinger. He tossed them overhand to me. I fumbled catching them and had to stoop to pick them up off the floor.

Matt said, "Time you got 'em back. What's with your fucking place anyway? Moving out or did Goodwill repo you?"

"I'm keeping to the essentials these days."

"Sure, whatever. How come you didn't return my calls?"

"I was out."

"Where the fuck've you been? I told you to stay put. What the hell's going on, Payton? I talked to my guy over at the Ninth, and he said the responding unit didn't have your name. Who'd you talk to on scene?"

"No one. I didn't stick around. I had a job to do."

"Yeh, right. I can see how busy you are."

"The job Owl hired me for."

"Job? What job?"

"Doesn't matter now, it's been taken care of."

"No. No-no-no, that's not how this is goin' to work. I ask questions, you answer. Now what job?"

"Tail job. So I—"

"You go off, leave him lying dead in the street? What kind of fucking head case are you? You call me an hour after—"

"How do you know when—"

"I told you, I called my precinct guy. He finally helped me track down where they took Owl's body. No fucking help from you there. As usual."

Heat seeped up my neck into my face. So much for the happy reunion. Nothing had changed in five years between us; it might as well have been the last time we spoke, after my final assignment for Metro.

It was a simple job, all I had to do was watch a door, a door without a handle that never opened, an outside utility door set flush in a blank two-story-high brick wall at the rear of the Baruch Houses apartment complex below Houston, from midnight to 5 A.M., Tuesday thru Saturday, in late March of 2003.

And still I managed to screw it up...

I was seated behind the wheel of an agency car, a blue Honda Accord, parked south of the access ramp to the FDR Drive.

It was temp work Matt had fielded to me to help me get by, never telling me what I was there for, except to verify that the door always remained closed.

It wasn't much of a door, especially after hours and hours of looking at it. If not for the outer hinges, it might've just been an immovable steel plate. The hardest part of the job was not falling asleep while listening to the sough of traffic on the FDR. But looking back, I'd've been better off if I had fallen asleep. That at least would have been understandable in the eyes of Matt, more than what actually happened.

It was about 4:30 A.M. when I caught sight of the girl rushing down the road, first in my rear view mirror and then as she passed by at an awkward half-run, a willowy white girl in her late teens casting quick looks over her shoulder. In the mirror, a car came into view approaching at a slow roll, a green late-model Impala with a rusted undercarriage and its headlights switched off. It passed by, closing in on the girl until a bend in the road ahead cut them off from view.

None of my business, literally. My business was to stay in the car, my job was to keep watching that door. But I didn't.

"There a problem here?" I called out.

Rhetorical question, because as I came jogging round the bend, the passenger door of the idling Impala stood open and a tall guy with straggly hair and a Pharaoh's beard was in the road trying to push the girl inside. She'd lost one shoe.

The guy favored me with a scowl and some choice words about my mother. The girl uttered nothing but a low, pleading *Nooo* as she shook her head from side to side.

Just as a goof really, I said to the guy, "Unhand her." Never expecting he would, but he did and the girl who'd been leaning back trying to pry herself away fell flat on her ass.

The guy took three quick strides to me. He looked like he meant business, so I cut out the comedy and raised my right hand fast. The telescopic steel baton sprang open to its full length with a satisfying snick and the tip sank deep into his crotch. He went down and over and did his lima bean impression.

I stood over him. My right shoulder was hit by something soft but heavy. Green and brown, it fell to my feet. A clump of grass and soil. The next hit me in the neck, not so soft.

I turned my head and the girl was digging her hands into the grass bordering the sidewalk to my right.

I said, "Hey, quit—"

She flung another clump at me. She had good aim. This one hit me in the chin, some of the dirt went down my shirt. I backed away, putting up my arms to block the next one.

But she'd found an empty quart bottle of Colt 45 malt liquor on the verge. Before she threw it I took off running. The bottle shattered at my heels.

My last look back, she was kneeling beside him in the road, cradling his head in her dirt-blackened hands. I had to admit they made a perfect couple.

When I got back to the agency car, my relief was waiting. Except he was anything but, a relief that is. He'd come early and found the car empty. For a beefy guy he had a surprisingly high-pitched voice as he laid into me.

I looked over at the closed door in the brick wall. It was still closed. I doubted it had opened while I was .gone, doubted it would ever open. But that wasn't the point, I understood that—whatever this surveillance had been meant to prove, I'd invalidated it and all the man-hours put into it. But I didn't need this guy screeching at me like a macaw parrot on crack.

I snicked open the baton again and held it up in front of his face. I wasn't going to hit him or anything, I just wanted him to shut the fuck up, and he did. I gave him the car keys. I closed the baton and handed it to him (I'd gotten it from the car's glove compartment), and then I walked away as he started shrieking at me again in his whiny falsetto.

Matt didn't shout when I called and told him all about it later that morning. He didn't even swear, which was the worst sign of all; Matt Chadinsky couldn't whistle without cursing.

I got my last check from Metro the very next day. It was messengered to me, probably costing more than what I got paid, but the messenger was the message. I was out for good and no mistake about it. The end.

Chapter Nine
YOU CAN'T PLAY IF YOU DON'T WIN

Matt yanked my noggin back to the present.

"So you going to fucking tell me what this is all about?"

"I already did."

"No, all you did was hand me a load of bullshit, nothing that justifies you leaving Owl lying in the street. He deserved more respect than you showed him, you shit-stain. George Rowell had friends in this city. Important friends. You better pray Moe Fedel doesn't catch wind of it, if he hasn't already."

"I'm not afraid of Fedel."

"Yeh, well you never were that bright, kid."

"Does…did Owl have any family? Who'll claim his body?"

"No. No family. He was an orphan, never married."

I took out my wallet, showed him the photograph of Owl and the girl. "So this isn't him and a granddaughter then? How 'bout a niece? Does the name Elena mean anything to you?"

"What have you gone, deaf? I told you, no family. The guys in the business, that's all he had, and that's who's gonna have to send him off. Owl lived for the job, always did."

"And died for it."

Matt stared at the picture of Owl, maybe lost in his own memories of the last time they saw each other, but my words finally sank in. He looked up.

"What's that fucking supposed to mean?"

"What did your guy at the precinct say about Owl's death? Everything kosher?"

"Kosher? Shit. Yeh, no meat and dairy mixed. Kosher!"

"Nothing off about it then?"

"I didn't ask. You told me it was a fucking accident."

"It was, but…"

"But what?"

"Owl was here working on something. A case for an 'old friend,' he said. He got a room at the Bowery Plaza two days ago. What's he been up to since? You're one of his oldest friends, didn't he contact you?" Matt had trained under Owl much the way I'd trained under Matt.

He shook his head. "I had no idea he was in the city. Haven't seen Owl in years, not since he retired. You still haven't told me what he came to you for—"

"He asked if I worked on the Law Addison job."

"What about it?"

"Just did I work on it, because he knew Metro had. I told him no, you hadn't called me."

"Damn straight, I didn't. I wanted that case closed, not fucked up."

"But it isn't closed, is it?" I said. "I was just reading up on it, and there was nothing about Addison's capture. He's still a fugitive."

"Yeh, so?"

I didn't push the point. "How did Metro get in on it?"

"Addison was arrested in May. The fucking judge set his bail at two million."

"How come so high?"

"You think that's high? For a guy like that? Made millions every year and probably had bank accounts in ten different countries? He was the biggest goddamn flight risk since Charles Fucking Lindbergh."

"Evidently. So how come he was granted bail at all?"

"Because judges are fucking morons. This one said

Addison's passport had been seized, his assets had been frozen, so if he wanted to flee, he'd have to do it on a fucking bus. What a bonehead. You know how much money Addison was playing with at his peak? Two *billion*. With a B. Of which $66 million is still unaccounted for. You can bet he had a nice chunk of that stored away in cash for just such a rainy day."

"Sixty-six million dollars," I repeated. "Shit, that's like eleven bionic men."

Matt didn't even crack a smile.

"After he pulled his breeze, the cops broke into his Soho loft and found open-ended tickets purchased on eight different airlines for flights to Vegas, L.A., Hawaii, Tokyo, and Thailand, as well as two false passports under an alias. And that's just the shit he left behind. Who the fuck knows what he took with him."

"And what was Metro's role in it?"

"The bailsbond agency was nervous, they hired us to keep tabs on him. Turns out with good cause. Addison put up some property in the Hamptons as collateral for the bond, but it wasn't until he got away that the paperwork finally went through. All the titles were faked, none of it was his. So the bailsbond agency is going to have to eat that loss."

"Unless he's found."

Matt narrowed his eyes. "What did Owl say to you about it? I mean, exactly, what did he say?"

"Said that Addison had some East Village connection. He took it for granted you'd called me in on it."

Matt made a fart noise. With his mouth, praise be; he was still sitting on my pillow.

"We'll manage without you," Matt said. "He'll pop up. Hell, it's only been four months. Guy like that, he won't stay hidden long, he can't. Likes living large. Only a matter of time before he's spotted."

"I kinda got the impression from Owl…" But I stopped myself, because that's all I really had, an impression.

"What?"

"Nothing. Only…he mentioned it in passing, that he'd stumbled on something."

Matt stared me straight in the eye for three beats, then slapped his knee hard.

"Damn! It would just be like that old bastard to pull one last rabbit outta his hat. He found Addison."

"Wait a second, I didn't say he—"

Matt stood up, headed for the door.

"I gotta get back to the office and check into this. Holy fuck, if—"

"Wait, I didn't say—"

"Yeh, I heard you. You didn't fucking say much at all. As usual. But Owl, he wouldn't have brought it up if it didn't mean something. He had a nose on him, I'll—"

Matt stopped short of the door, looked down at his feet, at Owl's briefcase where I'd left it when I came in.

He said, "I gave him that. For his seventieth birthday." He reached down and picked it up. "I'm damned if you'll have it."

I couldn't really object. He opened the door and I said to his back, "I'm sorry, Matt. I know what he meant to you."

He didn't turn round, but nodded his head couple times.

"Owl had a good run," he said. "Did it his way all the way down the line. No one lives forever."

I grunted. "Control yourself. You'll do yourself a mischief carrying on that way."

This time he turned around, and said evenly, "Fuck off, you fuckin' fuck-off."

Matt was never one to be at a loss for words. It felt like old times.

Only after he'd left and my office door shut did I realize I'd forgotten to congratulate him on becoming a father. And I still didn't know if it was a boy or a girl.

I switched the phone cord back to my receiver. As soon as I did, the phone started ringing. I picked up. "Yellow."

"Mr. Sherwood?"

It was my client, Paul Windmann.

"Yep."

He said, "She called."

"Who?" I was still thinking of Michael Cassidy and whatever she'd had to do with Owl.

"The woman who ripped me off. She wants to sell my stuff back to me."

"That isn't selling, it's ransoming. Don't pay."

"I have already."

"What, you saw her? When?"

"I haven't seen her. I sent her a payment through PayPal."

"Oh brave new world. How much?"

"That's not your concern. What I'd like is for you to make the pick-up for me."

"Sure thing," I said, trying to sound cheerful about it. "You're the boss. What's the address?"

"Number 27, Avenue C," he said. "Apartment three. Do you know where that is?"

"I think I can find it," I said.

I hung up the phone. I sat and thought a bit. Then I stood up and went to the kitchen area where my floor safe was located. I spun the combination, opened the door, and took out my gun.

A 9mm Luger, a black automatic with a dull sheen, which looked like it was made of plastic until you picked it up and felt the heft and knew it was serious. In twelve years, I'd only carried it three times in the course of work, never fired it except on a firing range downtown, and only once had to show it to some asshole who didn't believe I had it, hiking up to end a confrontation that was about to get ugly. But having a license to carry is a necessity of the job. Some clients expect it, others demand it.

In this case, I had no idea what to expect, so I was going armed. I had a stiff leather side holster for the gun, but I'd misplaced it a few years back, so now I had to stick the gun down the back of my pants, just like in the movies. It meant that I had to wear a light jacket over it, even though the day was way too hot. I would have to take a cab. If I walked to 27 Avenue C with my jacket on, I'd be a sopping mess of perspiration by the time I got there.

So I caught a cab. Back to Alphabet City, back to the apartment building on Avenue C, back to Mr. Andrew's apartment, where Jeff and the *diabla* were now living.

The gun dug into my lower back like someone was shoving it into me, prodding me forward against my will.

I got out a block away and walked the rest. The street door was swung wide, propped open by a stack of telephone directories. The inner vestibule door was held open by another stack, so I didn't have to ring a buzzer to gain entrance.

I walked down the first floor corridor, a breeze against my face and bright daylight spilling out from beneath the stairwell.

The light was from an open rear door into a back courtyard. I heard the sound of water spraying from a hose. I looked out and saw Luis, the forest-green-clad super, standing with his broad back to me, hose in his hand, the nozzle shooting a jet of water. He was rinsing out a plastic trash barrel lying on its side in an area of patchy grass and weeds, disjointed brick masonry, two or three torn window screens bent into parabolas, and scraps of yellowed newspaper. I didn't try to get his attention. I continued down the narrow hall. It seemed to get narrower as I got to the end. I knocked on the door of apartment three.

To the right of it, at chin-level, was a replastered hole in the wall about the size of a fist or a heart.

Didn't hear any footsteps, but as I stood there the white dot center of the peephole went dark as someone on the other side examined me.

Chapter Ten
SWING AND A MISS

From behind the door, a woman's voice asked, "What d'you want?"

"Making a pick-up."

"Who send you?"

"C'mon, open up. You know who sent me."

The white dot at the center of the peephole returned, but it was still a handful of seconds before a deadbolt turned and the door finally opened.

She was a tall young woman, twenty or twenty-one. She had a helmet of blonde hair and very pale ivory skin. Below her brown eyes were dark jaundiced pouches, a flattish nose, and a wide mouth now set in a tight straight line like she was biting down on the meat of her lips. She looked frightened. She said nothing, just reached out one bare arm from behind the door and handed me a black plastic bag. Something small and heavy swung like a pendulum at its bottom, but I didn't relieve her of it. I hadn't come here just to be handed a bag.

I'd never seen her before in my life, but I felt a vague sense of recognition. Trying to pin it down, I stalled her.

"Open the bag, show it to me."

"What?"

I didn't care what was inside the bag, but a dark suspicion was niggling at me and I wanted to see the other hand she was keeping out of sight behind the door.

"How do I know it's what I'm here for?"

"Please, take and go away. I want no more."

I heard it clearly then, the Eastern European accent that had been barely audible in the monosyllabic responses she'd given before. But no mistaking it now, nor the sound of her voice. She was the woman who'd left the message on my machine asking for George Rowell.

I've never had much of a poker face, even when the stakes were low, and I must've shown my excitement now. I spooked her and she yanked the hand with the bag back in and tried to slam the door in my face.

I gave it my shoulder and all my 155 pounds with interest. My enthusiasm got the better of me. The force knocked her down on the other side with a thump that shook the floorboards.

As I stepped into the dim apartment, she was scrambling to her knees. She'd dropped the plastic bag, but she'd held onto what she had in her other hand. A lethal-looking carving knife with an eight-inch blade.

My momentum carried me too far into the apartment to back out into the hallway. I retreated a step and my spine hit the door, shutting it with a smack.

It was a studio, what real estate brokers like to call a *cozy pied à terre*, with a kitchen area, a living room/bedroom area beyond, a tiny closet, and a door that presumably led to a tiny bathroom. The room was decorated mainly in glass and chrome, nicer than you might expect from the condition of the building—or of the young woman occupying it.

She was on one knee in front of me. She held the knife low to her chest, the point in line with my groin. More than an arm's length away, but still…

I reached behind, pulled out my gun, and pointed it at her.

"Don't move," I said.

The Luger's safety was on. I left it that way. I really didn't want to shoot her—didn't want to shoot anybody.

But I also didn't want a knife in the pecker. So I kept my
thumb ready near the safety.

This is the reason I hate guns: they end thought. Pulling
a gun preempts all other options. You've got a gun, you
don't have to think how else to work out a situation, just
hike up and unleash your piece. If I'd left mine back in
the office, I wouldn't be facing the task of convincing this
woman I wasn't a threat to her.

But I had my gun out now, so I had to make do.

I instructed her, "Put down the knife."

She shook her head no.

"Put it down. I'm not here to hurt you. But I'm not
here to get hurt either."

She looked me in the eye and then cast a long look at
the knife in her hand. She stopped pointing it at me.
Turning it sideways, she reached over and drew the edge
across her other arm. A shallow three-inch gash smoothly
opened across the back of her forearm. Blood humped
up out of the fresh slit, swelling from her wound thick,
wet, and dark.

"Christ, what are you doing?"

She said in her thick accent, "Put the gun down."

I shook my head. Correction, I shook all over. Head to
toe. She had shaken me. I was shook.

"Put it down," she told me. "Or I say *you* do this to me.
You come in here and you cut me."

I took a deep breath and exhaled.

"Look, go bandage that up, willya?" I said. "We can't
talk with you standing there bleeding like that."

She half-frowned, glancing at the wound, at the blood
from the cut trickling into the hair on the back of her
arm. Her nose wrinkled at the sight. There was something oddly familiar about the expression, though also
something strange about it: no show of pain, no emotion.
Her eyes empty, flat, as if saying, "What? You mean this?

This is nothing. I can do worse." And the tracery of scars on her arms showing that, many times before, she had.

She raised the knife again.

"Stop," I said, "you win."

I tilted my gun up so the barrel pointed at the ceiling. From where I stood, it looked like a capital L. L is for Loser.

But what was I supposed to do? I'd just seen her do worse to herself than I would've ever dreamt of doing. She was more a danger to herself than others.

Though lord knows she could still be a danger to others, starting with me.

I put my gun away in my jacket pocket. It sagged there.

She said, "Now go away."

"No. Not yet. And no more Ginsu demonstrations, either. Put something on that cut, then we need to talk."

She reached over to the sofa, picked up a crumpled t-shirt, wrapped it tightly around her arm. "Okay, talk now."

"I'm the guy you called this morning, asking about George Rowell. You left a message on my answering machine. My name is Payton Sherwood."

I reached in my pocket for my wallet, intending to show her my driver's license. Instead, the first thing in my hand was the photograph of Owl and the young girl. I brought it out, started to ask if she knew this man, when all at once I knew: it was her. The girl in the picture, Elena.

She asked, "Where did you get that?"

"From Owl," I said. "Are you Elena?"

She backed away from the question.

I said, "Look, relax. I put the gun away, didn't I? I told you, I'm not going to hurt you. I'm a friend. Owl hired me this morning. I was supposed to help him out with a job he was doing."

"Where is George? Why isn't he here? He doesn't answer at his hotel. Where is he?"

"Let's sit down first."

She raised the knife once more and stepped forward. I stiffened to keep my hand from reaching for my gun again.

"It isn't good news," I said. "Owl—George is dead."

This time the D-bomb hit its target.

Elena's face collapsed and I saw her hands start trembling.

"No. No. I do not believe—when did...?"

"This morning, around nine-thirty. He was hit by a car."

"No!" She was whipping her head back and forth.

"I'm sorry."

"Who are you? Why do you tell me this?"

I took out both my driver's and my investigator's license.

"See," I said, "I told you, I'm Payton Sherwood."

"How do I know you tell the truth? Those could be a fake, I have as good. You could be anyone."

"I wish," I said glumly. "And also that it wasn't true, but George Rowell *is* dead."

"How did it happen?"

"It was an accident."

"Did that woman have something to do with it? Did she?"

"What woman? Which woman?"

"The one with the green eyes."

"You mean Michael Cassidy?"

She looked confused. "That's a man's name. I said woman. With bright green eyes. She come this morning when George was here. We was having coffee. She just open door and walk in on us."

"What do you mean, walk in?"

"She has key."

"How come she had a key to your apartment?"

"It's not my apartment—my boyfriend house-sits, for owner. This woman, she say she is friend of owner."

"How long you been living here?" I asked.

"From June. Since owner has been away, traveling."

"Mr. Andrew? That the owner?"

"Yes. And he must have gave this woman the key."

"What happened when she came in?"

"She was drunk, or maybe drugs, she's laughing, crying. She close the door and sit down on the floor. She say she friend of owner, she come for help. She say someone try to kill her."

"Kill her?"

"She was drunk, talk talk talk like crazy. She keep saying, They try kill me with hot bag. I don't know what she means. How can someone be killed with bag that is hot?"

I thought I knew, but I didn't explain it to her. "Hot bag" was a street term used by addicts to describe a too-pure or even a spiked dose of heroin. The easiest way for dealers to get rid of an over-talkative junkie liable to roll over on them was by slipping him a hot bag.

I asked her, "What did you do?"

"I do nothing. She pass out. George look at her a long time. I think he recognize her. He start asking me all these questions."

"About what?"

"Same as you asked, whose apartment is this, who is owner…"

"And then what?"

"He walk around. Sit down over there."

She pointed to the other end of the room at the only non-modern piece of furniture, an ornate writing desk painted in white with twisted rose vines painted up each leg.

She said, "He open the drawer. Some of the owner's

papers are there. He look around inside. Then he take a
book down from shelf."

"Which book?"

She shrugged her shoulders.

I asked what color the cover was.

"White. Or maybe brown. I don't remember. He put it
back on the shelf." She gestured with the knife, its point
at shoulder height. "When he come back he had that look
in his eye, like when he knows something no one else
knows. Like when I first meet him…"

Her voice choked up. I reached out past the knife and
put one hand on her shoulder, caught between an impulse
to stroke her gently and one to shake her firmly. I wanted
to comfort her—but I couldn't indulge her grief just yet.
There was too much I still needed to learn. What Owl
had been doing in the city, what he'd come to see Elena
for.

I prompted Elena, squeezing her shoulder lightly: "Go
on. What happened then?"

"George say wake up, wake up, he get her on her feet.
He walk her to the couch. He talk to her, feed her coffee
—I make, full pot, and she drink, drink. I don't hear everything they talk, but I can tell he's using his persuasion
on her."

"His persuasion?"

"How he get people to do what he want. It was a nap
he have."

"Knack," I corrected.

"Yes. He convince her she'll be safer if she come with
him. He walk her out the door. That was last I see him."

"What time was that?"

"Little after seven in the morning."

"Why go out so early?"

"He'd been here all night. My boyfriend is away, work

all night at garage. George come over to help me to figure out…" She seemed to consider saying more but decided not to.

"Help you figure out what?"

"Not important," she said, and before I could ask again she went on, "Tell me truth, did this woman hurt him, is that how he died?"

"No. It was an accident. She wasn't even there. He left her back at his hotel room. She was waiting for him when I got there."

"Then it must be the other person, the one he say been following him."

"What do you mean? What other person?"

"You don't know? He tell me it's why he want to hire you."

"Told you when?"

"He call me when he reach hotel room with woman. He say he's picked up snake. No, not snake, what word he use…tail. Picked up tail."

"He saw someone tailing him?"

"He say it's just a feeling. But he trust his feeling."

I nodded, remembering the way he'd sensed me looking at him from my window. I trusted his feelings myself.

She said, "He tell me he gonna hire you to find out who's following him."

Owl had said he wanted me to tag someone following one of the people leaving Yaffa. He just hadn't mentioned that the person being followed would be him. And of course it didn't play out the way he'd planned. When the time for the meeting came, Owl was dead, so he never showed up at Yaffa; and either his tail knew this and never showed either or else did show up, saw Owl wasn't there, and left without my noticing. Unless I *had* noticed —unless the person Owl had been supposed to meet was

Sayre Rauth and Jeff had been his mysterious tail...? But no. Jeff had been so incompetent at it, Owl would've spotted him in a heartbeat and a half. Maybe the blonde kid, FL!P? He'd tailed *me* earlier—and he'd been there when Owl'd had his accident. Or maybe it was the Russians in their Grand Cherokee...?

Elena was saying, "I *knew* something was wrong. I been frightened since he don't call me..." And she started shaking again. I squeezed her shoulder harder, brought her back.

"Elena, I need to know, what was Owl helping you with?"

She didn't answer.

"Why was he here? Did you ask him to come?"

Nothing.

"Was it the problem you're having with your super?"

"What? I don't—Luis? He's a drunk. I know how to handle drunks."

"He said you punched a hole in the wall."

"Me?" She held up her small hand. It did look unlikely. "He do that himself," she said. "He drinks, and he forgets what he did—so he blame me. But he is harmless, he's no problem."

"Then what was George helping you with?"

She still didn't answer.

"Whatever it is, you know he wanted me to help, too."

She looked at me a long moment.

"What does it matter to you?" she said. "If George hired you and now he is... You don't need to do nothing more. It's over for you."

"It's not over for you," I said, the resolution warbling my voice, "so it's not over for me. George came out of retirement to help you. He told me he owed you a favor and he wanted to repay it. It's my job to repay it now. And in our line of work, we finish the jobs we're hired for."

"George owed me nothing," Elena said. "I told him this a thousand times. He did more for me than I ever did for him. He got me into this country. I wouldn't be here—wouldn't be alive—if not for him. This is better life than I could ever hope for if I stayed in Ukraine."

"That's where you're from? Ukraine?"

It was a stupid thing say. It put her back on guard just when she'd finally begun opening up. But a voice in my head kept whispering, Ukraine, Ukraine...something about Owl in the Ukraine... Then I had it.

"Hang on," I said, "does this have something to do with that case with the kidnapped American girl?" I looked her over. She was in her early twenties now, she'd have been about the same age as that girl when it happened—which was also, I realized, roughly the age she'd been in the photograph with Owl. "I remember hearing a story," I said, "about a case Owl had that took him to the Ukraine. Maybe ten years ago? I heard it from two different guys, actually. About how he helped rescue an American girl from a child pornography ring there."

She was nodding, the knife she'd been gripping all this time finally lowered. I saw that the t-shirt bunched around her arm was soaked a dark red, but at least the stain had stopped spreading.

"The way I heard it," I said, "he was hired by the grandparents of a missing girl who'd been abducted by her father. They'd sought custody after their daughter died the year before in a car accident. There were signs of sexual abuse by the father, as I recall, but the grandparents didn't press for criminal prosecution as long as he didn't contest their custody. They won the case—but lost their granddaughter. A month later the father kidnapped her and they both vanished without a trace.

"So the grandparents hired George Rowell. He tracked the girl down after photos of her surfaced on a child pornography website based in the Ukraine. He went over, learned that the girl's father had involved her with, what was it, a child modeling agency?" Elena nodded. "But not the sort of modeling agency you'd want your child working for. It was all porn, right? Photographing and videotaping naked girls between the ages of seven and sixteen."

"Six," Elena said softly. "There was one girl who was six."

"And you," I said, "how old were you?"

"Eleven," she said. "When I started."

I thought back to being that age, what had I been up to? Moving my lips to an *Encyclopedia Brown* at the public library, not disrobing in front of a camera.

I cleared my throat and asked her, "These people kept you prisoner? Locked up?"

"No. Not how you mean. We were…prisoners, but not locked up. Where I lived in my country, everyone was poor. These people, they offer us too much money for taking these pictures. Too much to refuse. And the girls, most didn't mind. It was only being naked. Not sex. Not for most of us. For some girls, it felt exciting, even glamorous. I never liked it. But I had no choice. It was too much money. Cristy—that was the American—she's like me, she don't like it either. But she does it, every day, because, well, her father says do it, the other girls, they do it, I do it, what she gonna say, no, I refuse? So they roll tape, they say, 'Pull, your panties down, darling, bend over, darling, blow a kiss, darling, sweetheart, princess,' and she do it. I do it. We all do it, with a big smile, show all our teeth."

I concentrated on keeping my expression neutral. I had to appear the seasoned professional—seen it all—

but it was a strain to keep my jaw from dropping open
and repeating over and over, "Omigod."

"Cristy," Elena said, "she was living with her father.
He would bring her to the studio for sessions. He give
her drugs before they shoot, pills, you know, make her
more relaxed. Then, end of day, he take her away again.
Never told nobody where they lived. But Cristy and I,
between shoots, we talk, we became friends. And she
told me where they lived. Then later, when George come
and say he's there to take her home…"

"You told him."

She nodded.

"It was like a movie, a spy movie. He need my help,"
she said. "He choose me. No other girl, he pick me. I was
in store shopping when he approach me the first time.
He pretend he need my help buying soup, read the cans.
He say, Oh, I'm so happy you speak English so good, can
you tell me what this says? And this? And he take me
down aisle where nobody is, and then he talk to me
serious, say he's gonna trust me, he's looking for American
girl and do I know her, will I help him?"

"And you said yes."

"Of course I say yes. He was so clever and funny and
brave. I liked him at once." Her eyes were bright with
memory, almost as if for a moment, for her, Owl was alive
again.

"All week, he say, he'd been watching the modeling
agency, the girls coming and going. He look for Cristy
and her father, but that week they don't come. He don't
know where they are. So I tell him I know where she
lives."

She smiled broadly, remembering with pride.

"George, he say, Help me get Cristy away from her
father, I tell you what to do. You frightened? Of course

I'm frightened, but I say no, I want to help. So he teach me a story I'm suppose to say to her father so he'll let Cristy go out alone. George tell me the story, make me repeat, repeat, till I get it right.

"Then he walk with me to their apartment. He hide while I ring bell. I was so scared! But when I hear her father's voice out the intercom, asking what I want, I know what to say, I say what George tell me: the agency want me to take Cristy out shopping, buy clothing for special pictures. I tell him they give me money for the clothes, and for him, too. He buzz me in.

"Upstairs, father takes the money George give me for him, tell Cristy get you coat, go out with this girl, come straight back, don't stop nowhere, understand? And Cristy nods, okay, okay, and go downstairs with me. We go four blocks, to a craft shop George showed me. As soon as we walk in, there's George, and Cristy's grandfather and grandmother are waiting, and they ask her, Want to come home? And she can't speak, she cries so much, she just keep nodding, yes, yes, I wanna go home. They put her in a car, go straight to airport.

"Then George say to me, you gotta go, too. You stay, they hurt you, 'cause you help me. I am last person Cristy's father saw with her so I am first person he'd come looking for, to ask what happened. I'd never be safe in my country. And George, he know this, he tell Cristy's grandma and grandpa, you get this girl out, too. They're very rich, they get me passport, visa. Week later, I am in United States, new name, new life. Not scared. Till now. Now I am scared again. First time since I come here."

"Why?"

"Someone find me," she said. "Someone from my past. From my country, from my old life. This woman."

"Who?"

She hesitated.

"One of the older girls. I don't remember her name."

I didn't believe her, but I let it pass for now.

"And how did she find you?"

"I don't know!" Elena said. "Maybe it is accident, just walking down the street. She's here in city now and she see me and find out where I live…and she's angry, I think she want to hurt me, because I got out while she and the others were left behind. So I call George, tell him this woman's bothering me, ask him can you help me? And he come. I feel bad when he show up. He look so old. He don't need my troubles, too. So I say go home, I take care of on my own, but George say, no, if you need help, I help. No way to turn him off."

I understood. I never could reach my off switch either.

"So I say, Can you get this woman leave me alone? And George say, yes, we just need something on her, get some lever…"

"Leverage," I said.

"Yes. And we get some. We get, and we are suppose to meet her at café, tell her what we got, George suppose to say leave Elena alone or we spill your beans. But now he's dead…"

Meet her at café? Well, that told me who the woman was. "That's what the meeting at Yaffa was supposed to be about?" I said. "Telling this woman to stay away from you?"

She nodded. "We were going to go together. But when I didn't hear from George, I didn't go."

"Instead you sent your boyfriend, Jeff?"

"You know?"

"I was there. I saw him follow Sayre Rauth."

"Sayre…? That what she call herself here? You meet her?"

"I have."

She tilted her chin at me. "And are you working for her?"

"No."

"Then why are you collecting this for her?" And she nodded toward the black plastic bag on the floor, the one she'd tried to hand me when I came to the door.

"A man named Paul Windmann hired me."

She smiled.

"Oh, Windmann. Did he enjoy his nap?"

"So that was you then? The woman he picked up and took back to his place?"

"Yes. It was George's plan. How we get the lever edge."

Elena beamed as she described how Owl had cleverly arranged it all. Setting up Windmann, providing the roofie, so they could steal his keys and break into Rauth Realty's townhouse, where Windmann worked as her second-in-command. George, bless his 84-year-old heart, had done the actual break-in. I could almost hear him crowing about it, chuckling over how he'd neither lost his touch nor fallen behind the times in terms of tools. Once he'd gotten inside, he'd plugged an ordinary iPod into the USB port on her computer and used it to siphon information off her hard drive. The iPod that lay at the bottom of the black plastic bag. The iPod Windmann had hired me to get back for him.

"But Elena," I said, turning the plastic bag over in my hand, "if you and George stole her files so you'd have something to hold over her head, why did you agree to sell them back to Windmann? Why were you ready to hand them over to me at the door?"

"Because everything's gone wrong!" Elena said. "I can't reach George, I don't know where he is, he don't call…I'm scared again. Maybe something happen to him, maybe if I stay something gonna happen to me. I know I have to go, run, get away. But for that I need money. So I contact Windmann and I sell the files back to him. Only thing I have left to sell, Mr. Sherwood. I'm not eleven anymore."

She stopped talking. The silence pressed down on her. On both of us.

"I need to know," she said finally. "Did George suffer? Was he in any pain? How…"

"He was dead by the time I got to him," I said. "Less than a minute. He'd hit his head badly. I think it killed him instantly. I don't think he suffered."

Her face went waxy pale and she ran for the bathroom door. She was sick.

I took the iPod out of the plastic bag and powered it up. Brought up the menu. The device had a 40 gigabyte memory, but only one song was listed on the screen. One song, when a machine like this can hold ten thousand. What was on the rest of the machine's memory? What sort of files had Owl found?

I set the bag aside and looked around the apartment. I opened the writing desk's drawer. Inside were pens, loose change, utility bills addressed to L. Andrews, pink parking garage ticket stubs probably belonging to the boyfriend. Hanging over the desk's chair was a pair of grease-stained coveralls with the name "Jeff" stitched on them. Through the open closet door I could see another couple pairs hanging.

I turned to the bookshelf Elena had pointed to earlier. Not searching for any particular title, just allowing my eyes to take them all in. One book on the third shelf down stuck out half an inch farther than all the others in the same row. Its spine was brown.

I pulled it out the rest of the way. It was a tall book titled *The Complete Guide to Tristan and Isolde*. Isolde. As in Enterprises, as in… I opened the cover and there in the upper corner of the first endpage was the owner's name written in blue ink: "Lawrence J. Addison." Law Addison.

And Michael Cassidy was the woman Addison had run off with when he skipped out on bail. The same Michael Cassidy who'd had a key to this apartment...

I could almost feel the gears shifting into place.

Owl wouldn't just have recognized her when she walked in on them—he'd have made the connection between her and her fugitive boyfriend. If Michael Cassidy is back here in New York, he'd have thought, Addison's probably with her, or not far behind. Or at least she'd probably know where he was.

So Owl must've confronted her, told her he knew who she was, told her that if he'd recognized her other people would, too; he'd have convinced Michael Cassidy that if someone was trying to kill her and she wanted to stay out of sight she'd be better off going with him than trying to hide on her own. It was something people said Owl had always been able to do, persuading people, getting them to follow his lead. It had been one of his strengths as a private eye, and now that he was a harmless-looking old man it must've been even easier for him—he could play on people's sympathy, and even the most beautiful young woman wouldn't worry about his intentions, about going back to this nice old man's hotel room.

I noticed that the sounds of Elena's retching had ceased. I went and looked into the bathroom. She was asleep on the bathroom floor, curled next to the porcelain toilet.

I looked at her cut arm. The blood-soaked t-shirt was brown now, not red.

I let her sleep.

With the black plastic bag in my hand and the hard-cover copy of the *Complete Guide to Tristan and Isolde* under my arm, I walked out of the apartment, letting the door swing closed behind me.

I'd come looking for answers. I'd found some, but now I also had a heap more questions. That was life, the deck was stacked; always the questions outnumbering the answers.

The corridor to the vestibule and the street door looked marginally different than when I had gone into the apartment. The telephone directories had been pushed aside and both doors shut. It was relatively quiet cut off from the street noise.

Daylight from the partially open courtyard door still came from beneath the slant of the stairwell, but I no longer heard the sound of the garden hose rinsing out trash barrels.

Before I left, I thought it wouldn't hurt to get some more information about Mr. Andrew from Luis. That's what I thought.

I started for the courtyard door and reached out a hand to push it farther open, but from the corner of my eye I saw something that registered as completely wrong.

Under the stairwell were more stairs, in shadow, leading down to a storage basement. A man was on them, but he was neither ascending nor descending, he was lying prone.

His workboots were toes-up on the top step, his head was awkwardly bent back over the seventh step down. Below his chin was a vivid, frown-shaped welt across his throat. Blood on his lips and red drool in his chin stubble. He was looking up, only he wasn't looking, not anymore. Nevermore.

It was disorienting for a second, like meeting someone face-to-face on an Escher staircase: going up/coming down? coming up/going down? Maybe he was really standing up and I was the one lying down.

Then, no maybe about it. The slant of daylight from the courtyard changed shape, the rhomboid widening. I turned, but not quick enough. Something crashed down on my head and I fell forward.

Last thing I was aware of: a steely sound, a sound like a roulette wheel at the moment when the croupier drops the ball in—No more bets, Mesdames et Monsieurs—and I was that shiny steel ball sent spinning in its narrow track, round and round and round, until finally I slowed and bounced and tumbled and landed in the double zero.

Chapter Eleven
INCH-HIGH PRIVATE EYE

I came to, not in darkness but gauzy half-light, wondering why my head hurt so much and why the mattress was so lumpy: what was it stuffed with, juice boxes and chicken bones?

I was lying on top of the dead man, the both of us in a heap at the bottom of the basement stairs. I scrambled off him. I must've landed on top and ridden him like a sled down the remaining flight of steps.

I crouched in a shadowy corner half-seated on a plastic rat trap, a black pentagon full of poison, staring up at the glare of daylight at the top of the stairs. No one was up there—whoever had hit me was gone—but I still gave it a minute or so before I moved again.

I looked over at the dead man. The super, Luis. The musty air of the chalky cellar was overlapped by the cloying vapor of alcohol. His bottle of tequila had broken, either in his fall or in cushioning mine.

Death has a stillness all its own, unmistakable for either stupor or sleep; by comparison the paint peeling off the walls was moving at a fast clip. All the same, I reached over and checked for a pulse just to make sure. Nothing.

I patted down his pockets and found a wad of bills in a money clip. A quick fan approximated it at eighty bucks. So not a robbery then, or at least not a successful one.

I tried to put the money back in the same pocket. It wouldn't go. Just one of the reasons you're not supposed to touch anything at a crime scene: things never go back the way they were. I slipped it into his breast pocket instead.

I stood, the wall at my back guiding me up.

I looked down at Luis. Another dead old man, my second that day, only this one wasn't an accident, at least not in the strictest sense of the word; someone had crushed his windpipe. It made me consider again Owl's accident and how strict that had been as well.

I brushed myself off. I touched the back of my pants. My gun was still tucked there in the waistband. As I climbed the stairs, halfway up I found the plastic bag I'd taken from Elena. The iPod was still inside it, so it wasn't all bad news.

But the book I'd been carrying was gone. Whoever hit me had stolen *The Complete Guide to Tristan and Isolde*. Unless, of course, the book belonged to the person who hit me, then that wouldn't be stealing.

I peered into the courtyard and the hallway but no one was around. I listened and thought and made a decision. I went back to apartment three. Though it had been closed when I left it, the door was open a crack now. With gun in hand—safety off—I opened it farther.

There was no one inside, living or dead. Signs of decampment and a hasty retreat. Closet door and dresser drawers hung open. Stray clothes on the floor that hadn't been there before. The pair of coveralls that had been draped over the chair was one of the things now missing.

With a murdered man within shouting distance down in the basement, I didn't want to spend any more time looking around.

But I did stop and pick up the phone. I pressed the redial button. On the other end, a phone rang and rang and no one answered, until finally on the twelfth ring an answering machine picked up: "You've reached E-Z

Parking Garage with accommodations available for short- and long-term parking. We're located at 446 East Tenth Street at the corner of Avenue D. The attendant is currently busy assisting another customer, but please leave a message and someone will get back to you."

I hung up without leaving a message, got the dial tone, then punched in *69 to get the number of the last incoming call. The call had come in at 1:12 PM and had a 212 area code. I wrote it on the back of a Con Edison bill addressed to L. Andrews.

The need to leave the building was building inside me like an uncontrollable urge. For all I knew whoever had hit me had also called the cops.

I drew the apartment door almost shut behind me, leaving it the way I'd found it, open just that crack, and went down the corridor to the entryway and street doors. I didn't stop to look back down at Luis but said a brief prayer for him in Spanish, pretty much the only Spanish I know. *Vaya con Díos.*

A block away I stopped at a payphone, dialed the local precinct, and anonymously reported a dead man in the basement of 27 Avenue C.

I walked home to the office, feeling a little nauseous and hoping it was a delayed reaction to my spooning a corpse and not an early warning sign of a concussion. A thick skull had always been my one saving grace, as well as a damning constant.

The case was coming together, I felt it wriggling in my hands like a newborn living thing, viscous and slick, squirming to get away from me. I needed to swallow a couple aspirin, smoke a cigarette, then sit down in my thinking chair and get a good grip.

Two people were standing outside the street door of my building when I arrived. A man and a woman in their twenties, both slender and of average height, dressed like upwardly mobile professionals; the man in a light-gray Ralph Lauren summer suit, the woman in a knee-length blue silk dress that could've come straight from the Fifth Avenue storefront windows of Lord & Taylor. The buzzer they were pushing was mine.

Shit, my three o'clock appointment with the couple who wanted the background check on their prospective nanny—what were their names again?—Mr. and Mrs. Dough.

Was it three o'clock already? Where does the day go?

I wasn't in the mood for Ken and Barbie and considered blowing 'em off, going someplace to get a cup of coffee until they tired of waiting, but I relented. My mom would never forgive me, turning away work.

"Good afternoon, sorry I'm late."

"Mr. Sherwood?" the young woman asked. Her husband was talking on a Bluetooth plugged into his ear.

"Yes. Mrs. Dough?"

She reached out her hand to take mine. Hers was a slender, soft, firm hand and she held mine for longer than I expected.

"Please, call me Jane." She had a spry Midwestern accent. "Mrs. Dough is my mother-in-law."

She laughed and I politely laughed with her.

Her husband's phone conversation ended and she finally let go of my hand as he joined us.

"Sorry about that, Mr. Sherwood, had to put out a little fire at work." He took the hand his wife had just relinquished. His was a loose, dry handclasp, like shaking hands with a feather duster. "Thank you for seeing us on such short notice."

"Yes, well, actually, this isn't, as it turns out, the best time for me right now. Tomorrow would—"

Jane looked stricken, I thought she was going to cry.

"Oh, please, Mr. Sherwood, if you would just hear our situation. It won't take long."

"Yes," Mr. Dough said, "we understand you're very busy, but my wife has been worrying herself sick about this, and I know it would help if we could talk it over with you now. We can pay cash up front."

It was more his wife's doe-eyed appeal than the talk of money that finally won me over.

"Come on up," I said, "I can spare you twenty minutes."

I unlocked the downstairs door and held it open for them. She went first, as her husband's cell phone rang and he stepped aside to answer it, politely ushering me ahead. I followed his wife up the stairs watching with each step her firm buttocks flex and relax beneath the thin fabric of her dress. It was a nice sculpted ass, she must've worked out. I was wishing Mr. Dough had stayed at work to put out his little fires in person. To keep my mind on business, I asked how old their child was.

"Three," she said.

"Two," he said at the same time from behind me.

"Annie will be three in November," Jane Dough said quickly.

Maybe I would've made something of that little discrepancy if I hadn't been so infatuated with her ass. She may not have had the raw flame-to-the-moth magnetism of Sayre Rauth, but…a fine ass is a fine ass.

At the top of the stairs, she stepped aside to let me pass and I went forward to open my office door.

"Right this—"

One of them hit me, a swift kidney punch that dropped me to my knees. Then one of them kicked me—maybe the same one—right between the shoulder blades. It knocked the wind out of me and sent me face-forward onto my office floor gasping for air and sucking up dust-bunnies.

They didn't even give me time for indignation or surprise as they patted me down, divested me of my gun, and handcuffed my wrists, not with metal handcuffs but with a plastic restraint, zipping me up like a trashbag.

I got just enough breath back to utter, "What the f—"

She kicked me in the side.

"Shut up."

Just great, I thought, I poke my nose in where it doesn't belong and someone hires these two to rough me up. I was stimulating the economy, creating new jobs.

Mr. Dough made a quick tour of my office, drawing the curtains, looking in the bathroom and around the corner of the kitchenette. He nodded an all-clear to her. She opened up her purse and took out a cell phone and dialed a number with the tips of her tapered, tangerine-sorbet fingernails.

He dragged me by the ankles into the center of the room and sat me up. Dust down my front. I had to clean the place one of these days. Definitely before my next bodily assault.

"Keep quiet and don't move," he told me. He brought one of the club chairs over in front of me. The woman sat down in it.

She said, "There's someone who wants to speak to you."

She held the cell phone in front of me, aimed at my face.

It had a brightly lit, inch-square LCD screen, and it was displaying the face of a bald-headed man with a short black goatee and little piggy eyes over a flat nose with nostrils flaring like an angry bull's. He was a barnyard amalgam and I recognized him at once.

Maurice "Moe" Fedel, the former NYPD detective who'd retired to start Fedel Associates, Risk Management Consultants, one of the biggest detective and security agencies in the city, with branches in Philly, Baltimore, and D.C. He was one of George Rowell's oldest friends;

they'd started as sparring partners when Fedel was still on the force.

I'd never met him in person, but I'd seen him a few times on TV when visiting my folks. He was a frequent and outspoken guest commentator on their favorite 24/7 cable news network.

He was wearing a blue shirt with a stiff white collar like those cones vets put on dogs so they don't bite their stitches.

His husky shout sounded tinny over the phone's tiny speaker.

"So, you're Sherwood?"

I looked above the videophone at the woman holding it. "What is this? You want me to talk to an appliance?"

"Hey! Don't talk to them, dummy, talk to me!" The inch-high face shouted in its mini-bellow. "I'm the one asking the questions and I asked are you Sherwood?"

I didn't say anything.

Moe said, "What are you, stupid? John, tune him up!"

The man walked behind me and lifted my pinned arms up over my head, twisting until fire shot into my shoulder sockets.

The woman sighed, said in a bored voice, "He's Sherwood."

Moe said, "I know all about you, Sherwood. You're a fuck-up, a joke in this business."

"Saw my résumé on HotJobs.com? I gotta update it."

"Wise-mouth and smartass. I heard about you. All I want to know is why Owl came to see you this morning."

"Who?"

"George Rowell. I know he was at your place this mornin'. And now he's dead. And you're going tell me what happened or it's going to get ugly."

"It's ugly already. You're the best argument I've seen for going back to rotary phones."

"Tell me what—"

"Fuck you," I said. "Instead of asking what he came to see me for, ask yourself why he didn't go to you, Moe. What was it he didn't think he could trust you with? Or maybe you were too busy playing with your toys to help out an old friend. Ask yourself that, but first get these two turds out of my office!"

The phone must've been a cheap model, because the face on it seemed to have tinted purple.

"You're done in this city, asshole! You hear me? *Done!*"

Bang bang bang.

Chapter Twelve
A PROCESS OF ELIMINATION

Someone's fist hammered on my door. It was the prettiest sound in the whole wide world.

BANG BANG BANG.

"Open up! C'mon, Sherwood, I know you're in there."

It was Matt Chadinsky. He banged some more.

He bellowed, "What's with the closed curtains? Whatcha doin' in there, pullin' your pud?"

It cost me a kick in the ribs, but I croaked out a loud, "Just a second!"

"That I believe!"

He banged on the door again, three times hard. He wasn't going away. My playmates had to eat it.

"It's my probation officer," I said. "He'll probably need all your names, what should—"

Moe Fedel said, "Okay, you guys get out of there. But, Sherwood, we're not finished. Not by a long shot."

The cell phone videoscreen went to black.

John Dough lifted me by my shoulders to my feet.

Jane Dough brushed off my shirtfront as her partner cut the plastic wrist restraints behind me. She patted me gently on the chest.

"No hard feelings," she said. She'd dropped her Midwestern accent, replaced now by an easygoing New York twang. "Just business, right?"

I massaged my wrists, working out the lingering bite

of the restraints, and tried to think of a cutting comeback
for her, but couldn't. My heart wasn't in it. So then where
was it?

I said, "So none of this—all this was a set-up. Jane's not
even your name, is it?"

"Jane Doe and John Doe, get it?"

"Yeh, I got it." I rubbed a bruised rib. "So then…you
two aren't really…"

"Looking for a background check on our nanny? No,
sorry to disappoint you."

"I was going to say married."

Standing by the door, John Dough laughed.

"I think he wants to ask you out. Must like the way you
roughed him up."

She arched an eyebrow at me. I felt a little like I was
back in high school.

Matt banged three more times on the door.

"Open up, I need to piss!"

"So what's your name?"

She turned around, let her eyes roam my dilapidated
office before they rested back on me. She shrugged.

"You're a detective, figure it out yourself."

"I will."

She nodded her head once, then turned to her partner,
who opened my office door and stood to one side. She
stepped into the hall. He waited a moment then followed
her out.

I heard their footsteps echoing in the stairwell as Matt
walked in. He looked around my darkened office, at all
the drawn curtains.

"What? Don't tell me I missed the fucking slideshow?"

I went around opening the curtains again.

"How'd you get in?" He hadn't buzzed.

"In?" he said, his face a mask of mock innocence. "Oh,

your downstairs door. I used this." He wiggled the pinkie of his right hand. "You should have your landlord put a better lock in. Your forehead's bleeding."

I touched it and it stung over my right eye. Bright red blood filled in the arches and whorls of the fingerprints of my forefinger and thumb. I headed for my bathroom.

Matt said, "You should apply—"

"I know what I should apply."

"Oh, right. I forgot. This is what you do best."

I wanted to wish him into the cornfield just then, but I was imagining I might need his help. I ran a towel under cold water and pressed it to my forehead until the bleeding stopped.

When I came back out, Matt was standing behind my desk.

I went to sit down and he didn't move.

"Do you mind?"

Matt shook his head. "No. I don't mind."

I squeezed by him. By the time I was seated he was on the other side of my desk.

"So, who were those two?"

"Don't you know?" I asked, airing out a nasty hunch.

He narrowed his eyes. "How would I know?"

"They work for Moe Fedel."

"No shit."

"They wanted to know what George Rowell came to see me about."

"No shit."

"Yeh, no shit." I walked up to Matt, stopped a foot away. "The shit part is how'd Moe find out Owl came to see me this morning? Unless you told him, Matt."

I faced him. He was a head taller than me and a foot wider. Trying to read his expression now, I realized I'd never really looked this closely at Matt Chadinsky before.

Never had to, never thought I had to; he was always just Matt, I knew who he was.

Looking at him now was like seeing a stranger. I never noticed that mole on his left temple before or that the whites of his eyes were dullish gray like pearl-inlay, nor that his ears were slightly crenulated like arugula.

He didn't utter a word, just looked at me like I was something he'd picked out of his teeth but couldn't remember what he'd eaten that was that shade of green.

I said, "You sicced Moe Fedel on me and he sent those two glamour ops of his over here to pull my teeth. Then you show up, pounding on my door, all Mighty Mouse, here-to-save-the-day."

He squinted at me. "What, are you high?"

"I don't hear you denying any of it."

"Deny what, you paranoid piece of shit? You've gone off the deep end. Why would I rat you out to Moe?"

"He was pretty quick off the mark setting up those two to rough me up."

Matt's mouth twisted into a sour smile.

"Those two roughed you up? What'd they fucking do, rap you on the knuckles with their goddamn Blackberries?"

"You didn't answer my question."

"I also didn't tell you there's no fuckin' Tooth Fairy. Some things you're just supposed to know."

"So how'd he know so quick that Owl came to see me?"

"He didn't have to know, you cockfart! He runs one of the biggest detective agencies in the city, he found out. What did you fucking expect? One of his oldest friends— a private investigator—gets hit by a car and killed practically on your fucking doorstep. All he had to do was open the Yellow Pages to make a connection."

"I don't buy that," I said, but I was unsure. "He knew too much when he talked to me."

"Or too little. Why else would he dispatch those two

and 'rough you up,' except to haze you, rattle you, and get you to talk? He was just wavin' his dick around and you swallowed the bait. I warned you, Payton. But no, you don't want help. You know better. You're always the smartest fucking guy in an empty room."

I thought about it, going over again in my mind what Fedel had actually said to me, and in a way it fit.

An ex-cop, Fedel knew the way to work information out of someone was to act like you already knew everything and then just sit back and listen for the contradictions. Had I ratted myself out? I wasn't sure. It still bothered me, though, Matt's showing up in the nick of time.

"So what're you doin' here, Matt? I don't see you for five years, then twice in one day. My star must be in Uranus."

He ignored the feedline, which made it only half a joke.

"Need to talk to you," he said. "I was waiting across the street for you to get back. Saw you go up with those two, then all your curtains shut. Thought I'd investigate."

I found where they'd put my gun and where I'd dropped the plastic bag with the iPod in it. Nobody wanted my goodie bag. I went to my desk and dropped everything in a drawer.

"So what'd you need to talk to me about?"

He sat heavily on the edge of my desk, his buttock knocking over my cup of pencils and pens and spilling them out. He didn't pick them up, I had to. I shook my head, lamenting, "Oscar, Oscar."

He said, "Law Addison was spotted today, here in the city."

"He's back?"

"I shit you not."

"Where in the city?"

"Right round here. Fucking Tompkins Square Park, y'believe it? Only two hours ago."

"Who by?"

"One of my people clocked him coming out of a bakery, but my guy was on another job. Lost sight of him before he could signal his back-up."

"How'd he know it was Addison?"

"Addison's the one that got away over at Metro. We've got his ugly mug tacked up next to every goddamn coffee-maker. But it's nothing positive yet—otherwise I wouldn't be talking to you, asshole, I'd be giving it over to the cops. Addison's a fugitive."

"What did they say at the bakery?"

"What?"

"He was coming out of a—"

"We're on that. What I need from you is what Owl said to you about Addison."

"Why?"

"Because he must've fucking seen him too. Why else would he pull his name outta the air?"

"I asked him if he'd found Addison. He said he didn't."

"Then why—"

"He didn't find Addison, but he did find the woman Addison ran off with."

Matt didn't say anything, but his mouth hung open like he was straining to get a breath out, or else haul some-thing from out of his memory. "Michael Cassidy? Owl told you that he—"

"No, never got the chance. But when I went over to his hotel room, he had her stashed there. She hit me on the head and booked."

"Where is she now?"

"I don't know."

"Shit. So did you get anything out of her? Fuck, I can't believe you let her get—hit you on the head!?"

"I didn't know who she was, I only just found out."

"What were you doing in Owl's hotel room anyway?"

"What?"

"What were you doing in Owl's hotel room?"

"What was I...was doing...where I was where—"

"Yeh, yuck-yuck-yuck, funnyfuck. Knock off the Abbott and Costello. How'd you get in?"

I wiggled my little pinkie at him.

He snorted. "You sure it was Michael Cassidy?"

"She's hard to take for anyone else."

Matt nodded. "So both of them came back."

"What's he look like, Addison?"

"Mid-30s. Six-two, about two hundred forty pounds. Towhead, looks like a Swede. But according to my guy, says he's lost weight, looks trim. Shit, what did I tell you, no way that guy could stay under wraps for long. Probably thinks it's blown over, the idiot-fuck."

"He's such an idiot, how come he's so rich? Not to mention still walking around and not in a cell."

"Give it a day or two, he'll be in a cell."

"What would he come back to the city for anyway? It can't just be for the cheesecake."

"If that junkie girlfriend's still with him, maybe they're in town to score some dope. I always figured she'd lead us to Addison one way or another, either by ending up on an ER gurney or a slab."

"An O.D. like Craig Wales?"

Matt ignored that. "Or maybe he left behind a stash of cash," he said, "and now he needs to replenish. How did she look to you, still on the needle?"

I shrugged. "Didn't find any of the utensils, not even an alcohol prep. Nothing in the room. Heard a phone conversation, though, from outside the door, that sounded like a score, so I wouldn't be surprised if she were."

Matt, reluctantly eating crow, said, "Look, I know I

didn't ask you in on this Law Addison thing to begin with. Maybe I should've. Maybe it wouldn't of mattered. But you're in on it now. Understood?"

"Ordering me that you're hiring me?"

"What was Owl's connection to all this? Did you find out what he was working on? Anything that might be a lead to where Addison is stashed now?"

I thought it through: Owl comes to the city to help Elena deal with Sayre. While he's with her in the apartment, Michael Cassidy walks in. She has keys because the apartment belongs to Law Addison, under the alias of L. Andrews. Owl tags her and puts her in his hotel room for safekeeping. On the way, he picks up a tail. Then he decides to bring me in to flush out whoever's following him and...

That's as far as my imagination took me. But other new factors had to be taken into account. Luis' murder was one. Had Addison also returned to the apartment, been spotted by his good friend the super? Luis would've made a big noise about that, a noise Addison couldn't afford being heard. That strike across Luis' throat suggested that silencing him may have been a motive or intent in the man's death.

Finally to Matt I said, "No."

To hell with him, it was my case now. And it was breaking.

He must've read my mind. "Same to you, pal."

"Pal? You're only here because I might have a lead on something that would look good on you. Don't pretend you're doing me any favors. Do your own damn spadework. I'm busy."

"What about that client?"

"What client?" I'd lost track.

"The one who turned up on your doorstep, what's his

story? Think he might've been sent here by Michael Cassidy? To feel you out?"

"Separate affair. I do have other jobs you know. And I'm on the clock, so if you don't have anything else to peddle me…"

"I'll pedal you, I'll land the whole bike on your head. Go on, Payton, go it alone. But remember when you blow it, it won't be me you'll be entertaining with your wit. The cops'll want to know why you withheld information on a couple of wanted fugitives."

"And who'll tell 'em, Matt? Not you, right?"

He said nothing, just leveled a bland gaze on me.

I asked, "What's the reward for information leading to his capture or arrest? How much does Metro stand to pocket?"

He stood up from the edge of my desk, the sudden displacement of weight jarring the pens and pencils cup, spilling them over again.

He shook his head.

"Call me when you calm down. There's no talking to you when you get cranky like this. I think you need your nap."

His nap-time jab reminded me of what I'd forgotten to say to him before.

"Congratulations, by the way."

"Huh?"

"I heard you're a father now. Boy or a girl?"

"Yeh," he said and walked all the way to the door before he stopped. He didn't turn around, he spoke looking up toward the ceiling.

"I've got a son."

"That's great, Matt. And how's Jeanne doing?"

"Fine. She's digging being a mommy. I think it gives her something she was missing for a long time."

"And you? Gives you something too?"

Matt's shoulders bunched up, like maybe he was laughing silently, or crying.

Then he said, "Hey, Payton, remember that geek who used to work over at Metro. The one used to fix the copier when it—"

"Chuck R. Dyer," I said. I'd just been thinking about him that morning and his picture in *Time* magazine.

"Yeh, him. That's the one. Chucky. I used to call him Chucky all the time, after that movie. You know, that cocksucker's a fucking billionaire now?"

"Yeh, I did know."

"It got to me. Knowing that, you know, that this pisser who used to come in and sanitize the phones at my job—*he's* a fucking billionaire. And what do I got?—*hemorrhoids!*"

I snickered, couldn't help it.

Matt went on. "You know for a while I used to tell that little anecdote exactly the way I told you just now. Always got a laugh, too. Then one day, I'm having one of my liquid lunches with a client, and I tell it to this guy. And he starts giggling, sort of sputtering. And it hits me like an aluminum bat, he's laughing at me. This fucker's laughing at me. I wanted to crush his fuckin' face in, ya know?"

"Dale Carnegie would be proud."

"Only it was me. I told the story, I *made* this guy laugh at me. Made me want to crush my own face in. So I stopped telling that story. Stopped drinking until I passed out every night. Checked myself into this detox clinic a cousin of mine runs upstate. I got off the booze for good."

I was sorry to hear that, not for his sake, but for nostalgia's. Some of my fondest memories from working at Metro were of our bull sessions at the local bar after a case had wrapped. I'd enter, weak and weary, and Matt— he still had his mustache back then—would already be at a table with two dark, frothy pints of stout in front of him.

I'd walk over, saying, "Good idea." And he'd grin in wide-
eyed innocence, and reply, "Oh? Did you want one, too?"
But those days were gone. Soon I'd be alone with only my
own vices for company. Made me wonder—were all the
sad, solitary drunks in bars merely social drinkers who'd
lost their society?

Matt continued, "Giving up drinking saved my fucking
marriage. Jeanne was threatening to leave me—she didn't
want to raise a child in an alcoholic home. That's what
finally did it. Becoming a father changes things. Changes
everything."

"So I hear."

He waved his hand down through the air, like he was
fanning away a fart that blew back on him.

"You don't get it, Payton. The point of the story is—"

"There's a point? Cool."

"Would you listen?"

I said nothing. It reminded me of another of Matt's old
axioms that he'd drilled into me at Metro: Whenever you
look, see; when you listen, hear.

Matt said, still not turning to face me, "Life's not a joke,
Payton. But your life can *be* a joke. Stop joking around.
Before it's too late." And on that upbeat note, he left me.

I sat and thought, but not about what he'd said. My
brain was ticking away on Law Addison. There had to be
a nice big reward for information leading to his capture.
The kind of money people would do anything for, and—I
admit it—I'm people. I thought it would be fun to collect.
On top of that, it'd be a Botox shot to my sagging practice
if I brought him in.

But Matt was right, I didn't know enough to figure this
out on my own, how it all fit together. I didn't have the
resources at my fingertips. But I knew someone who did,
and she was home. I could hear the clomp of her boots
above my ceiling.

Chapter Thirteen
BURNING BRIDGES

I went upstairs to Tigger's door, knocked, and answered her "Who's there?" with "Me, returning your set of keys."

The door opened.

She said in a hushed voice, "Quiet, everyone's sleeping. Nana and papa fell asleep on Rue's floor by her bed. Retz nodded off on the can, so shhh."

As soon as I saw her, I got a lump in my throat.

She'd been my neighbor in this top-story loft apartment for over ten years, was here when I moved in. We'd had an instant connection, pals at first sight. Maybe if I'd been younger, I'd've tried to make it more. But she was seventeen at the time and I was too old for her. Funny I used to think twenty-eight was too old.

I still didn't know the whole story of how she'd come to New York City, she'd never put forth the information, but she'd dropped enough hints for me to sketch in the outlines. She'd come to the city at fourteen or fifteen, running away from a home life that made resting her head on the hard edge of a sidewalk a more comfortable cushion. She'd mixed with rough people in those early years and become one herself. She began working raves when she was sixteen; it turned out she had a natural talent as a techie. By the time I moved in she was going on eighteen and already had her union card, working Broadway shows in the city and sometimes on tour.

Deeper than that I'd never dug. I deliberately avoided it. Tigger knew what I did for a living, invading people's pasts and ferreting out the truth. It was work in the pursuit of which you developed certain "skills" of mistrust, deceit, emotional insulation, and healthy paranoia. But what's healthy professionally can be poison in a friendship. Stay in the business long enough and these skills harden into personality traits you can no longer turn on and off. After a while, you can't meet someone new without dissecting them; you start assuming all the faces you meet are masks.

But I had never done that with Tigger. And never wanted to. Somehow it was important having one person in my life I didn't treat as suspect, not even the least-likely variety.

Of course we'd also both been young back then, and the temptation to probe hadn't been so great. The past hadn't been that important to us; too much was going on in the now that needed sorting out. But soon the past was all I would have of her.

She must've seen some of the thought on my face, because her bushy brows knitted.

I swallowed the lump and forced a smile. Be happy. I needed her help, not her sympathy. And most of all I needed her computer.

Tigger had a much more sophisticated computer set-up than I ever would—a NASA console by comparison. The whole thing was separately powered by a solar panel unit she'd mounted up on the roof. Con Ed never saw a penny. She could set up shop on a desert island, that one.

In the past year, after becoming a new mother, she'd quit working in theater and turned to graphic design, something she could do from home. She'd been successful at it, too. Too successful. It was enabling her to buy a house in the country and leave the city, and everyone still in it, behind.

Part of my discomfort over losing Tigger was selfish: I

used her on a regular basis as a sounding board and pro-
curer of information. She was my Huggy Bear. She knew
parts of this city I didn't know existed and the sort of
people who inhabited them. I would miss that almost as
much as I'd miss her.

To make up for that impending deficit, I was going to
wring as much out now as I could.

She must have seen the greed in my eyes.

"Is this for a case? Finally got a client?"

A client? Just to show her up, I gave her a tally of
my clients so far that day. Four in all. If she was shocked,
her face didn't betray it. She was the quintessential New
Yorker, never batting an eyelash. Though she did squint
hard when I was telling her about Mr. and Mrs. Dough
knocking my stuffing out and interrupted me to ask, "Wait,
is this true?"

"Dunno, I'm just telling you what happened."

I stopped giving her the rundown of my day at the
point where Matt walked out, for fear of lapping myself.

"Four clients in one day," I said. "That's more than I've
had all year. And it all started with George Rowell. Everything that's happened…there's got to be something that
connects it all. I can't chalk it up to coincidence."

I got no argument from her. I was a little disappointed.
Never could anticipate what her reaction was going to be,
but usually she was contrary.

This time she said, "You're right. There *is* something
that connects all these things. Links all of them together."

That tone of voice—complete conviction, complete
self-confidence…she saw something, she knew the answer!
I could feel my heart start thudding like a boot kicking the
back of my chair in study hall.

I asked, "What is it?"

"It's you, Payton," she said. "You're the connection.
Your perception frames them all and imposes a pattern,

which precludes you from ever perceiving them as what they might well be, merely a random set of unrelated events."

"Oh," I said. It was a letdown. "Well, thank you, *sensei*. But that doesn't really help me."

"I call 'em as I see 'em," she said, and leaned back in her rolling chair. "So let's get to the important part: Which of these women is it that's got you panting?"

"What?"

"Come off it, I've seen that look in your eye before, like the pilot light's gone on. You don't get that look over a man. Only a woman. And not an ugly one either. So give—is it Little Miss Pilates with the nice bum and the fake name or is it the Suicide Girl with the *Ninotchka* accent and the scars?"

I gave. "Neither," I said. "It's the bad guy." I'd told her about following Sayre Rauth from Yaffa and then speaking to her outside her townhouse, but I'd confined myself to the what, where, and when. This time around, I added in the how. And what a how it was. I hadn't realized how much she'd made my blood boil or how obvious it was that she had. Tigger smiled as I told her of the effect Ms. Rauth had had on me.

"Who'd've thought one of the city's hottest women would be working as a realtor?" she said. "Not one of your top ten sexiest jobs. Which firm did you say she's with?"

"I didn't say. She's got her own, Rauth Realty. That's what the townhouse is, their office."

Tigger's smile vanished. "No such company."

I grinned. "Sez you. I was there a few hours ago."

Tigger shook her head resolutely. 99% of the time there was no arguing with her, because 98% of the time she was right.

"I know all the registered realtors in the area. Trust

me, for the last year I've been talking to half of them, the other half I e-mailed. And I never heard of a Rauth Realty, at least not here in the city. Certainly not in this neighborhood."

"Oh. Well, maybe I got the spelling wrong. Or maybe she's not registered."

"Uh-huh. You want to tell me a little more about what she's like?"

"I…she…"

"Oh, so it's like that, huh? Well, be careful, Payton, you know how you get. Don't stick your neck out too far over her—or any of your other parts that are liable to get chopped off."

"Don't worry. I think she's okay."

"So you think this Elena's just lying about her?"

"Not lying, necessarily—but not telling the whole story."

"Sure you aren't just thinking with your dick again?"

"And what's wrong with that? It's my divining rod."

Tigger snorted and turned to one of her computer screens. "More like a compass needle."

"Pointing dewy south."

She laughed. While I had her in a good mood, I started asking her what she knew about some of the other people and names I'd come across. "You ever hear of a girl named Michael Cassidy?"

"Hear of her?" Tigger said. "I saw her last night."

"Excuse me?"

"Michael Cassidy: red hair, green eyes, famous daddy, fourteen minutes into her allotted fifteen? That Michael Cassidy?" I nodded. "She was at that premiere afterparty where Craig Wales overdosed."

"You were there?"

"I set up the lights, favor for a friend. Left before the big foofaraw went down, but I've been checking it out this morning on the web."

She rode her swivel chair like a magic carpet over to her desk and the bank of computer monitors. There were three. They shared the same screensaver, an elaborate Lionel Train set-up with tracks that extended across all three monitors. When the engine passed from one to the next, it entered a mountain range and disappeared, a suspenseful moment as it traversed the empty gap between screens, only to appear finally on the next one over, chugging renewed puffs of greasy smoke.

Tigger rattled the mouse and the little world of perfection vanished from the monitors.

Tigger's computer was already logged onto the Internet, constantly online. It was freakish, but in this regard Tigger was no longer the freak. Not that I'd ever dream of saying something like that to her face.

"There, look." She pointed at the center monitor.

A site containing a transcript of the late Craig Wales' text-message blog accompanied by cell phone snapshots of the party that people had uploaded. In the background of one shot I could see Michael Cassidy arguing with a short woman with a deep tan and peroxide blonde hair. "That's Coy d'Loy," Tigger said.

"Coy d'Loy? Sounds French."

"If by 'French' you mean made-up. She's one of a current crop of It girls."

"What, you mean It, like popular young women of the moment, or *IT*, like Pennywise the clown?"

Tigger laughed. "Bit of both. She runs this rabid public relations firm called The Peer Group. Almost went under a few months ago—she was one of those who got taken in by that crooked money manager, Addison—but she took money from a silent partner to stay afloat, some bruiser with ties to the Russian mob."

I was only half-listening. Another face in the background had gotten my attention, at first only because he looked so out of place. The crowd was mostly composed of people in their twenties, but this man was in his late sixties, a stubby old man with bulbous features and no chin, black hornrim glasses, and a stiff gray pompadour. I'd seen him someplace else and it bugged me I couldn't remember where.

That image was the last picture of the night taken by Craig Wales, followed by his final live-blog entry, a message that he was going off with "MC." "OMG, used to spank to her TTS. ML!"

Guess ML stood for "more later" but that was the last he ever note. Twenty minutes later, he was dead.

"They went off to shoot up together," Tigger said, "but he didn't come back from it. Stuff was too pure or else it was doctored with something."

A hot bag. Elena's words echoed in my head. "Where did you hear that?"

She clicked over to a site called D-O-A.com. It linked to a leaked preliminary M.E. report on the death of Craig Wales. She printed it out for me. Then we skimmed a stream of blogs commenting on the actor's death, from *Perez Hilton* and *Page Six* to *Smoking Gun* and *Hooded Armadillo*, but no one had picked up yet on Michael Cassidy in that photo.

It was exhilarating, knowing that little bit more than was being reported. It's why I never trusted what I saw or read in the news. Not that what was reported was wrong, just nearly always only a sliver of the truth.

Now for part two of my little quest. I handed Tigger the iPod.

"Can you take a look?" I said. "Supposedly Owl used it as a portable hard drive, sucking down info off Sayre's computer."

"And you want to look at it," Tigger said, "because nothing says love like spying on a lady's files."

"I want to look at it because what's on it might help explain how Owl wound up dead."

"Okay, then," she said. "Let's see what's on it." She plugged the iPod into a USB shell in front of the right-hand monitor and her computer began a virus check on the device.

Tigger flashed me a grin, her nose ring tinkling in contact with her two front teeth, giving off a silvery *ping*.

She said, "I feel like Nancy Drew."

"*The Clue in the Crumbling Cock*," I chimed in.

"Get out, that isn't one." She laughed. I was a bad person, but still my bad jokes tickled her. Hell, I'd miss her.

After a few more seconds of chugging away, her computer gave the device an all-clear. We leaned our heads together as the contents of the iPod opened up on her screen.

Stacks of files folders appeared, 183 in all.

Tigger blew a feathery lock of hair from her brow.

"So, you know what you're looking for here?"

"Nope." I looked and looked and kept looking, reading the names of the folders one by one. Many were just meaningless series of characters like L77JPLEQIN.

Tigger said, "Look, I'd like to help, but my peeps will be waking from their naps soon, and I know someone's going to want her snack."

"I hear you. Let's take a shortcut," I said. "Can you sort all the folders by date? Oldest first?"

It was done before I'd finished asking her for it. Tigger studied the screen and said, "Interesting. The two oldest are from 2001, but after that there are none that are older than last year."

I had her open the first folder, the oldest one, dated 2/4/2001. It contained one item, a single Excel file.

Tigger double-clicked on the icon and a spreadsheet

opened up. The field headings were all in Cyrillic characters, except for a logo at the top: TWEENSLAND. The alphabetical entries in the columns below were written in English, though. Names, addresses, phone numbers, credit card numbers, e-mail and IP addresses. The names all looked to be male; the addresses covered some two dozen states. There was a column of dates (1999 through 2001), another showing durations in minutes, and one containing what appeared to be usernames, aliases like *yancy77* and *popeyespappy*. The final column was what looked like a comments field filled with tidbits like "school principal," "deputy sheriff," "doctor," "seminarian," and more, entries like "softball coach," "scout master," and "two boys, Mike & Joseph."

It all looked so innocent, unless you knew what you were looking at. Which Tigger didn't—I'd told her about seeing Elena, but not what Elena had told me about the childhood Owl had rescued her from. For all Tigger knew, Tweensland was second cousin to McDonaldland.

Tigger started printing up the spreadsheet for me.

"Shit, Payton, there's ninety-two pages of this. You're going to owe me a ream."

I smiled at her. "Saucy wench, and you a mother now."

She giggled through her nose, it came out a snort.

"Let's see what's in the other 2001 folder," I told her.

She clicked to open it. Inside were over forty mpeg files. Video. Before I could say anything, Tigger double-clicked one at random. "Wait!" I yelped.

Had it been my computer, there would've been a time lapse of anywhere from five seconds to fifteen minutes during which I could've stopped it or at least given her a more coherent warning. But Tigger's computer was a hundred times faster and more modern, and so with ruthless efficiency the video clip sprang to life on the screen.

In the upper-right corner of the picture appeared super-imposed the same logo from the Excel file: TWEENSLAND. A line at the bottom said *Copyright 1999*. The time-counter on the computer's media player showed that the clip ran just over nine minutes.

A rangy twelve-year-old girl with shoulder-length chestnut-colored hair entered the frame beside an afghan-covered couch. She mumbled something, but it wasn't in English, nor was the reply she got from a coaxing female voice from behind the camera's lens.

Sweeping her hair out of her face, the girl looked into the camera, then unbuttoned and stepped out of her loose-fitting blue jeans. They fell in a heap at her bare feet. She tugged her brown sweater up over her head in a single cross-armed motion, ruffling her hair and revealing early breasts, small and nubby. Her skin was pale and smooth and iridescent; the curving innerwall of a seashell. Behind her on a small table stood three narrow cylinders on end—one flesh-colored, one kitchen-utensil white, one silver-enamel like a child's toy missile—and an uncapped bottle of baby oil. She lay down naked on the couch and reached for—

Tigger shut down the media player and the image instantly vanished—from the screen, at least. I had expected something like it but still been unprepared. I was frozen, transfixed—like a butterfly pinned to a collector's board. Only 20 seconds into the clip, longer if measured in heart-beats. I felt wrung out, twisted.

Tigger didn't say anything. I didn't dare say anything. Her printer went on spitting out the 92-page document.

She pushed back her swivel chair, steadied it, and stood up. She walked into her kitchen, where I saw her bend to take something from under her sink. She came back carrying a claw-head hammer.

I was tempted to defend my head with my hands, but

she walked right by me, plucked the iPod out of the docking cradle and dropped it on the floor. She squatted beside it and smashed it with the hammer. I didn't stop her. After five direct hits, it was ground up pretty good.

I said, "I think you got it."

She turned on me in a flash, such a look of black fury on her face, I did cover my head suddenly with my hands, afraid that she might lash out indiscriminately.

She shook the hammer like Thor.

"Payton, whatever you're involved in, take it out of here!"

"Look, I had no idea—"

She raised the hammer and I shut up. I heard her baby daddy groan in the bathroom, but if any of the others had woken up, they remained quiet.

Tigger said in a tense whisper, "People lose their kids for having shit like that on their computer, and you brought it in here—"

The last page sent to the printer stopped abruptly. The sheet of paper came out only three-quarters complete. The machine made a frustrated grinding sound, like a gnashing of teeth, before finally spitting out the interrupted page unfinished.

I took the pages from the tray, squared them on the desk like a deck of cards. Tigger put her hammer down on the nearest mousepad. We both just breathed in and out for a bit.

She said, "Sorry, Payton, but—"

"It's okay," I said. "Everyone has lines they don't cross. Or they should."

Tigger asked, "Was it important evidence?"

I shrugged. "I saw more than enough."

The girl's nakedness flashed in my mind again and I re-squared the printed pages.

"What's going on anyway?" Tigger asked. "All the

dates are like seven or eight years ago. Is the outfit that made those videos still in business?"

I shook my head. If the stories I'd heard were true, the head of the modeling agency had been arrested shortly after Owl left the country and the whole operation shut down.

"I think we're looking at a different sort of business now," I said. "I think someone's using this info to contact former customers. Maybe asking them how much they value their wives, their bosses, their parishioners never finding out what sort of videos they like looking at."

"Someone," Tigger said.

"Sayre," I said.

"Well, I'm no fan of blackmail normally, but if your girl's out there blackmailing pedophiles, making their lives hell, she's aces in my book." Her voice dropped. "But I don't know, Payton. I don't much like this. I just hope you're on the right side of it."

"Me, too," I said. "Listen, Tig. I'm sorry about—"

"—the mess? I made it." She prodded some of the fragments that had once been an iPod. "But do you see now why I'm moving out of New York? I don't want my daughter growing up in the middle of…all this."

There are bad men in the suburbs, too, I almost said. But didn't. Why piss in her bouillabaisse?

I thanked her, apologized again, told her I'd call her later. But I wouldn't, not unless she called first. I'd brought kiddie porn into her home—unintentionally, but I done it. I'd tainted her sacred trinity of computers with it. A stain, worse than any physical one I could've left. She would have found it easier to forgive me puking on her rug.

It felt like my bridges were burning, behind me as well as in front. But more important to me than making sure I landed on the right side when the smoke cleared, was not getting stuck anywhere in the middle with flames rising at either end.

I scooped up the bits of smashed iPod onto the stack of printed pages. I felt like that hapless rube left holding the bag at the end of the magic trick involving the handkerchief, the pocket watch, and the mallet. *May I have a volunteer from the audience? Now, sir, we've never met before...*

I walked away, leaving Tigger in front of her computers. The screensaver reappeared on the monitors, but the little train would have to roll over a lot of track before that other image was completely erased.

I went back down to my office.

No more Googling for answers. I was sick of what the Internet had to offer. I was going to get my information the old-fashioned way.

Earn it.

Chapter Fourteen
RESULTS MAY VARY

It was four o'clock. I called Paul Windmann to tell him that I was coming to return his stolen iPod. He said it wasn't a good time, that he'd come to my office later and get it.

I said I'd see him in ten minutes and hung up.

I put his four orange 50 Euro notes in my pocket in case he wanted a refund. And I took my gun, if the money wasn't enough.

Outside my building, the blond kid, FL!P, was loitering, seated on the brass-covered Siamese standpipe. He was holding his skateboard with two hands, scraping one edge against the concrete. Engrossed in what he was doing, he didn't see me until I was flagging down a cab. He ran over shouting, "Hey, dude, wait. I got something to give you."

He reached into a pocket of his baggy pants and tugged out a square cream-colored envelope and handed it to me.

The envelope was blank except for the embossed return address: The Peer Group, on West 21st Street in Chelsea. Peer. I remembered the call I'd answered in Owl's hotel room, the message that Michael Cassidy should call the pier office. Not pier, Peer.

The P.R. firm Tigger had mentioned, run by the un-French Coy d'Loy. West 21st Street in Chelsea. It was the same block as on those sales handbills I'd found in Owl's pocket.

The envelope's flap was unsealed. Inside was an invitation to a film festival screening that evening and the afterparty being held at The Wiggle Room on Rivington.

I folded it into my pocket.

"You'll go, right?" he asked. "I'm supposed to find out."

"Find out for whom? Your sugar mama?"

"Look, you goin' or not? It'll be worth it to you."

A cab pulled to the curb. I got in, but before I shut the door, I asked the kid, "You sic those three heavies on me? The Russians looking for Michael Cassidy?"

"You know where she is?" he asked eagerly, his eyes lighting up.

I slammed the door and gave the driver the address for the Crystalview, leaving the kid standing there.

I leaned back, reread the invitation. It was for a screening of *Reneg*, the new film by Ethan Ore.

The Peer Group. Chelsea. Michael Cassidy's ex-husband. Yeh, I'd be going to the movies tonight.

The cabbie let me off right in front of Windmann's building, just below the Holland Tunnel entrance, on Washington Street between Vestry and Debrosses. I'd never seen it before, but I'd read about its construction. One of the luxury condo high-rises that had gone up in recent years on a newly redeveloped waterfront, an area so beautiful it made you think you'd stumbled upon a completely different city.

The Crystalview had been open for business for over a year, but a postman friend of mine told me that so far they only had a twenty percent occupancy, or what only amounted to four full floors of the twenty-story stovepipe-shaped monstrosity.

Security cameras in the lobby, but no doorman and no one behind the obsidian-topped maplewood front desk. If eighty percent of their units were empty, they probably didn't have enough to cover the expense of a full staff yet.

To let people in, there was a fancy, high-tech house-

phone system by the front door, with a keypad and a direc-
tory showing apartment numbers with spaces beside them
for names, most of which were blank. I found Windmann's name and entered the corresponding number on
the pad. No answer. I tried again, but still no response. I
guessed he didn't want to see me. Well, too bad, I was
going to see him.

I entered the numbers of a few other units with names
showing, but no one else answered me either. Maybe the
place was a *Marie Celeste*.

An elevator door opened and a Chinese deliveryman
stepped into the lobby. He left a stack of menus at the
front desk, then held the door open for me on his way out.

I considered taking the stairs up to Windmann's, but his
apartment was on the nineteenth floor. I'd never make it.
I hadn't eaten anything since Wednesday dinner. I'd been
operating solely on stored fats and the buzz of the hunt.

My lonely elevator ride up to nineteen was uninter-
rupted. I felt the oppression of all those empty units
around me as I rose by and above them. Unhaunted spaces.
It gave me the willies, that vacancy, that vacuum, like a
potent sample of the nothingness that may attend us all
after death. Then my ears popped and I yawned some to
clear them. I hated elevators.

Ding. At the nineteenth floor, I walked down the hall
past five closed doors until I got to Windmann's and
stopped.

His door was ajar.

As a kid, I never got that pun, the door is a jar, whenever I came across it in one of the jokes-and-riddles books
I used to pore over, trying to figure out the answers. At
first I didn't understand it, but even once I did "get it," I
never thought it very funny.

I didn't think so now either.

I'd been encountering too many partially open doors

today. Normally in New York City that didn't happen so often, especially not with a pneumatic-hinged door like this, which should've closed silently of its own weight.

I could see why it hadn't: a corner of the inside front mat stuck out and blocked it. I couldn't tell if it had been placed that way intentionally or was just something that happened to happen.

After all, accidents happened.

I took out my gun and, keeping to one side, eased the door open with my fingertips before poking my head in. Nothing, no movement, no sound. A tall urn with three umbrellas in it stood under a hall mirror.

I entered crabwise, letting the door shut behind me, re-straightening the floor mat so it closed completely this time.

I inhaled through my nose and smelled it. An acrid odor wafting on the climate-controlled air. Sulfurous, it prickled my nostrils. The residue of a certain kind of burning. Cordite. Gunsmoke.

I lifted my gun and, very carefully, slid a live one into the chamber, trying to be quiet about it. But within that silent apartment it was like chiseling my name in stone.

I looked, I listened, I waited. More silence, more stillness, not even a reassuring gurgle from the pipes in the walls, everything was triple-insulated.

I walked forward, my sneakers whispering softly. There was a dusty outline on the parquet floor as if a narrow rug used to lie there.

At the end of the hallway, I came to a perfectly ordinary, empty room, lit a caustic orange by late-afternoon sunshine.

I stayed in the mouth of the hallway and helloed a few times, listening after each hello like I was measuring the depths and outer reaches with sonar. I got no response.

After a while, I felt a little silly, but only a little. I'd have felt a lot sillier getting shot. That stink in the air wasn't Etruscan Musk, a gun had gone off recently. So I waited some more before finally going in.

No one home. I walked around. No one in the kitchen or bedroom, or bedroom closet or bathroom. I returned to the living room, at a loss for what to do. Wait with folded hands? Start poking around? Raid the fridge?

I was drawn to the south-facing floor-to-ceiling window of high-stress glass. It overlooked the skyline of lower Manhattan and, at this height, provided a view of Ground Zero.

Prophetically named. Seven years later, still nothing more than ground, a zero. Just two days before, the first steel beam of the memorial museum had finally been put in place. Great, I thought, now if only they can agree on the curtains. What really should've been done was transform it into a memorial park. At least now it would be something, instead of a pit, an unfilled hole, an open grave. Not an idle allusion: the people who died that day were crushed and their remains remained, now permanently a part of the island itself.

I'd won $50 on a scratch ticket the night before and cashed it that morning. How lucky can you get? Saw the first tower hit on TV, thought it had to be a hoax. Tigger was already up on the roof standing against the maddeningly clear blue sky. Not one single fiber of cloud to obscure the southern view. No hoax, it was all really happening. Then it happened again. Later, when I had binoculars to my eyes and Tigger asked, "Are those ribbons? What are those swatches of color falling from the south tower?" I put the binoculars down, and with the naked eye they did look like bright ribbons or banners fluttering in descent, and the falling glass and tumbling *metal shards only a tinsel and confetti cascade. Tigger wept. I couldn't. Nothing surprised me after a while, until the next morning when the sun came up—I'd have taken odds that that was no longer a sure thing. I went out for the paper at dawn. Had to go to Grand Central for it, walking thirty blocks up a vacant First Avenue empty of traffic but teeming with ghosts, an invisible legion of thousands marching shoulder-to-shoulder toward their common commute. Along the way, every available surface—bus kiosk, plywood construction wall, payphone window—was papered with MISSING posters. Once upon a time, a missing poster would've quickened my pulse with the hint of a case, the scent of a chase. But no one was missing, they just weren't coming home.*

I felt dizzy, had to steady myself, my palm on the window glass. I felt the choppy throb of a news copter going by. I turned away. Get a grip, Payton, work, work it out, work is the answer. I asked myself, What would *Blue's Clues* do?

I went over and looked behind the couch, a big mahogany affair with fluffed-up cushions upholstered in wine-dark brocade.

And there he was.

Paul Windmann lay on the ground collapsed in the shape of a backward dollar sign. His body on a long narrow rug, the sort found in entryway halls. One corner of the rug was still bunched up where someone had grasped it to drag it and its load out of sight behind the couch. Done quickly before he bled out, since no marks of it showed on the floor. On the rug however, a wide blot of blood now surrounded him like a crimson moat.

In the fleshy hollow just below his chin was a raw bullet hole, an entry wound. Another corresponding hole was at the top of his forehead below the hairline. A not very big exit wound, a small caliber, I guessed.

Only I didn't have to guess, the gun glinted between his thighs. A square, silver-plated .22 neat as an Art Deco ashtray, exactly like the one I'd seen in Sayre Rauth's hands.

I sighed and shook my head. I had no interest in tampering with evidence. But that wasn't going to stop me.

I straddled Windmann's body, careful not to step in his blood. It was like playing a twisted game of Twister, trying not to put right foot down on red.

Tucking my hand inside my sleeve, I picked up the pistol. Its snub barrel was warm, and reeked. I flicked its safety on before sliding it into my back pocket.

I was disturbing a scene that a moment before might've passed for suicide. Now it was nothing but murder. The angle of the shot told me something, though. There'd been a struggle over the gun and Windmann had lost. Everything.

I left the place without searching further. This time I skipped the elevator and headed for the stairs. And walked directly into the view of a security cam mounted in a corner of the facing hallway.

I was in a cold sweat about it for a second, except there was nothing to do but tuck my chin in and pray. Walking underneath, I saw its cables hung loose in their factory-sealed plastic. It hadn't been hooked up yet.

A block away from the Crystalview, I found a payphone and dialed Paul Windmann's number, let it ring twice and hung up, just so my office phone wouldn't be his last incoming call in case anyone dialed *69.

Then I caught a cab, because my legs were feeling wobbly.

There was a small television screen fitted into the back of the driver's seat displaying a Channel 7 newsfeed. It ran an update on the death of Craig Wales, providing the latest tidbit: the police, it said, were searching for a

woman suspected of providing Wales with the fatal dose.
I switched off the TV and rode in silence.

The driver took an unexpected turn, swinging us cross-
town on Twelfth Street between Seventh and Greenwich
Avenues. It was a narrow ancient lane of unpaved cobblestones, picturesque but bumpy as hell. Maybe the cabbie
thought I was a tourist.

With every swerve and hard bounce, I felt the gun in
my rear waistband and the other in my back pocket
pressing against me, two loaded guns shoved in my back.
I fought the urge to take them out and recheck their
safeties.

I had the driver drop me a block from my building. I'd
become wary of my street door. No one was waiting outside it for me though.

I checked the opposite side of the street as I got
closer, watchful for any sudden movement. But it was the
end of a workday in Manhattan—there was nothing but
sudden movements. People running to make buses or to
beat that other guy to a disgorging cab. I gave up.

At the Siamese standpipe where FL!P had been seated
waiting for me before, I saw curved white scratches on
the sidewalk made by his whetting the edge of his skateboard like honing a tool.

I unlocked my street door and stepped in. Nobody
jumped me in the vestibule. It was a good start. How I
meant to go on.

The stairwell was empty. I climbed up. Eye-level with
the upper floor, I peered through the railing, but no one
was there either. I went the rest of the way up. My office
door was locked. I opened it, looked in. There was no one
inside. I entered and—

Jumped a foot as the downstairs doorbuzzer buzzed.
Shit. Couldn't even sit down.

Chapter Fifteen
HOT KISS AT THE END OF A WET FIST

I pushed the intercom's SPEAK button, said, "Yes?"

I pressed LISTEN and heard street noises, then a woman's voice asking, "Payton Sherwood?"

I pressed SPEAK again.

"Yes, who is it?"

LISTEN.

"Sayre Rauth."

SPEAK.

"What do you want?"

LISTEN.

"I thought more about...hiring you. May I come in?"

"Are you a good witch or a bad witch?"

SPEAK.

"Come on up."

I buzzed her in. And waited.

I breathed in and out, and braced myself for setting eyes on her again. I'd be cool, reserved, not betray with a single look or gesture the effect she illicit—no—elicited from me. Standard operating procedure was to never show how you really felt. Unfortunately, I've never been good at concealing my feelings. Easier not to feel at all.

Two short raps. I opened my door.

As soon as I saw her, I started bleeding again. She stood before me dressed in an airy, chocolate-brown silk blouse, a short pleated black skirt, and tasseled calf-high calfskin boots. She smiled at me and gave me a hungry look, and the cut in my forehead started to trickle. A droplet ran down and around my brow, then continued to descend along my left temple like a rivulet of sweat.

She must've seen it, but she didn't say anything. She must've seen even more, but if she did, she didn't give it away.

I excused myself, turned, and headed for the bathroom. Over my shoulder, I invited her in. "Be right with you."

I splashed cold water on my face and dried it. The cut had already stopped bleeding, wasn't very deep. To be on the safe side, I put on a Band-Aid. It made me look tough, in a cartoonish sort of way, like Sluggo from the comic strip *Nancy*.

When I returned, Sayre Rauth was still standing on the threshold, hadn't come in yet.

She raised both her arms up over her head.

"Want to frisk me? I might be armed."

"Skip it. I've softened my stance on deadly force. Come in, nunchucks, machetes, grenades, and all."

She looked disappointed, or at least she didn't put her arms down right away.

What the hell, I knew she didn't have her gun on her, it was in my back pocket. And I didn't need to pat her down to pinpoint her other lethal weapons.

She finally walked in and stopped in the center of the room and surveyed it.

"This is your office?"

"I also live here."

"Alone?" She cocked an eyebrow.

I nodded.

"You aren't married, then?"

"Not then, not now."

"Perhaps you are in a…relationship?"

"If so, no one's told me. Let's stick to business, Miss Rauth. Have a seat," I said. "But I gotta tell you up front, we're all out of toasters."

"What?"

"Nothing." I sat behind my desk. "It's just…you're like my fifth or sixth client today. Hell, I've lost count."

She crossed her legs. I watched the occasion; parts of me celebrated it. She said, calling my attention back up to her eyes, "Business must be good."

I lifted up my hand in mid-air and tilted it side-to-side like a life raft on choppy waters.

"It fluctuates. And there's the mortality rate to consider. Hiring me could be hazardous to your health, by the way."

"I'll risk it. Do you mind if I smoke?"

"I insist."

She smiled and shook some of her hair out of place. "Half the time, I don't understand you."

I lit a match for her cigarette but a breeze from the window blew it out. She used her own lighter and exhaled a steady stream of smoke through her nose.

"The other half of the time, I think you make fun of me because my English is not always so good. When I am nervous."

"Sorry, it's nothing personal really. Just my own private syntax."

"Sin tax?"

"That too. Mind if I bum a smoke?"

She offered me her pack of cigarettes. Foreign label, brand I never heard of. I lit up. Its dark-brown tobacco tasted like something that'd been scraped off of someone's cleats. I coughed, but only to the point of tears, no blackouts or brain aneurysms to speak of.

"So. You want to hire me. For what?"

"To find my sister."

"Your sister. She's lost?"

"We've lost touch. But…I believe you are in contact with her. Her name is Elena."

"Ah, yes, your sister, Elena. How come you want to find her?"

"It's complicated. She may be responsible for a robbery the other day. I think she stole property belonging to me, and some…sensitive data involving clients' personal information stored in my computer. Data I'd very much like to recover."

"Is that why you sent your associate Windmann to hire me?"

"Paul?" She didn't try to deny it. "I knew nothing about that until after he came to see you. Paul was listening over the intercom while you and I were talking earlier. He thought he was helping me by coming to speak to you. He thought you might be, well, Elena's…"

"Elena's Paul? Yeh, well, he did more than check me out. He hired me to do a job."

"What was this job?"

"He wanted me to get back something he claimed had been stolen from him."

"And did you…did you get it back?"

I slid the stack of printed spreadsheet pages across the desk to her. She only looked at the top one, didn't pick up a single page or bother asking what it was.

I said, "Why don't we cut out the missing sister story and start from scratch."

"Scratch?"

"Starting with the modeling agency you were a part of back in the Ukraine."

"You know about that?" She shrugged her right shoulder. "Okay, but I warn you, my story still may shock you."

"I'll risk it."

"You won't look at me the same way."

"I'll risk that, too."

She told me her story. It was much the same as what Elena had told me, and told in the same matter-of-fact way. At least this time I didn't have to fake a heard-it-all-before reaction.

She tried hard to explain to my western sensibilities how something like Tweensland could've come into existence and lasted so long.

"We answered an ad in the newspaper. Many girls came with their parents. The day you arrived you saw a clean establishment, a big studio with expensive equipment. A dozen men and women working there. It all looked very legitimate, and the money they promised, they delivered. They paid us by the hour, as much as twenty, thirty dollars an hour. It was a fortune, and no one questioned how they could afford to pay that much. They didn't want the money to stop coming.

"In the beginning they photographed you in dresses, pajamas, bathing suits. It wasn't until a couple of days later—once they'd gotten you comfortable—that they started saying now how about one more with it off?

"We were told to keep quiet and, in return for our silence, we got money, too—nearly as much as our parents were receiving, and all our own. Plus clothes and make-up, and food of course. It was heaven for a twelve-year-old girl—except for the fucking."

"Elena said most girls just posed naked," I said, "they didn't have sex."

Sayre drew on her cigarette, let the smoke out slowly. "I'm sure she'd prefer to remember it that way. Maybe she does remember it that way. I've got a hundred hours of video says otherwise. Maybe I'll show it to you sometime."

"No thanks," I said.

"The secret was well kept," she went on. "The girls knew, the owners knew, and the customers, of course. The parents knew or should have known, but if any of them ever complained, they were bought off. Or else blackmailed. They'd signed releases to have their daughters photographed; they could go to prison, too, lose their jobs, their families.

"But it rarely came to that. People took the money and kept quiet. It was a bad time for everyone."

I said, "Mostly for the girls."

She shrugged. "We weren't digging ditches or shoveling coal. There were worse things. I knew girls my age who made money having sex with their older brothers' friends. Less money, less clean, more dangerous."

"You almost make it sound like the agency was a good thing," I said.

"No, it was not a good thing. But there were no good things for us. Just bad and worse."

"How did you get out?"

"I enjoyed the camera, knew what it wanted. By the time I was thirteen, I was working behind it. I'd become the lover of the website's designer, Raphe. I assisted him, helped pick out photos, decide on themes, coach the other girls. At the same time, I learned as much as I could about the financial side of the operation, the start-up fees and monthly charges; how the money came in and where it went.

"It was very profitable, but I knew it couldn't go on forever. Problems started when some of the girls they'd used earlier on but were too old now began complaining. Word got around. There was talk of an investigation. The official in charge was contacted. It was decided a girl should go over to him and give a thorough and satisfactory...report. On her experiences with the modeling agency, you understand. I was that girl. And I was *very* thorough. More than satisfactory.

"It bought the agency a little more time. But only a little. More officials were becoming aware of what was really going on. Tweensland was an international enterprise and pressure was being applied by other countries.

I didn't want to be around when it came crashing down, so I made certain preparations. A good thing, too. Because—"

"Because the shit hit the fan," I said. "When Elena helped that American girl, Cristy, to get out."

"Yes. That was a big mistake."

"Whose? Elena's or Cristy's?"

"Tweensland's. They shouldn't have used Cristy. An American? People care about Americans. You can fuck Ukranian girls, Georgians, Latvians, Albanians, Kazakh, Serbs, Poles, no problem. But you put one American girl in front of the camera, you've dug your own grave. She was pretty, she was popular with subscribers—but it was a big, big mistake."

"But you don't consider what happened Elena's fault."

"*Her* fault? Of course not."

"She thinks you're angry at her."

"I'm not."

"She thinks you hate her. That you want to hurt her." She smiled sadly.

"Not at all. I'd like to help her if she'd let me. But instead she steals from me. Steals information I need that's very private. Very, very private. Information that's worth a lot of money, but only if it remains private."

She sat a minute not saying anything, then stood and walked around to my side of the desk. Leaning over me, she asked, "Do you know why I've told you this, Payton? All my dark secrets?"

I hazarded a guess. "Because you're going to kill me?"

She laughed huskily and shook her head. The sound filtered through the blades of her hair, languid and low.

"I don't kill men. I have other means." She leaned closer, including me within her silky aperture of hair. My immersion in her fragrance was a sweet asphyxiation.

"There are better ways," she whispered. "Ways more

favorable to both parties, more...agreeable. Wouldn't you agree?"

"I wooden. I mean, I wood. I—" I shut up. She had eyes.

She had more than eyes. Her lips on my lips.

Coming up for breath, she smiled down on me with that kinked-up joker's grin I'd just been tasting. Strands of her hair caught in my chin stubble like Velcro.

She said, "I'm sure that together, you and I, we can come to terms of mutual, mutual—"

I pulled her back down before she went reaching for my Roget's Thesaurus.

She might've just been auditioning me to take the place so recently vacated by Paul Windmann. A new front man for her operation, another not-quite-honest someone, maybe less ambitious than the last one, who'd apparently struck out on his own before getting struck down. She might have been fitting me for a suit of stripes or a burial suit. But right at that moment I didn't care.

She'd seduced Eastern Bloc government officials at age fourteen—what chance did I stand at resisting her at twenty-two? So why fight it? Make love, not war. And how.

She raised her arms and I lifted her blouse up and over her head. I had her turn around. I placed one hand on the back of her neck where her silky hair grew low, starting at the top nub of her vertebra.

My hands traveled forward and my fingers traced along the edge of her breasts, down her ribs, across her belly, around her back. Her buttocks tensed and she rolled round. Her face was flushed.

She laid her hands on my shoulders and shoved me down like I was the plunger of a detonator wired to high explosives.

My mouth slid along her belly while my hands went

beneath her skirt and felt her thighs and her bare buttocks. She wasn't wearing panties. She'd come prepared,
if that was the right word for it. Screw it, I was beyond
words.

My fingers and mouth found her and we were lost in
our separate and joint pursuit.

In a few minutes, I knew she liked me at least a little.
Much of it could've been faked for motives of her own, or
maybe just out of habit. But some things couldn't be
faked. I was sopping wet with her.

She raised my head by the hair and looked me in the
eyes.

"I want to see you."

And she did.

And so did the neighbors across the street because we
never got around to drawing the curtains.

Naked on my daybed a quarter-hour later, sticky and
sweaty and sated, she finally told me how she'd gotten
out of her country.

"I blackmailed one of the officials I'd met with and
convinced him it was in his best interest to rush through a
student visa for me. I came to America, bringing with me
a laptop I'd stolen from Raphe. It had copies of all his
files, all the business information about Tweensland.
That's when I decided to start my own company, Rauth
Realty—and for capital I contacted some of the website's
former customers to request their help."

It was the strangest pillow talk I'd ever been party to.
She told me how she'd started shaking down the website's former customers. It wasn't so easy. She had to
research them first, find the ones with the most to lose,
updating their records with current addresses by going
through their local newspapers in the library or online.
Then she'd had to contact them.

"My English was not very good, so it was hard. But in

time, it got better. And it was even a little fun," she said, and laughed to herself, her pert breasts jiggling. "The *fear* in their voices when it hits them what I'm calling about. These *men*. The stammering, the limp threats, and finally the pleading. They all end up sounding like little girls themselves.

"Soon I had enough money in an online bank account to start going to classes to learn the language better and reduce my accent. I was in America now. Here surface is everything. I came up with the name 'Sayre Rauth.' I hired Paul Windmann. I rented the townhouse."

"Sounds like everything was going peachy. So what went wrong?"

"Elena," she said.

"What about Elena?"

"I saw her. Just one day on the street. I was surprised —I look very different than I used to, but she…she looks the same. I followed her. She was living on First Street then; the place she is now on Avenue C is new. I found the name she was using and the name of the man she was living with. I ran a credit check on them and what do you think I found?"

"Lots of debt?"

"The opposite. A joint savings account they had totaling over seventy thousand dollars."

I whistled.

She nodded.

I said, "So naturally you wondered where that money had come from. Were you afraid she was running the same set-up as you, shaking down former customers?"

"It crossed my mind."

"That would really screw everything up, wouldn't it?" I said. "After all, the whole point of blackmail is exclusivity, the promise that no one else in the world knows. If more than one person knows the secret, why pay up?"

A quote from Benjamin Franklin popped into my head: *Three can keep a secret, if two of them are dead.*

Sayre nodded. "As you say, if it was true. I needed to know. So I contacted her. Politely, I swear to you. But she was spooked, started making threats. And then the robbery."

She propped herself up on an elbow and pulled some strands of hair out of her mouth.

She asked, "How much money would you need to live on for the rest of your life?"

"The rest of my life? Darlin', the way today is shaping up, probably what I got in my pockets right now."

"I'm being serious."

So was I, but I'd play her game of what-if if she wanted. Only problem was: all far-reaching numbers are relative, all currencies in flux; to have given her a truly honest answer, I would've had to project a figure phrased in gold ingots.

In my experience, money wasn't everything. For instance, I always got a much better return when I bartered in information. It provided a higher yield.

But she wanted a number, so I said, "Five million."

She huffed. "Dollars?" She frowned. She blew hair out of her eyes. "That's a lot of money. Too much, I'm afraid."

I stretched out, airing my matted armpit hair. "Sorry, but at least now you know what you're working for."

"Why so much? I would think from the way you live that—"

"Look, I never haggle. It's part of my charm."

"I only asked—"

"And I answered. Now let me ask you one: Did you kill Paul Windmann?"

"What?" Her mouth formed a moue. "Paul is—"

"Paul *was*," I corrected her.

"When...when did this happen?" She dug an elbow

into my chest, raising herself to look down at me. "I saw him at one."

"Uh-uh-uh, answer my question first."

"What question—did I kill him? Payton, you think I—ha! Funny time to be asking me that, don't you think?"

I could think of a funnier time to have asked it, but then again I wasn't in it just for laughs anymore.

"Answer the question."

"No. I didn't kill Paul. Are you satisfied?"

"I was satisfied before you answered the question."

"Was he shot?"

"Why, missing any bullets?"

She turned her head away, so all I saw was her long dark hair. With her face averted, her voice sounded thick. "I loaned Paul my gun this afternoon."

"You did what?"

"He said he needed it for protection. His keys were taken in the robbery. He was arranging to have all his locks changed, but until then…I gave him my gun." She turned back to me. "Now tell me, was he shot?"

"Yes."

I didn't know a word of her native tongue, but just then I learned about half a dozen of the worst ones you could say in it. When she simmered down, she asked, "Was my gun still there?"

"Yep. Looks like there was a struggle for it and it went off in his face."

She grimaced, but her voice held a note of resignation.

"And you thought it was me?"

I thought a lot of things. I thought she had a motive: Windmann wanted those files on the iPod for himself, either to take over her operation or, more likely, to blackmail her, threatening to expose her to some of those men on her list. A good enough reason enough to kill. I thought she was capable of killing anyone she set her sights on. But I didn't think she was stupid.

I said, "Nope."

I wriggled out from underneath. I stood and walked over to where my pants had ended up. I fished her gun out of my back pocket and tossed it to her. She caught it one-handed.

I said, "If you shot him, you wouldn't have left that behind."

She sniffed the barrel and reared back, her nose wrinkled. She looked at me. "I... Thank you."

"Don't mention it."

She grabbed the daybed's quilt and hugged it to her, laying the gun on top of it.

"It is very...considerate of you," she said.

"Stop. You'll make me blush."

"Why did you take it from the scene?"

I shrugged. "I wanted something to hold over you."

"But not anymore?"

I shook my head. "If I were you, I'd get rid of it right away. It's better than even money that's the gun killed Windmann."

She asked, "Do you know who did kill him?"

Maybe the woman who stole his keys and used them to steal the data. Elena. Though she'd seemed to be more of a knife woman.

"Not yet," I said. "But it's nothing for you to worry about. I, on the other hand..."

"What are you doing?"

I was putting on my pants.

"What's it look like?" I said.

"Where are you going?"

I shook floor dust off my shirt, put it on again and started buttoning.

"Sorry—but I'm on the clock. Got one more lead to check out." She had, god help me, a hurt expression on her face. "I wasn't expecting anyone…" I started. "Look, I'll be back in a couple hours. Stay. Help yourself to… uhm, there's water in the sink."

She held up her gun and pointed it at me, while pointing out to me, in a voice as dark and velvety as moonshadow, "I could *make* you stay."

She would have been doing me a favor.

Chapter Sixteen
MEAT MARKET

At the turn of the 20th Century, the Meatpacking District on the lower west side of Manhattan was a bustling distribution center for slaughtered livestock, back when there were still boats docking actively at many of the Hudson River's piers. But once transporting produce over roadways became more economical than doing so by water and the piers fell into disuse and disrepair, the life of that section of the city faltered and fell away.

Around the turn of the 21st, it was a veritable no man's land, though that's a bit of a misnomer, since one of the few trades to flourish there in the 1980s and 1990s was freelance male prostitution.

But now the early part of the new century had arrived and the area had undergone enormous changes. It began with many of the defunct and abandoned meatpacking establishments being bought up for art spaces and studios. Bars and lounges sprouted to cater to the people leaving the art galleries. Then trendy upscale nightclubs arrived to accommodate the people getting out of the bars. Finally, multi-million-dollar condominiums rose up to house the people who frequented and owned these businesses.

Except for those condos, on the surface little of the neighborhood had changed. But now outside the buildings instead of idling refrigerated trucks waiting for deliveries, there were air-conditioned limousines making pick-ups. Adding a bit of extra color tonight were two local news vans with roof-mounted satellite dishes. The media had been attracted by the film festival's association to the overdose death of Craig Wales, like sharks drawn by chum.

The screening was at the Lyndsford Gallery on Bethune and Washington Streets. In front of the main entrance was a red velvet cordon rope outside a door manned by a six-foot-two, 250-pound behemoth wearing a plain black t-shirt, a pair of stiff black jeans, and an expression that oscillated between hostile scrutiny and indifference.

I was glad I had an invitation to hand him for admission.

Once I was over the threshold, a perky redhead dressed in a neck-to-toe black leotard and miniskirt lightly grabbed me by the arm. I didn't protest, curious to see where this might lead, but just as quickly she let me go, leaving something behind on my wrist.

"What's this for?"

"If you go out to have a smoke, you can get back in."

I thanked her and looked at the plastic bracelet she'd fastened on my wrist, like the one I'd found inside the wastebasket in Owl's hotel room. Different color, but same make, same manufacturer. Different night, different color, but two pieces fitting together.

Looking at my hand, I realized I hadn't washed up after leaving my office—after leaving Sayre Rauth—and I grinned stupidly, remembering her sweet sounds, her fingers let loose in my hair. My jaw was sore and my tongue—

Someone bumped me from behind and I moved forward.

The wide, brightly lit lobby was almost full. A nice turnout, no doubt a result of all the press coverage the festival had received in the wake of Wales' death. People were there to see and be seen. I was just trying to see,

myself. Looking for a skinny woman with beet-red hair
and mesmerizing green eyes or a tall blond man who
looked like a Swede. I didn't see either one.

Instead, I faced a pond of strange faces talking, drinking
from plastic cups, eating hors d'oeuvres from paper nap-
kins, laughing, arguing, acting up, posturing and posing.
People wearing sunglasses indoors, sporting slide-rule
sculpted beards and haircuts set to expire at midnight.
I waded in among them, picking up snatches of their
conversations ("You know Prentice? Well, he's dying."
"*Why?*"), bits of gossip ("Stole his mother's jewelry to get
the money to finally cut his film"), and just plain inanities
("What's the name of that gray I like?").

Most of the guests were dressed in anonymous black
suits and dresses, while a few were decked out in unusual
eye-catching getups, as if sporting costumes from different
genre flicks—a period piece, a sci-fi techno-thriller, a
horror movie.

"Crabcake?"

"Wha?"

I turned. A tanned young man with curly sideburns
held a silver tray aloft, balanced on his fingertips.

"Nibbles!" I said, reaching out with both hands.

I swear the guy shrank back in alarm. I scooped up
four, left him two. Such a look! You'd think he'd been up
all night preparing them himself. I crammed one in my
mouth and shooed him away, because I saw a woman carrying a tray of chicken fingers coming by. I didn't want
her to think I was taken care of. I tried to catch her eye as
I ate another crabcake.

I guess I was looking the wrong way. An unfriendly
hand clamped down on my shoulder. I stuffed the other
two crabcakes in my mouth and turned.

Jane Dough, Moe Fedel's lovely rowdy, looking tough

and terrific in a dark blue pantsuit, had hold of me. From her left ear protruded something like a black bendi-straw.

She said, "I'll have to ask you to leave."

I said, "Mlff-mifuf wuhlff-mmulmuf. Mulmluff?"

She rolled her eyes. I chewed and swallowed.

"Working security?" I asked. "Moe must be under-staffed. How 'bout putting in a good word for me? I'm affordable."

"Go quietly."

"Go? Hey, I just got here, I—"

"—please," she said, a wintry smile on her face while her eyes continued to scan the crowd. "Just go now without a fuss. No scenes. Don't forget, I can take you."

I snorted. "You know something, Jane? You're nothing but a bully."

She met my eyes, but only briefly and barely, like when a sweater sleeve catches on a sliver of wood.

She smiled smugly.

"So, haven't found my name out yet?"

"Why bother? Whatever it is, 'Jane Doe' suits you better."

She didn't like the barb. She bared her teeth and whispered something into the tip of her bendi-straw.

I saw a pair of heads in the crowd revolve toward me and settle. Two stocky guys worked through the mob until they were on either side of me.

Jane, her eyes roving again, told the pair, "Show him out."

But before they could, up popped in front of me a Malibu-blonde whose black roots came up to my chin.

She was all-around tanning-booth golden, the color of a Thanksgiving turkey done to a turn, and smelled of cocoa butter. She wore a shimmering tasseled dress like a gun moll in a road company production of *Guys and*

Dolls. The low-cut top hugged tight across her chest, prominently outlining her breasts. They had the shape and gravity of two clutch purses full of nickels.

"Payton! You made it."

Jane was taken aback. Her eyes stopped scanning the faces in the crowd, went wide with disbelief.

"You know this man, Ms. d'Loy?"

"What? Of course, are you stupid? He's my *guest*! Who are *you*?"

"I'm—"

"I don't care. Payton," she linked my arm and towed me away, "come with me and meet people."

I craned my neck back, "See ya round, Jane."

I asked Coy d'Loy, "Do you know that woman's name?"

"Who? What, *her*? She's no one, just additional security we've put on. Had to because of—" she dropped her tone lower, then compensated by raising the volume of her voice "—the tragedy. What happened to poor Craig."

Heads turned and I noticed a smile tug on Coy d'Loy's cheek, wrinkling her too-tanned flesh like the skin on last week's butterscotch pudding.

She led me to a corner table where three people were seated. Two of them I knew, but wished I didn't. The skateboard kid FL!P dressed in a plain white t-shirt and chowing down on chicken fingers. And the Russian thug with the black satchel-handle mustache who'd choked me demanding to know where Michael Cassidy was. He was pouring himself a shot from a bottle of Stoli as I approached.

The third person at the table was an attractive young black woman in a shimmering copper-colored dress that conformed to her firm figure like electroplating. I gave her my full attention and she returned it with an amused grin.

Coy d'Loy said, "Now Philip here you already know." She indicated the blond kid, who didn't look up from his plate of food. "And I believe you've also met Gladimir."

The Russian shot me a hard look as he downed his drink and muttered, "Ya."

I said, "I've had the displeasure."

"Yes, well, I understand there was a slight misunderstanding earlier today between you two," d'Loy said. "Hopefully we can work past that. But first, I'd like you to meet Moyena. Moyena, Payton."

I shook her hand and she dazzled me with a smile.

"Moyena is my newest associate. We at The Peer Group are expecting great things from her. You wouldn't believe the trouble we had luring her into the fold."

"Just playing hard to get," Moyena said, a touch of irony in her low, lazy voice. "Nice to meet you, Payton."

"Back at you."

She tilted her head to one side and commented, "You're actually quite handsome, Payton." Like somebody had been contesting the fact.

Coy d'Loy tittered in agreement. "I was just thinking the same thing."

I wasn't surprised; I always get a bit more attractive when I'm working on something. A subtle form of lycanthropy triggered by the scent of prey.

I asked the Russian, "How 'bout you, Gladys? Still think I'm pretty?"

The blond kid laughed through his mouthful of chicken.

Gladimir stared hard at me with his nearly black eyes, like he was measuring me for a four-ply plastic trashbag. He poured himself another shot.

"Okay," I said, "so we all agree I'm the best looking boy since Michelangelo carved the David. What am I doing here, Ms. d'Loy?"

"Call me Coy. And, please, sit down. Would you care for something to drink?"

I shrugged. "A bottle of beer, if the cap's still on."

"Very good. I'll join you. Philip, do the honors."

It wasn't a request, but an order. The blond kid hopped to it; with his all-consuming dream of being famous one day, he knew which side his bread was buttered on, and now so did I. Ms. Coy d'Loy was calling all the shots.

When he was gone I asked her, "What's with the kid? Relative of yours?"

"Philip? No, no relation. But he proves himself very useful to the group. He's been with us several months now and I have no regrets for taking him on."

"Where'd you pick him up, Boy-Toys 'R' Us?"

She patted my hand, a little too sharply I thought, more like a slap.

"I see I'm going to have to watch what I say around you. No, he just showed up at the offices one day in April, looking for a job. I took him on as a trial—completely off the books, of course. And he's proven himself useful. He's very ambitious. Wants to learn the business from the ground up. That always helps."

Helps what? I thought, but didn't ask because he'd returned with our beers, two Pacifico Claras. I popped my cap on the table's edge. Coy d'Loy didn't even look at hers, just left it unopened on the table.

"So," she said, "you must be wondering why I arranged to meet you this evening."

I took a swig of my beer.

"Not really. I can make an educated guess. You want to lay your hands on Michael Cassidy. You think I can help."

"You got it in one. That's right."

"The question's why. What's she to you?"

"We represent Ethan Ore. He's worried about her.

With his new film ready for release, we can't afford to
have our client distressed or...worse."

"What's worse?"

"If you know anything about Michael Cassidy, you
must know she's hardly a stable person. There's no telling
what she's capable of, what harm she could do to him.
And I don't mean just professionally. She's been known to
be violent in the past. Especially when she's taking drugs."

I said, "Sounds like it's a good thing she ran off with
another man then." I didn't mention names.

"Maybe. If she'd stayed away. But we know she's back
in the city."

"What makes you so sure?"

She gave me a withering smile.

"Please, Payton, let's not waste time. We won't make
any headway if we don't put all our cards on the table."

I shrugged, took another pull on my beer.

"I'm not disputing it, I only asked how you know."

She sighed.

"Maybe it will simplify matters if I tell you that the Peer
Group also represented Craig Wales. Last night, Michael
Cassidy appeared at the premiere of Craig's film. You
see, there was a scheduling change. Originally, Ethan's
movie was to be screened last night, but he was bumped
back because we decided it was a better slot for Craig's
film. But Michael Cassidy didn't hear about the change
and she showed up to confront her husband. She stayed
and attended the afterparty. I think you know how that
ended."

"She and Wales went off together to shoot up and he
ended up overdosing on bad junk."

"Exactly. It should've been her."

"What do you mean by that?"

"Just that she's the junkie—isn't that what junkies are
supposed to do? Poor Craig was just experimenting.

To the best of my knowledge, it was his first time using heroin."

"Tough break," I said, then drained the rest of my beer. "He should've stuck to wine coolers. You going to drink that?"

She slid her unopened beer over to me. I opened it and drank.

She said, "Before any of us knew what had happened to Craig, she'd slipped away. I believe the police are looking for her in connection with his death, as the supplier of the drug that killed him."

"Then maybe you should be talking to them instead of me."

"I don't think so. A man came to the Peer Group offices this morning, saying he was acting on Michael Cassidy's behalf. He wanted our help in contacting Ethan. You see, Ethan had moved and changed all his numbers during her...absence."

If she wanted to dance around the subject of Michael Cassidy running off with Law Addison, it was okay with me. I was thinking of the handbills I'd found in Owl's pockets, sales fliers for two stores in Chelsea located on the same street as the Peer Group's offices.

"What's that got to do with me?"

"Please. We know he's an associate of yours. When we told him we couldn't possibly give Ethan's information to anyone but Michael Cassidy *personally*, he walked out. I instructed young Philip here to follow him, hoping he'd lead us to her. Instead, he went to your office."

"Not quite all the way to my office," I said.

"No, not quite."

I asked her, "Did he explain to you why Michael Cassidy couldn't go in person to your offices? No? Well, it seems she thinks someone tried to kill her last night. Whoever it was got Craig Wales instead by mistake."

She frowned at me. "Do you believe that?"

"Enough of it."

"It sounds to me like a junkie's paranoid dream. You see that, don't you? You understand why it's so important we get to her before the police do. She needs professional help."

"Police are professionals."

"Medical help."

"Oh. So what medical school did you—"

"Enough!" Gladimir bellowed. I guess the vodka had done its trick. He reached a bear's paw across the table, grabbed a hunk of my shirtfront, and twisted it. "Tell us where she is! Now!"

For a second I considered smashing my beer bottle across his face. Except it was still half full and I hated to waste.

I grinned at him instead. Smiles cost nothing.

"Gladimir, comrade, buddy," I said, "hasn't Coy here told you why she really wants to find this woman? From that look on your face, I guess not. She isn't interested in helping Michael Cassidy—all she wants is to get a line on the guy who ripped her off. Law Addison, the man Michael Cassidy ran off with."

I don't know how much of it Gladimir was processing, but it interested him enough that his grip loosened up on my shirt.

He turned to Coy d'Loy. "What's he saying?"

"I've no idea."

"Then try this on for size," I said. "Up until this past Spring, the Peer Group—like many of its clients—was heavily invested with a financial outfit called Isolde Enterprises, run by a man named Lawrence Addison. The problem is Addison turned out to be a con man and an embezzler and he did a disappearing act with all their money. The way I heard it, the business almost went under, until someone stepped in and bailed them out, becoming a new silent partner. Sound familiar? I make that new partner to be you, Gladimir."

"So?"

"As ye reap. Ms. d'Loy had no choice in the matter, because it looked like she'd never be able to recoup those lost funds. All of Isolde's assets are frozen pending Addison's trial, a trial that will never take place unless Addison is apprehended. Which was an unlikely prospect until Michael Cassidy resurfaced yesterday. Now suddenly the chances aren't so slim."

Gladimir let go of my shirt entirely and sat back in his seat. "I don't understand."

"What do you think is going to happen if the Peer Group gets all that money back? How important are you going to be to her business then, Glad? If she turns up Addison with Michael Cassidy's help, how long's it going to be before she sets out to sever her ties with you?"

I let the question hang there, and so did everyone else. It was a rhetorical question anyway.

What I was saying seemed to penetrate into Gladimir's skull. He frowned so that the curve of his lips matched that of his downturned mustache.

He asked Coy d'Loy if this was true and she denied it too quickly to be convincing. He stood and towered over her. For a second, I thought he was going to hit her and I'd have to break the beer bottle across his face after all, so I chug-a-lugged what was left, down to the foam.

But he didn't smack her, just turned and strode away.

She didn't try to stop him, instead leveled her gaze on me.

"Now that he's gone," she said, "maybe we can work out some sort of deal. A finder's fee if things turn out the way they should. Say five thousand dollars?"

"No thanks, Ms. d'Loy. I've already got a job. You

happen to be part of it. But thank you for the beers all the same." The ceiling lights dimmed, brightened, dimmed, and brightened. "I think it's time to go to the movies."

I stood up, turned and looked down at Moyena.

"It was nice to have met you. Sorry we spent the whole time talking shop."

"No problem. I found it fascinating. Now if I ever need a private investigator, I'll know who to call."

"Be good," I said, then fell in with the crowd filing into the main screening room.

I was careful picking where I sat down inside, choosing a seat directly in front of two frumpy older women who appeared the least likely in that crowd to have murder in their hearts. But what did I know?

The houselights dimmed everywhere but directly in front of the translucent screen. A young man stepped onto the small stage and faced the crowd to a small round of applause.

He was slightly stoop-shouldered and had small lozenge-lensed eyeglasses and a mini Art Garfunkel afro. He introduced himself as Ethan Ore and said he hoped everyone would enjoy his effort. He bowed his head and stepped to one side as the little theater went to black and the movie began with the bold-lettered title, RENEG, emblazoned on the screen.

It wasn't my kind of movie, but I followed it enough to tease out the story. The film centered around a young couple, a talented young actor/director married to a heroin addict, and their joint struggles with getting her off the drug and his to make it as a serious artist. A real flight of imagination, this one.

There was a funny sequence among the prevailing pathos in which one potential producer turns the husband down for an upcoming project because he finds out the wife is a notorious heroin addict, while a second pro-

ducer turns him down for another project upon finding
out the young man himself is not sufficiently tied into the
underground drug culture—unable even to help the guy
score a dime bag of weed.

In one scene, presented in a split screen, the husband
tells a friend how much progress his wife is making kicking
the habit; meanwhile she's shown alongside, cooking up a
spoon of smack under a highway underpass.

It was a drama full of long pauses and I couldn't say I
enjoyed it much. As the movie drew to a close, the wife—
after experiencing a hallucination in which a stray feral cat
spoke to her in the voice of her dead mother (provided by
Olympia Dukakis)—checked herself into a rehab clinic
to finally get clean. When she provided her medical history to the admissions nurse, it came out sounding like a
penitent murmuring in a confessional.

It was a powerful scene, with a really moving perfor-
mance by the young actress, and I thought it should have
ended the film.

Instead there was an additional three minutes tacked
on. That's both how it looked and how it felt; even the
medium was different, changing from film to digital. It
jarred the senses and sensibility.

It was a one-camera shot, the scene focusing on the
woman's husband at the rehab clinic on visiting day. He's
seen sitting in the waiting room before switching to the
office of the administrator, who tells the husband that
the wife wants to discharge herself from care and return
home.

"Is she ready?" the man asks.

The administrator tells him, "My professional opinion
is no. She's made great strides, but it's still too soon for
her to be released. Falling back into her old patterns
would be inevitable."

But it turns out it's not up to the administrator or to

the doctor, the decision rests entirely with the husband. Because she checked herself in voluntarily with his help, unless he co-signs her release, she cannot leave.

The scene ends with the husband walking back to his car still carrying the magazines and candies he'd brought to give to his wife, and talking on his cell phone saying, "I think I can make that three o'clock meeting after all." The End.

The houselights came up to applause and murmurs.

Ethan Ore stepped out on the stage once more to take a short bow and invite everyone to the afterparty.

I was already working my way to the aisle so I could intercept him on his way out.

"Mr. Ore?"

"Yes?" He was looking past me, searching faces, probably for financial backers and prospective distributors for his film.

"It's about your wife."

That got him looking right at me, and looking a little afraid.

"Michael? What about her? Who are you?"

I told him who I was, that I'd been in touch with his wife, and that I needed to talk with him in private.

"I can't right now, I have to...I can't right now. Are you going to the afterparty?"

I said yes. He said he'd speak with me there, then eased himself around like someone performing a vertical limbo.

Outside, some people were climbing into limos while others were competing for taxicabs. I decided to walk.

I stopped at a newsstand and bought a pack of American Spirit cigarettes with the last ten bucks in my wallet; I was living large. I lit up and smoked.

I'd learned a lot, but there was still a lot left to learn, and I was getting a creepy feeling I wasn't even asking the

right questions—been asking the wrong ones all day—
and that I was running out of time. It was silly. What dead-
line was I trying to beat?

It was half-past seven, dusk. The setting sun in the
hazy western sky was the same salmon color as the end of
my cigarette.

I turned away from it and walked east, following my
shadow, a long narrow stain spilling out in front of me.

Chapter Seventeen
THE WIGGLE ROOM

I decided on the way to stop by the office first.

When I walked in, Sayre Rauth was gone. I sat down behind my desk to check messages (none) and discovered that the printed pages of the Excel spreadsheet were gone, too. My first thought was that Sayre had probably taken them in order to destroy them, but then I realized something I probably should've hit on sooner.

If Owl had taken the data from her computer in order to pressure her in some way, it wouldn't have been enough just to copy the files. How much good was a copy, after all? Some—but the thing that would've made it really worth a lot as leverage was if after copying them he'd purged the originals, deleted the files from her hard drive. That way, assuming she hadn't backed up her files, his copy would be the only copy. If she ever wanted her hands on the files again, she'd have to do whatever she was told. When you consider the risk Owl had taken by staging a break-in, you had to figure he'd have taken this extra step to ensure it had been worth it.

So now Sayre Rauth had her files again—the spreadsheet anyway, not the videos. But the spreadsheet was the key to the kingdom. I sat and smoked another cigarette. It started my stomach working and I went into the bathroom to take a dump. But before I even sat down, I noticed I was out of toilet paper. I went into the kitchen, but I was out of paper towels as well. The best I could manage was a stack of coffee filters. I brought them with me into the bathroom and sat down to empty out.

The funny thing was…

The rising stink stunk sweetly of Sayre Rauth.

I'd ingested her, her saliva, her slick sweat, her warm and tangy effluvia. Savoring her flesh; inhaling her exhaled breaths; absorbing her through my pores. More than just the scent of her perfume was left on me and in me.

In all likelihood I'd never see her again. She'd gotten what she wanted.

Did I care? Did I ever.

I stubbed my cigarette, quickly rinsed off in the shower, then dressed to go out.

Before heading over to the Wiggle Room, there was a stop I had to make.

It was balmy outside, the air hazy as if seen through gummy eyes. The sun had dropped below the rooflines and evening was pooling in the valley of buildings, but the streetlights hadn't come on yet. Getting dark earlier now; in three weeks, it would be autumn. But some of the thrill of summer still remained.

Though it wasn't the weekend yet, the city was already festive. Thursday was the new Friday night, the night that native New Yorkers went out to party, a day before the out-of-towners and tourists congested the streets and the club lines.

Car horns bayed like penned-in dogs calling to each other in the night, one horn triggering off four others.

I walked down Second and turned left onto Tenth Street, then right onto First Avenue, making an Etch-a-Sketch-style diagonal line toward my destination in Alphabet City.

Walking by Coyote Ugly, I was accosted by a pint-size girl in a black leather halter top and miniskirt who was standing out front delivering a "step right up" spiel, trying to drum up business for the bar. I guess the sign declaring FREE SHOTS WITH EVERY PITCHER wasn't getting it done. I was in a hurry, I had things to do, so I tried to slip by her quickly. But she wouldn't be denied her fun, and I was too damn polite to just ignore her.

She yelled out to me, "Spell cop!"

"C-O-P."

"Spell shop!"

"S-H-O-P."

"What do you do at a green light?"

"Stop."

"GO!" she shouted and laughed and waved me away like a traffic cop gesturing, *Move it along, bub*.

Only it made me stop after a few strides and think about just how easily I'd been fooled. Some glitch in my brain, I guess. I wondered what other blind spots I wasn't seeing.

The streetlamps flickered to life as I crossed the avenue and turned down Ninth toward Tompkins Square Park.

The road, black during day, was now lit stark orange by the city lights, and the surrounding buildings were darker silhouettes, looming shadows of various sizes.

I walked around the park instead of going through it. On Seventh Street, I passed three old Latin gentleman on the sidewalk seated on lawn chairs in front of a color TV attached to a power cord coming out of a ground floor window. They were watching the baseball game, Yankees at Tampa Bay. The cheerful announcer rattled off the balls and strikes of a behind-in-the-count batter. "One away."

Somebody's air conditioner from high above dripped water on me and I jumped like it was death's own bony finger tapping me on the shoulder.

At Avenue B, I turned right and headed down to Fourth

Street and the townhouse where I'd first spoken to Sayre Rauth.

All the windows were dark. I went through the gate and up the steps to ring the bell. I waited, but got no answer. When I looked to the left, the brass plate was missing from beside the door. No more Rauth Reality, or Realty, or whatever it had been. Gone now, and I guessed so was she. I wasn't completely surprised.

I left, went back to Avenue B, walked down to Houston Street and across it. A fire engine rolled by, its speakers blaring the War song, "Low Rider." I walked by Katz's Deli and turned right onto Ludlow, down past Stanton, until I came to Rivington Street. The Wiggle Room was on the southeast corner.

The afterparty was a private affair with a burly neckless doorman keeping out the general public. It was a good thing I'd remembered to bring the invite along. I flashed it and he let me pass.

Inside there were more people than had attended the actual screening. The bar was to the right. I made straight for it, but had to wait ten minutes before the bartender took my order. And then there was an uncomfortable moment when I tried to pay for my 7&7 with a 50 Euro note. It was the only cash I had. Fortunately, a German guy at the other end of the bar agreed to change it for me, handing me two twenties and pocketing the difference. *Danke schön*.

I was about to start making my way through the crowd, to the rear of the bar, in search of Ethan Ore, when, all smiles, he walked through the front door arm in arm with Moyena. I kept my back to him and watched him in the bar mirror until he was just behind me. I turned.

"It's time for our talk," I said.

It took him a second to place me, but as soon as he did the smile melted from his face.

"Oh. Yes, but…wait here. I have to…I'll be right back."

"Don't be long."

I waited, sipping my drink—it tasted faintly of dish-washing liquid—and listened to the bar chatter.

A tall skinny white guy with a wispy chin beard like Shaggy from Scooby-Doo was talking a mile a minute at a well-dressed Asian man who looked half-asleep.

"A million people fucked-up! Why? Cuz there's no meaning to their lives! Why? Corporations have bled the taste out of life! Why? So they can sell you *things* that'll bring it back! Like the antidote to the poison they're poisoning us with! But they'll never *cure* you. Why? Cuz there's more money in *treating* the illness than curing it! Why?"

I stopped listening, I already knew the answer.

I downed the rest of my drink and was thinking about going out to have a smoke when Ethan Ore finally reappeared.

"Sorry about that."

"You might be," I said, "after you hear what I've got to say."

"What do you mean?"

"Your wife's in a lot of trouble, Mr. Ore."

"She's not my wife. We're separated."

I didn't argue the point.

"When was the last time you spoke to her?"

He thought for a long moment and didn't meet my eyes.

Finally he said, "She called me this afternoon, about three o'clock."

"You know she's back in the city?"

He nodded.

I asked, "Is Law Addison with her?"

"What? Why would he be with her?"

"They ran off together, didn't they?"

He didn't answer the question. I got tired of waiting.

"There're people looking for her who think she did. But frankly, I'm beginning to wonder."

"Wonder what?"

"Do you know where your wife is right now?"

He shook his head.

"Where was she when you spoke to her?"

"She wouldn't tell me. Do you know?"

"Yeh, I do," I said, amazed—not for the first time—by how many lies you sometimes have to tell to get to the truth.

"Where is she?"

I said, "We'll come back to that later. Maybe. If I tell anybody, it should probably be the cops."

"Why would—" He stopped himself, looked side to side, then, lowering his voice, asked, "Why would the police want to know? What has she done this time?"

"There's a good chance she's going to be arrested in connection with the death of Craig Wales. She provided him with the drug that killed him. She might even be charged with murder."

"No. It wasn't her fault."

"How do you know that?"

"She told me. She said someone tried to kill her by giving her bad drugs. Too strong or something. Only it was Craig who shot up first and it killed him."

"Who does she think is trying to kill her?"

"Law Addison, who else?"

"Why?"

"He must've found out she—"

The bartender came over, a big bear of a man with a black Rasputin beard streaked by gray. He saw my empty glass, none in front of Ore, and asked, "Another? And how 'bout you?"

Ore ordered a vodka tonic and I had another 7&7. It

was weaker than the first. Ore downed three-quarters of his drink in two swallows.

I prodded him on, "Must've found out what?"

"That she had…double-crossed him."

"How?"

"Well, she didn't go off with him the way they planned."

"So you know she never really ran off with Law Addison?"

"I know now. I didn't at first. I mean…I really thought she had gone with him. That's what the police told me, it's what the press kept reporting. What did I know? We hadn't been living together since the end of last year."

"So when did you find out the truth?"

"Not until, like, the end of July. I got a call from this rehab clinic up in Ithaca, telling me Michael was a patient there, asking me to come up. It wasn't until I visited her that she told me the truth herself, that everyone had it all wrong. She'd never run away with Addison. All that time she'd been at this hospital getting herself cleaned out. She wanted us to get back together."

He shook his head and finished off his drink, then started chewing the ice.

"Did she tell you why she didn't go with Addison?"

He nodded.

"Someone talked her out of it. She'd been on her way to meet him. They were going to drive to some place in Pennsylvania where he'd set up a fake identity or something. He was packing up his car. She was waiting for her dealer to drop off a load of drugs. But instead of her dealer, this other guy showed up."

"Who?"

He shrugged. "I don't know. Maybe the same guy Coy told me showed up at the Peer Group offices this morning. He knew all about her, all about Law's plans to skip out, and he told her how they didn't have a chance. That they'd only get caught and she would go to prison for aiding and abetting a fugitive. She was pretty strung out at the time and this guy offered to help her out."

"Help her out how?"

"He told her he'd keep her out of it. He saw what bad shape she was in, she was hitting rock-bottom. He arranged to send her away for treatment, to this clinic up near Ithaca. And she went. And that's where she's been all this time, in rehab."

"Why didn't you tell the police any of this? They still think your wife's a fugitive."

"She begged me not to, and…and I was trying to complete my film. I couldn't afford to be dragged into some… God! I still can't afford to be connected with any of this. I wish she'd never come back here. I wish she'd just stayed where she was or else…" He didn't finish the thought.

But it reminded me of his film's final scene, the one that had seemed tacked on, in which the husband refused to co-sign his wife's hospital release.

He gripped my arm suddenly and spun me on my bar stool.

"Look, you're working for my wife, right? Tell her I need her to go away again. Just for a little longer until I get my film straightened out. She called me this afternoon for money. Tell her I'll pay her anything. But I can't afford for her to be here now. She'll fuck everything up, I know she will. She always does."

"I think she's got bigger problems than that right now."

"Please," he said. "Tell her I still care about her. Tell her there's a real chance we can get back together. Tell her anything! But please help me keep her away."

From behind us, a voice said, "Keep who away? I hope you don't mean me?"

We turned and faced Moyena. She was smiling, but had a troubled look in her eye. She placed a hand alongside Ethan Ore's cheek.

"Ethan, are you okay? You look sick?"

"What? No, I'm fine. We're just talking about the film."

"Well, there are more important people you should be talking to right now. I've got a man from Lionsgate at the table in the back. He wants to meet you."

Ore's distress seemed to evaporate.

"Really? Where?"

He slipped off his stool and let Moyena lead him away. Neither one of them said a word to me in parting. For that matter, I was distracted too. My thoughts were in a jumble.

Someone put a buck in the jukebox and Patsy Cline's "Crazy" started playing.

I felt a little like that myself. I'd been looking at things the wrong way all day. I was trying so hard to see things right that it took me a few moments to realize there was someone talking to me.

I looked to my right and faced an old man seated on the barstool next me.

"I'm sorry, what did you say?"

He was a stubby old guy with bulbous features and no chin. He wore black hornrim glasses, and on his head was a stiff gray pompadour. He looked vaguely familiar. He was about the age of one of my dad's golf buddies, but I doubted it. Given the crowd, I wondered if he was a character actor, someone I might've seen in a commercial or soap opera on TV.

He said, "Oh, I was just asking if you were one of these creative people. A film director, maybe."

"Me? No."

"What do you do?"

I lied and said, "I'm a writer."

"Oh, well, there you go, that's creative. I thought so. What do you write?"

"A little of everything."

"Really? What are you working on now?"

"Oh, I…don't like to talk about it while I'm still writing it. It dissipates the energy you should put into the work when you talk too much about it beforehand."

The old man nodded his head judiciously.

It sounded good to me, too. Hell, maybe I would try being a writer. Nahh. I was broke enough as it was.

The old man bought me another drink. While he was paying for it, his back to me as he counted out his money, a couple of guys passed by and one of them pointed his way. The guy said to his friend, "Hey Rick, isn't that your Mr. Gower guy?"

Rick saw me looking at him and told his friend to shut up.

The name rang a bell. The bar's cash register opened.

"Down the hatch," the old man said, handing me my drink. We clinked our glasses.

I took a sip. It was stronger than the last one, not a 7&7, more like a 14&3.

Mr. Gower. The name echoed in my mind. Mr. Gower. I took another sip.

Don't hit me, Mr. Gower, that's my bad ear.

I had it. That's why it sounded so familiar. Frank Capra's *It's a Wonderful Life*. I've always been good at Trivial Pursuit. It was the name of the shopkeeper George Bailey worked for as a kid, and later he appears as a disgraced wino in a bar.

I took another swallow of my too-strong drink.

Because Mr. Gower was an ex-pharmacist who Jimmy Stewart hadn't been around to stop from mixing up a prescription with poison.

I stopped the rim of my glass against my lips and it

tapped a tooth. I felt funny. And not the good kind of funny.

I was also remembering where I'd seen this old man twice before on separate occasions. The first time that morning, almost running into him in the lobby of the Bowery Plaza on my way out. The second time on Tigger's computer monitor, "I was in the background in a photo taken by Craig Wales before he died."

I turned to the old man and asked, "Whadyousay?"

"I said nothing."

"Fuck."

His face seemed to balloon out of proportion and fritter. His ears looked much too big, like tiny fetuses on either side of his head. I didn't like looking at him, but I couldn't stop. It was fascinating, like communing with a sentient lava lamp.

"Diden you jes..." I lost my train of thought, it had derailed and flung passengers and luggage all over the tracks.

I looked around for the conductor and instead saw the blond kid FL!P by my side.

"You don't look so hot, dude."

"Nigh...Thor...neither do I."

The old man said, "We should help him get some air. Take his other arm."

I said in Brooklynese, "Out you pixies go. Through the door or out da winda." Shit, now what movie was that from?

They escorted me outside, but it didn't make me feel any better. I couldn't figure out why I was still hearing Patsy Cline singing. If I was hearing it at all. It could've just been inside my head like everything else.

I tried to put my feet up and rest, but I was still standing.

Somebody or somebodies huddled me into the back seat of a car.

"Wear...?"

I forgot what I'd been about to say.

Couldn't have been very important then.

Nothing was very important then.

It gave me a chance to close my eyes and forget.

Sweet forget, how I've missed you.

Chapter Eighteen
HIDE NOR HAIR

I came to in a strange room. It reminded me of what it was like to be a baby again, you fall asleep one place and hours later wake up somewhere else entirely.

I sensed I wasn't alone. I cranked open my eyes. When you live alone, you're used to waking up alone, so waking up now with two people staring down at me was disturbing.

I tried to sit up, but I couldn't. I was strapped down to some makeshift operating table. Also disturbing.

Why had I immediately made that snap judgment of 'operating table'? Because of a chemical smell in the air? Or the greenish glow from a fluorescent ceiling fixture? Or was it the fact that the old man, Mr. Gower, had a pair of latex gloves on and was opening up the package of a brand new syringe?

The blond kid, FL!P, was fidgeting on a metal stool, playing with a set of scales on the marble countertop.

. Mr. Gower said to him, "I'll need your help with this part." He fitted a new needle onto the tip of the syringe.

FL!P hopped off the stool.

I said, "Whoa, whoa, whoa, hold up." I was trying to gather my wits, but it was like reconstructing a blown-apart dandelion. "What's on the menu?"

Mr. Gower said, "Lie still, we are going to ask you some questions."

"Ask away. Don't delay another second. But whatever you're doing there, stop! You don't need that, whatever it is. I'm more than willing to tell you whatever you want to know."

Gower ignored me, spoke to the blond kid.

"Roll up his sleeve."

I started to struggle. It was only a makeshift set-up, how sturdy could it be?

Pretty damn sturdy. I only got about a centimeter of give out of the straps.

"Hold up!" I said. "Listen, kid, this isn't good, don't do this."

"Just tell us where Michael Cassidy is," he said.

"Done!" I said.

"You know where she is?"

"Of course." And this time I wasn't lying, because suddenly I *did* know. Knew all along, I guess, just never put it together. Amazing how the threat of death can galvanize one's mind. Something that had been bothering me earlier finally came into sharp focus. The stuff emptied from my pockets after Michael Cassidy hit me on the head in Owl's hotel room. Now I knew exactly what'd been missing: the room's magnetic card key.

"Where is she, then?"

"I'll take you to her," I said. "Right now. Just get me out of this thing. There's no need for—"

"His sleeve," Mr. Gower blandly repeated himself.

"But," FL!P began, "I...I think he's telling the truth."

Mr. Gower remained perfectly still, holding the hypodermic needle shoulder-high, thumb on the plunger, while at the other end a milky dribble hung suspended. He smiled benignly.

"This will only make certain that what he tells us will be the whole truth. It's perfectly harmless, I promise you. I believe he might even enjoy the trip."

"Don't listen to him, kid! Undo these straps and I'll take you right over to Michael Cassidy and...and...Law

Addison, too!" I said in desperation, falling back on lying since the truth wasn't setting me free. "Yeh, that's right, both of them together. Right now."

Mr. Gower shook his head sadly.

"See what I mean? That's a lie. We'll never know the truth unless we do it my way."

"What do you mean a lie? How the fuck do you know?"

"His sleeve."

"Stop saying that!"

He stopped saying it, but only because the blond kid was capitulating. He had his hand on my sleeve and was tugging it back, revealing my bare, exposed, naked arm.

"Okay," Mr. Gower said, extending the needle "this will only take a—"

"Look out, kid!"

I don't know why I shouted it, reflex I guess, seeing that needle as Gower aimed it at the kid's upper arm. I had no love for FL!P, but I absolutely hated needles. *I* didn't want to get stuck by one and didn't want anyone else to get stuck either.

Why he believed me, I don't know. Must've heard something in my voice, the urgency, because the kid responded like a whip, flinging himself backwards. He landed on the floor, skidding out of view, screaming up, "What the fuck, old man! You almost stuck that into *me*!"

"I told you to hold him still," Mr. Gower tried to explain. "You moved."

"You tried to stick me! What's in that?"

"Harmless, I tol—"

"Then stick yourself with it! Sh-uh'ya!"

"Please talk sensibly, just come back here and hold his arm again."

"Hold this!"

FL!P sprang back up on his feet, holding his skateboard close to his chest like a narrow shield. Then suddenly his arms shot forward with the skateboard jutting straight out. Its edge caught Mr. Gower below the chin in the soft flesh of his throat.

I heard a crunch.

Mr. Gower dropped the syringe. Mr. Gower made hissing noises and scuffled his feet. Mr. Gower sat down on the floor. He didn't get up again.

The kid was wild-eyed, he was mumbling, murmuring, "Y'see that, y'see that, motherfucker?"

I didn't want to interrupt, but I urged steadily, "Undo the straps, undo the straps." He must've heard me, because he dropped his board and his fingers began working at the buckles. I heard the wheels of his skateboard freely turning, the steely sound of its ball bearings a familiar one to me, the same sound I heard before something hit me in the basement stairwell.

The kid kept mumbling, "Y'see that, y'see that?"

Yeh, I saw it. And I saw how the wound looked on the old man's neck, same as the one I'd seen on Luis' throat.

Unrestrained, I sat up on the table, rubbing my wrists, and asked, "So who is—who was this guy?"

"I never met him before tonight. He came up to me at the party, said he had a way to get you to tell where Michael Cassidy and Law Addison were hidden. He knew all about it, so I thought, what can I lose? All he wanted was help lugging you up here. But he didn't say nothing about shooting you up with drugs. Or me!"

I stood up, looked around the place as I worked the circulation back into my wrists. It was a mini chemical lab with scales, test tubes, beakers, and Bunsen burners. In addition to equipment were the varied and variegated ingredients for cooking up drugs, including nail polish remover, industrial pesticide, and several household cleansers. There were also piles of tiny glassine envelopes, the sort the post office gives with stamps, and for the same reason: to keep out moisture. The envelopes contained chunks of white powder, the finished product. It was scary what kids will ingest in any white powder form, never stopping to question what made up the substance they snorted, smoked, shot up, or swallowed in a pill, just as long as the longed-for numbness ensued.

Mr. Gower, or whatever his name really was, looked to have been some kind of low-level cook. And judging by how he'd showed up at the hotel this morning, he was probably the person who'd been on the other end of the phone when I'd walked in on Michael Cassidy. He must have been one of her drug suppliers, quite possibly the one who'd concocted the hot bag that took Craig Wales' life. And he'd been ready to do the same thing to FL!P, and then surely to me, too, once I'd given him whatever information I had. I wouldn't be shedding any tears over his death.

There was a knock at the door then. A knock that developed into a heavy pounding. BANG BANG BANG.

The kid turned to me, "Who's that?"

"It's probably whoever told Gower here to off you and me."

The knocking got louder, then stopped being a knock. The doorframe trembled. Whoever it was was trying to kick in the door. Three or four more like that and he'd succeed.

I spun around, saw a window with a fire escape outside it.

"That way," I said.

We flung it open and crawled out onto the rusted fire escape. We were on the third floor of an apartment building. Outside it was full-on night, the streetlamps blazing orange.

The kid scrambled down and I was right on his heels. He didn't bother releasing the ladder at the bottom, just grabbed onto the last rung and dropped down to the sidewalk below. I did the same, and as soon as my feet touched pavement I started running.

The kid was fast. Ordinarily I never would've been able to keep up with him, but I'd heard other feet coming down the fire escape behind us—its whole framework shaking—and it gave me wings.

I wasn't even sure in what direction we were running until we ran out of island. We were on East Sixth Street and East River Drive when I yelled to the kid to hold up. He was headed for the overpass that traversed the drive and gave access to the athletic fields of East River Park.

He stopped halfway up the walkway ramp and looked back. Not at me. He seemed to be searching in the distance, back the way we'd come.

I needed to get close enough to grab him. If what I now believed was true, he'd not only killed Gower, he'd killed Luis, too. Gower could rot for all I cared—but I was going to see FL!P got nailed for Luis.

But as I got to the foot of the walkway, he saw something that spooked him. He started running again at full tilt, all the way across the cement overpass and into East River Park. I almost lost him in the dark, but as I reached the park I saw furtive movement off to my left. I headed in that direction.

Several years ago, the retaining wall that ran along the edge of the park had eroded and begun to crumble into the East River, and the asphalt promenade that lay over it started caving in, producing potholes which grew into sandy sinkholes. For safety, the city had erected high chain-link fences closing off the worst sections, making them off-limits until they were repaired. But of course they'd never gotten around to repairing it, too many other things needed patching up. It was the same all over the island. This was an old city that suffered too much weight bearing down on its thin shell of civilization. It had started collapsing in on itself like a star on its way to becoming a black hole.

Where I'd glimpsed FL!P moving was inside one of these fenced-off areas of the park. A crescent-shaped section of grass and trees about eighty feet across and thirty feet deep at its widest, that was cut off on the landside by an eleven foot high chain-link barrier. On the river side was the promenade's waist-high wrought-iron fence.

The enclosed area was in shadow, but I could just make out the humps of two unoccupied cement benches inside. I saw movement again beside one of them.

I looked around for a way to get in. Far to my right, where the fence started to angle in toward the promenade's railing, I found a five-foot-high gap someone had clipped in the chain links with wirecutters. Not recently, done some time ago, probably by kids looking for a private place to do drugs or make love, or both. The gap swayed slightly though there wasn't any breeze. Which suggested FL!P had passed through it moments earlier. I stepped through myself, careful that none of my clothes snagged on the sharp edges.

I measured my steps, breathed deeply and softly, until I found the kid crouched down beside one of the benches. He sprang up as I got closer.

"Oh, it's you."

"Relax," I said. "Nobody's coming. We lost him."

The kid shook his head from side to side.

I said, "Thanks for helping me back there. Quick thinking the way you handled the old man. It's a shame you left your skateboard behind."

"Oh, fuck." I guess he'd been too busy to notice.

"Yeh. It's how the cops are going to pin you for murder."

"What?" He whirled round to face me. "No way. You

saw, he tried to stick me with that needle. I was defending myself. Self-defense."

"Oh, absolutely. But I didn't mean him, I meant the man whose life you ended this afternoon. The super of that building. You really shouldn't have done that, y'know."

It was dark and I couldn't see his face all that well, but I heard the distress in his voice.

"I didn't—"

"Don't bother denying it, kid. I know you did it. Soon the cops will know too. Your fingerprints are all over that skateboard, and those bruises on both their necks are going to match up perfectly. You're done."

"They'll never be able…there's no way they'll know it was me—"

"Sure they will. See, I'm going to tell them."

"What?" His voice became very small, like a worried mouse in a Beatrix Potter book.

I told him how it was. "I liked that old guy. And I'm not really that fond of you."

"But I…I saved your life!"

"And I said thanks."

"Please don't…don't tell. I didn't mean to do it."

"Why did you?"

"It was an accident. I followed you there and I was just listenin' outside the door. I thought it's where Michael Cassidy was. Then that old bastard saw me. I tried to get away, but he grabbed me by the arm. I didn't mean to— he just grabbed me and I wanted him to let me go. It was an *accident*. Please don't tell."

He started to cry. It was the first time since I'd met him that he sounded his age. I almost felt sorry for him. Almost.

"Yeh, an accident," I said, "just like Owl, this morning, falling into traffic."

"That…" He sniffled. "That wasn't any accident."

"What do you mean?"

"Somebody shoved the old guy in front of that car. I saw the whole thing. I even—" He shut up.

"You're making it up. I don't believe you," I said, but I was lying. It was the only thing that might've explained why Gower had tried to stick him with the needle instead of me. Someone wanted to silence the kid. Which meant he knew something, had seen something.

The kid pleaded, "No. No, really. I saw it. Honest! They were talking and then that black car came and—I couldn't believe it—he shoved the old guy right in front of it."

"Who did?"

"Look, I'll tell you, okay? But we gotta trade."

"Trade what?"

"I tell you and you let me go."

I said nothing.

"Come on, you gotta let me go. Will you, if I tell you?"

I thought about it, but there wasn't much to think about. The cops would probably land him without my help anyway, so what did I have to lose versus what I had to gain?

"Okay," I agreed.

"You'll trade?"

"I said all right. Now tell me. Who was it?"

He sniffled some. "I don't know his name."

"Then what the fuck are—"

"I can describe him!"

"Okay, so describe him."

"That's easy. You must—"

He stopped talking, his head tipped back. For a second, I thought he'd gotten beaned by a badly thrown Frisbee, I saw something go flying off after skimming the top of his head.

Only it *was* the top of his head. It landed about three feet behind him.

Hearing the shot was an afterthought as I ate gritty macadam, trying to will myself flat as a sheet of paper. My body hit the ground before the kid's landed in a loose-limbed pile. Then a second shot rang out and a spurt of dirt hit my face. Shit. It stung.

I'd been wrong when I said we'd lost our pursuer. It wasn't exactly a new experience for me, being wrong. Unlike getting shot at in the dark. Never served in the military, so this was a new one on me, one I could've gladly gone my whole li—but why bother thinking about it? I'd lost my cherry.

Shit shit shit.

I was trapped in here. Around me on three sides was the chain-link fencing, eleven feet high, and the only exit the open gap through which the kid and I had entered. If I tried to go back through that gap or to scale the fence, the gunman would see me and kill me. Unfortunately the only other choice was the fourth side of this little enclosure—and that direction held nothing but a fifteen-foot drop to the foul, fast-moving water of the East River. The current would pull me under like a hundred cold hands.

Shit.

As I glanced about, I felt my skin prickling. There's an undeniable thrill in being hunted. Whether it's race memory, instinct, or perversion, since childhood we've all enjoyed the game of hide-and-seek. And there was an atavistic part of me that wanted to enjoy it even now. But seeing a boy's head shot off would dampen even the most ardent player's enthusiasm.

Shit.

I started to crawl along on my belly, making for the promenade's railing and the water's edge.

I could hear the rattle of the chain-link fence. The shooter was looking for the opening I'd passed through, and it wouldn't be long before he found it.

Shit. Or have I already said that?

In danger and in lovemaking, our bodies are transformed. Blood flows rapidly to all the necessary parts, our muscles expand and our joints become more fluid. We're at the height of our efficiency, like it's what we were meant to do. It makes all the other activities in our life seem like a ridiculous waste of breath. Meaningless fillers between love and death. But to be honest, I'd much rather been home watching TV.

Fuck.

I finally reached the railing and could see the East River beyond, its choppy surface dark silver and oily. Off in the distance were the lights of the Williamsburg Bridge, full of cars which were full of people, all too far away to do me any good except as an extravagant nightlight. One that wasn't going to keep the bogeyman away.

I started to pray. Nothing elaborate, just "God help me" over and over again. My grandma used to tell me it was all you ever needed to say.

There was a gap beneath the lowest part of the fence railing where the ground was crumbling away. Just wide enough for me to squeeze through.

I didn't hear the rattling of the chain-link fence anymore, just footsteps. He'd found the opening. He was here.

I slipped over the side, dislodging pebbles and chunks of asphalt into the water below. I kept my hands tight on the base of the railing. The last thing I wanted was to land in the East River, it was as sure a death as a bullet. So I just hung there, my legs dangling over the swift moving current of the night tide.

But I couldn't stay in one place. I was in a direct line with where the kid's dead body lay. I wouldn't be hard to find and I wanted to be hard to find.

God help me.

I began working my way, hand over hand, farther down the fence railing.

I was wishing I'd thought to blacken my fingers with dirt so they wouldn't stand out so clearly. But I'd had a lot on my mind.

God help me.

I'd gone only about three feet when something dark appeared at the railing above my head. I looked up.

Into a face looking down at me.

I thought I was dead.

But it was the face that was dead.

Then the shoulders and the arms and the chest of a dead body. It was the kid who wanted so badly to be famous, being hoisted over the railing and pitched down into the anonymity of the East River. He made hardly any splash at all.

I just hung there for a long time, not daring to move, risking only shallow breaths. My fingers felt fragile as ice, I imagined them cracking and splintering away into tiny shards.

But I didn't let go. I hung on.

It's what I do.

And eventually I bucked up, started moving again, hand over hand down the railing. I took some of the weight onto my feet against the wall, while minimizing as much as I could the scuffling noises I made.

I lost track of my progress, and of time, until I finally came to an outcrop of building extending out over the river. It was a water-treatment facility. The air was perfumed with an aroma like Tide laundry detergent.

I heard shouting as I climbed up and back over the railing. A skeleton crew of workmen had spotted me and were threatening to call the cops.

I took off running.

Chapter Nineteen
NOBODY ON

I went north, slowing down to a walk when I got to the FDR Drive overpass at Stuyvesant Town. I crossed the street and entered the huge housing complex and disappeared into its winding, dimly lit paths, finally emerging again at 14th Street and Avenue B. I looked west. High above the rooflines the illuminated clock tower at Irving Place read a quarter after two.

I was tired and shaken—badly in need of a drink—but I didn't go back to my office, not right away. There was one person I had to see first, one person who could be the key to all of this, and now I knew where she was, where she'd been all along.

If I was right, Michael Cassidy had taken the magnetic card key from me for one reason: after I'd left the hotel room, she'd returned and used the card key to get in again, and was probably still there. Only one way to find out.

So I headed back to the Bowery Plaza, on Third Avenue and St. Marks Place.

But I was too late. Parked in front of the hotel were an ambulance and a police cruiser, and just pulling up, one of the white and gold O.C.M.E. vans. Office of Chief Medical Examiner.

I kept my distance, not wanting to get involved, but needing to know what had happened. I saw a bearded young guy sitting cross-legged at the corner begging for spare change. He had a paper cup hanging by a string at the end of a short stick. He held it up to passersby as if it was a fishing pole. Up and down both arms, he had solid sleeves of tattoos, but whoever had done the work had used cheap ink. The interlocking images were hopelessly smudged, leaving his flesh muddied dark blue and purple as if with post-mortem lividity. I dug a quarter out of my pocket and dropped it in his cup.

"How they biting?" I asked.

"Not bad." He reached into his cup and took out my quarter, and also a linty penny that was in there. He tossed the penny away on the sidewalk.

I said, "Gotta throw back the little ones."

He grinned. One of his canines was chipped in half.

I asked, "You know what happened over there?" I pointed to the hotel with my thumb.

"Yep. Some lady killed herself in one of the rooms. Shot herself in the head. Heard one of the cops talkin' to the ambulance guys. S'pose to be someone famous, but I ain't never heard of her."

"What was her name?"

"I dunno. Don't 'member. Why?"

I shrugged. "Just curious." Then I walked away.

Suicide? I didn't buy that. Which left what? And who? Law Addison maybe? Finally disposing of a junkie ex-girlfriend? Or her husband, Ethan Ore, for the same reason and maybe one more: he might get a good movie out of it. But who else?

I tried to put it together in my mind. I'd seen the old guy Gower entering the hotel lobby that morning as I was leaving. He must've been making a delivery to Michael Cassidy. If he'd known where she was, then so had whoever had tried to kill me, and long before I'd figured it out. Ahead of me the whole time. No wonder he hadn't hunted harder for me in the park, I was no threat to him. Not as much as the kid FL!P had been or Michael Cassidy

herself. They each knew his face and now they were both
dead.

The kid's last words to me echoed in my brain.

"That's easy. You must—"

I must…I must what?

Nothing came to me. And I felt like nothing ever would.
My head was swimming and my soul was afraid. I walked
back to my office in a daze. I hardly even noticed my
favorite sight in the city, the brilliantly lit Art Deco spire
of the Chrysler Building in the distance, looking so much
like the kind of rocketships we once expected our fan-
tastic future would hold. Now it might as well have been
only a scale model.

Seated behind my desk again, I lit up a cigarette, and
smoked. It didn't help. But it didn't hurt.

I opened my desk drawer and found where I'd tossed
my gun. I also found the sealed envelope that contained
the stuff I'd grabbed out of Owl's pockets that morning.
Had it only been this morning? Felt like it'd all happened
months ago.

I tore open the envelope and shook its contents onto
my desk.

The receipt for George Rowell's hotel dated 9/2/08.

The broken plastic wristband from the wastebasket.

The two sales leaflets for the men's discount clothing
store and the Persian rug wholesaler in Chelsea on West
21st.

The pink pasteboard receipt for a parking garage.

Parking garage?

I looked at it like I'd never really seen it before. Maybe
I hadn't. I'd broken one of the rules—Matt would kill me—
back at Metro, Matt had always tried to drum into me the
golden rule: *When you look, see.*

Why in the world did Owl have a parking garage
receipt in his pocket? He hadn't driven into the city, I'd

found his round-trip bus ticket from New Hampshire in
his briefcase. So what the hell was this?

I looked.

And I saw.

It was one half of a parking garage claim check issued
by E-Z Parking Garage at 446 East 10th Street. The same
garage where Elena's boyfriend Jeff worked.

A standard parking garage receipt, it listed alphabet-
ically all the various makes and models of cars: Acura,
Audi, BMW, Buick, Cady, Chev., Chrys., Corvet, Dodge,
Ford, For'gn, Honda, Hyundai, Infiniti, Jaguar, Jeep,
Lexus, Lincoln, Mazda, Mercury, M-Benz, Mitsubishi,
Nissan, Olds., Peugeot, Plymouth, Pontiac, Porsche,
Saab, Subaru, T-Bird, Toyota, Volks., and Volvo, as well
as boxes for Convert., Sta'wgn, Van, and Compact. As
well as a listing of colors: Black, Blue, Brown, Gold, Gray,
Green, Orange, Red, Tan, White, and Yellow. Also in-
cluded were spaces for the location of the vehicle, noting
floor level and parking space.

This receipt had two holes punched in it: "Blue" and
"M-Benz."

A blue Mercedes-Benz.

Its location: third floor, space 17.

I turned over the receipt. Printed on the back was the
date and time the car was checked in. May 10th, 1:51 PM.

Thinking back to the info I'd found on the web about
Law Addison, it seemed to me I'd seen a mention of his
driving a sky-blue Mercedes-Benz.

Even the date rang a bell. Addison had disappeared
on May 11th, the day after the date on the receipt.

This wasn't Owl's parking garage receipt—it had belonged to Law Addison. Owl must've found it in the
writing desk in Elena's apartment. I'd seen a batch of
stubs in there myself, but I'd figured they all belonged to
Jeff—he worked at a garage, after all. But one of them

could certainly have been Addison's, if he'd been in the habit of parking his car at the garage where Jeff worked; that explained how they might have known each other, the millionaire and the grease monkey. And they must have known each other, since Jeff had somehow wound up house-sitting for him while Addison made his run for the border.

Speaking of which…if this receipt was for Addison's Benz, that meant Addison had never claimed his car before going on the run. Why? Because the car was too hot, too recognizable for him to flee in? Or was there some other reason?

I got out of my chair and started pacing the office, coming back to my desk every other turn to stare down at the pink receipt.

This meant something, I knew it. I didn't know what, but it meant something.

Goose-pimples rose on my arms. Excitement tingled in my nostrils.

I took my gun out of my desk drawer and slid it into the waistband at the back of my pants.

Suddenly I wasn't tired anymore. I didn't need a nap or a drink. No longer fatigued, I was electric.

I was at the office door with one foot outside when my phone rang and yanked me back.

I picked up the receiver. It was Sayre Rauth. She didn't sound happy.

"Payton, I need your help."

I laughed.

"You don't need anybody's help. You're too damn good."

"Please, listen."

"If it's the rest of your files you want, you're out of luck. They were destroyed. All that's left are the papers you took off my desk. You've got it all."

"That's not why I'm calling."

"Don't tell me it's to say that you love me and can't live without me."

Apparently not, as she didn't say anything for a long time. It reminded me why I hated talking on the telephone. You were never able to see the other person's face, as if the words were all that mattered.

"No, Payton," she said. "It's Elena. I'm worried about her. She left me a message that she wanted to see me. I went to her apartment. She wasn't there, but in the hallway...I saw yellow tape, police tape, all around. Someone there told me a man was murdered this afternoon. Payton, do you know where she is?"

I thought about it. "I might. You remember her boyfriend Jeff? The one I told you followed you from Yaffa?"

"Sure."

"You know where he works?"

"The garage, right? Over on Tenth Street? Is that where she is?"

"If I had to make a bet," I said, "I'd bet on her running to him, and I remember her saying he works nights. I'm headed over there right now. I'll call and let you know what I find out. Where are you?"

She hesitated, just a fraction, before she said, "My office. But don't—I'll call you. In an hour? Or I...I could come by your place?"

I didn't hesitate, not a fraction. I'd had all the seduction I could handle.

"Call me in an hour." I hung up.

It was past three AM, but scattered in the streets were still the sounds of late-night revelry, street-corner drunks hooting and laughing. Somewhere blocks away a bottle smashed, thrown forcefully to the ground. Such a tiny sound, but universal; anywhere on the planet it expressed the same demand: *Know I'm here!*

The air was piss warm and, because of the orange glow

of streetlamps, had a urinary hue, too. And not good piss, either, not clean piss, but that syrupy orange kind. Not even human. Cat piss. The kind you can't get out, ever, no matter how much you scrub. Whatever's marked by it has to be tossed out. Can't be saved.

Only occasionally as I walked was the humidity relieved by sharp gusts of breeze that went as soon as they came. Short windbursts like an engine revving, as if in the dead of morning a storm was on the way.

Chapter Twenty
BETWEEN C & D

The E-Z Parking garage was located on East Tenth between Avenues C and D, just across the street from a small lane called Szold Place, which ran along the side of one of the city's outdoor public pools. All closed up for the season.

I stopped and surveyed the parking garage from the pool side of the street. Three floors of parking with a big elevator shaft in which cars were lifted to the upper floors. Each of the partitioned levels had gaps overlooking the street with heavy black netting to keep the birds out, heavy black netting covered in starbursts of white birdshit.

On the second level could be seen the fronts of cars facing out behind the netting. But at the third level, the spaces were all empty, no cars.

The garage was closed, its metal roll-down gate snug to the ground. Its cave-like interior seemed to be lit by nothing but emergency exit door lights, a dim red gloom bleeding around the rounded concrete pillars. This was no way to run a business. Supposin' I needed my car in a hurry? Just supposin'.

But as my eyes became adjusted, I saw there was another light inside as well, on the ground floor. A pale light showing in a small glass-enclosed office just to the right of a closed metal door with a punch clock beside it.

I rattled the cage wall of the gate, producing a ripple.

A shadow crossed the light in the office and a black silhouette faced me, like those ghosts in Japanese horror flicks.

The ghost went away and a few seconds later I heard a noise far off to my left. A door had opened. I went over to it. Elena was holding it open.

Her eyes widened when she recognized me and she tried to shut the door again. But too late, I was inside. I closed the door behind me. The small areaway was lit by only a single bare 60 watt bulb dangling overhead from a cord.

I asked, "What are you so afraid of?"

"I...nothing, I thought—"

"That I was someone else? Who are you expecting?"

"I don't *expect*, it's just. I don't want trouble—"

"What sort of trouble are you afraid of?"

"Nothing. No one."

"Is it Sayre Rauth? Because you've got nothing to be frightened of there. I've talked with her. She isn't after you."

Elena backed up a step, keeping me at arm's length. Her expression was wary and more than a bit sad. "She get to you, this woman, and you believe her lies. Like all men."

"She told me she wants to help you."

"She help me before, when we're in Ukraine. I know her help, I don't want it."

"Well, she's not here now, I can tell you that. And *I* certainly won't hurt you."

She shook her head. "Go, please. I don't want you here."

"Sorry, Elena. I'm not going anywhere till I get some answers."

"Then at least come to office, I need to be near phone."

"Okay, I can do that." I followed her, keeping my hand lightly on the gun butt in my waistband. She led me to the glass-enclosed office where only a desk lamp was lit, illuminating a blotter with a few pens on it and several pink parking receipt tickets like the one I had in my pocket.

Elena sat behind the desk and commenced to stare at the telephone, willing it to ring.

I shut the door and stood with my back to it, looking out through the glass walls like a fish in a tank, staring into the darkened vacant parking garage and its patches of red gloom.

I said, "Tell me something. What happened after I left your apartment this afternoon? I went back a few minutes later and you were gone."

"I wake up in bathroom," she said. "I hear loud crash outside, feel floor shake. I wait a minute, go out into hallway to look. Nothing. Then I look down in basement, and I see you, you and super, at bottom of stairs. You look like you are dead, both of you. So I run—I pack quick, a few things, and I run."

"Yeh, well, I'm not dead. Luis is—but so is the guy who killed him. You don't have to worry about him."

She shook her head. "I will never go back to that apartment."

"No, probably not," I said, thinking of Sayre's description of the building wrapped in crime-scene tape. Thinking, too, that if Addison was in town again he might want his *pied à terre* back. "Did you know the man you're house-sitting for is a wanted fugitive?"

"What?" Her eyes shot up from the cradled phone receiver to my face.

"The police," I said, "they want to arrest this man, along with anyone who's been helping him. By house-sitting, say."

"We don't help him," Elena said. "We don't even house-sit for him—we sit, yes, but it is for Jeff's boss, he give us the keys, say go live there free, just pick up mail, pay phone, electric, nobody will know. So we do. But we never once see Mr. Andrew. We don't help him any. I don't think he even know we are living there."

"Jeff's boss gave you the keys?"

"His new boss, yes. The man who buy parking garage, he give them to Jeff and tell him move in, watch over apartment, keep it safe."

"When did this new boss buy the garage? Just recently?"

She nodded. "June. He come in, he fire all the workers, everyone but Jeff. So now Jeff works like dog, seven days, all day. I never see him. I don't think it's worth it, even with the extra money."

"What extra money?"

She tilted her chin down and didn't say anything.

"Look, Elena, honest, I'm trying to help you. But I can't unless you answer my questions. What money?"

She peered at me from under her brows.

"He give Jeff special bonus, for all the extra work he gonna have to do. Seventy thousand dollars. Too much money, I think, like back home when they pay us extra for modeling because they need us also keep our mouth shut. But Jeff explain to me that things is different here, they sometimes pay you seventy thousand dollar to work in a garage. I don't know. It's not sound right to me, but he say, so…" Her English, never great, was getting worse as she became more agitated. I had to strain to make sense of what she was saying.

"This money," I said. "The seventy thousand dollars. That's what got Sayre worried. She discovered how much money the two of you had in the bank, and figured you had to be doing something illegal."

"No, nothing illegal, we done nothing!"

Maybe you haven't, I thought, but what about your boyfriend. I asked, "Where is Jeff?"

I could see it pained her to answer. "He was here, but he leave more than an hour ago." She glanced over at a clock on the wall. "Hour twenty-five minutes."

"Did he say where he was going?"

She shook her head.

"No, just said he need to see his boss. He said he'd just be couple minutes, or will call me if it's longer. They talk on phone, Jeff and boss. He was shouting, so I hear."

"What were they talking about?"

"Money. Always money. Jeff say seventy thousand not enough if he got to work all the time, seven days, every week, on and on. He say just close down garage, be better. I think. I didn't understand. He was shouting and…something about closed-off top floor of the garage. Jeff say boss tell him he pick him up out front and they drive somewhere to talk."

The closed-off top floor. I thought about the pink ticket in my pocket. Addison's car had been parked up there.

I told her, "Wait here."

"Where you go?"

"The top level," I said. "I want to check something out."

She said, "You need take stairs—Jeff say he turned off elevator for night."

"Good."

I found the stairs by following the red lights of the EXIT signs. Beyond the door the stairwell was lit by fluorescent fixtures, which made my climb brighter but no more cheerful.

I opened the door at three and came out in a vast, empty space. I couldn't see a single car. Just concrete walls, concrete floor, concrete ceiling; I was surrounded by giant slabs of it as if in a tomb.

My footsteps echoed in the chamber as I walked along toward the far end. About ten feet in, I found a bend in a dividing wall and on it a junction box with four light switches. The first I tried lit up a quadrant behind me to the left. Empty. I switched it off and tried another. This one lit up an area on the other side of the dividing wall. I went around to look.

In the far corner, a single vehicle was entirely enclosed under a cloth cover pulled down to its wheels, snug as a hood on a kidnap victim's head.

I circled it until I found a bungee cord release, then loosened the cover and dragged it off the car.

It was a sky-blue Mercedes-Benz.

All the windows were open a crack. I lifted the handle of the driver's door and it was unlocked.

Both the front and back seats were empty. There was a strong smell of gasoline fumes. I looked down and saw a strip of oily rag on each of the floor mats. Just one strip, deliberately placed on each of the four mats.

I opened the glove compartment. As usual, no gloves— but strangely, nothing else either. No car registration or owner's manual, not even a pair of sunglasses or a peppermint. I swung it shut.

I sat in the driver's seat, let my hands hover over the steering wheel without touching it. My feet could barely touch the pedals. The man who drove the car was a good three inches taller than me, making him something over six feet.

I reached under the steering wheel and found the lever that unlatched the trunk.

I watched it rise in the rear view, smooth and inexorable as the coffin lid in a vampire flick.

I walked around to the back of the car and looked in.

"Shit—" I jumped and did a little sissy-pants jig. "Shit."

I'd been expecting something like it, but my imagination didn't do the sight justice. I couldn't look directly at him at first, had to build up resolve, casting glances first at the periphery, the thickness of the layers of plastic he was cocooned in, the negative space around his body. In the corners at the bottom of the trunk, beside his head and his feet, were several open cans of Raid and other insecticides.

Finally I got myself under control and looked straight at him. Like all horrors, it wasn't worse than I imagined, just different, more specific, alive with details my mind never could've conceived.

I had to unwrap him. It wasn't the right thing to do, it wasn't the smart thing to do, and it sure wasn't the tasteful thing. But I had to unwrap him and know for sure.

The thick sheet of plastic was slick with something oily. I smelled my hand. It stunk of pesticide, insecticide, and—I sniffed again—citronella.

The plastic was folded and tucked under his body and once I shifted him a bit it came open like a flower.

What the plastic revealed was a desiccated corpse. Not much face left to make a positive I.D., it looked like it'd been crushed in, but only after death since there'd been little bleeding. However, I could see that he'd had blond hair, long limbs, and had probably looked a lot like a Swede. No doubt in my mind, it was Law Addison, dead in the trunk of his own car. His daring flight from justice had never gotten off the ground.

There was more of him left solid than I would've thought possible after four months. But I saw a possible explanation. Like the outside of the plastic, the body was slathered with insecticides and citronella. It would've kept the flies away and retarded decomposition.

He was dressed in a blue shirt. The one wound I could

see that *had* bled was in his chest near his heart. The
dried blood splotch around it was black and flaky. There
were other wounds, about a dozen repeated punctures in
the lower chest, belly, and groin, strikes at all the major
organs and intestines. But none of those had bled. All
had been delivered post-mortem.

Like the insect poison, it looked like another measure
to impede decomposition, by releasing the build-up of
interior gases which so quickly aid in the corruption of
flesh and the reduction of the body into sludge.

It all pointed to workman-like improvisation, but by
an informed hand. Someone who knew what he was
doing and didn't want a stinking car trunk full of dead
man soup. Instead he had something more along the
lines of a modern mummy.

I poked around gingerly, looking for the bulge of a
wallet on Addison's body, but no luck. Shifting his husk, it
felt like all his weight was concentrated in the middle,
around his waist. He was wearing a brown leather belt. It
looked wider than most belts. It had probably been snug
back in May, but it was loose now, and I gave it a little
tug. It was heavy. Heavier than leather and its brass
buckle would explain.

I unhooked the belt and pulled it off him in one
motion like someone starting a lawn mower with a rip-
cord.

Dangling from my fingers, it felt heavier still. Heavy
as a deep-sea diving belt. I located a tiny zipper on its
underside and opened it. It was lined with gold coins.
Krugerrands. By quick estimate twenty of them. By
quick arithmetic, over seventeen thousand dollars, if not
more. I zipped it back up and draped the belt over my
shoulder.

Law Addison had tried to make his getaway, was all
ready to flee. But something had stopped him. Someone.

A lot of things made sense in a hurry. This discovery was like the last marble that tips the scale and starts the peppery march of a hundred other marbles cascading. A few minutes ago, I hadn't even known what had happened. Now I knew what—and I also knew who.

The realization gave me a sickening lurch, like losing your grip while climbing a sheer rock face. Falling backward into utter nothing, a gluttonous void. In front of you, vanishing rapidly, is the view of your last good firm handhold, getting smaller and smaller as you plunge. All around, the air is whistling and just behind you, out of sight, growing larger and larger in the corner of your eye, lies the end of all suspense.

Chapter Twenty-one
'TIL WHEN-NEVER

Two sounds brought me back to the now. One a sound like dragging and the other like a squeaky wheel. I tried to trace its echo in the desolate top level of the garage. My eyes fastened on the rounded concrete corner of the dividing wall, beyond which was the stairwell.

The dragging sound stopped briefly, but the squeaking continued. Then footsteps began, sharp and direct slaps bouncing off the concrete walls of the chamber. Getting closer.

I unpacked my gun, held it in my right hand hanging loose down by my thigh, and waited, watching that corner.

A thick shadow appeared and behind it a man.

"Payton? What the fuck?"

"Hi, Matt. What you doing here?"

I wasn't trying to be funny, I guess I was just a little punchy, and he sounded so…normal.

"Oh. Trying to clean up your mess."

"*My* mess?"

"Yeah, dickhead."

He came forward, dragging something behind him like a laundry sack, but it wasn't a sack. It was alive, it was Elena. Duct tape wrapped several times about her mouth, all around her head and hair. Her wrists and ankles were bound the same way. The squeaky sounds I'd heard were just her muted whimpers.

Matt stopped advancing about eight feet away. He dragged Elena up beside him in one pull, his hand wrapped around the back of her blouse.

He said, "I had it all settled so neatly, things were finally fine. Then you start nosing into it. You're as bad as Owl was."

I gestured—with my left hand, not the one holding the gun—at the open trunk of the car and Law Addison's body in its chrysalis of plastic sheeting.

"How did this happen, Matt?"

"I did my job. That's all. Metro was brought in by the bailsbond agency. We were supposed to keep an eye on Addison, in case he got antsy. Which he did. Unfortunately, he slipped our tail—the assholes I had watching him lost him. Better believe I fired their asses on the spot. Same way I fired you five years ago. Remember?"

"Yeah," I said. "I remember."

"So then I had to track this Jethro down. And that's what I did.

"We didn't know about the 'L. Andrew' apartment down on C, but we did know about the junkie girlfriend. Easiest thing in the fucking world for me to roust her connection and let him know he was looking at a federal beef unless he called me immediately the minute she got in touch. Sure enough, she phoned him up, looking to score a stockpile before going away. And he called me like the good little pusher he was. He told me when and where, I went in his place, and when she got there, instead of her delivery she got me, reading her the riot act."

"I heard about that," I said. "From her husband. You bum-rushed her out of the city and got her tucked away in a rehab clinic upstate. Same place you went for your detox treatment, I bet, that place you said your cousin runs."

"Not bad, Payton. I shouldn't have let that slip. But you get under a guy's skin, y'know."

"*De nada*," I said. "But explain this to me. You hid Michael Cassidy away and pumped her for info—fine. She spilled to you where Addison was and you staked out his hidey-hole—fine. But how's all that end up with him in the trunk and you owning *this* place?"

"Well, this place is where Addison ran to when he finally made his move," Matt said. "I was getting ready to bust him—swear to God, I was maybe two hours away from kicking in his door and putting the cuffs on him— when he walked out with three suitcases in tow and jumped in a cab. Of course I followed him, I figured he was making a run for the airport. But instead he came here. Took the elevator up with his luggage. I took the stairs. When I got here, he was over there—"

Matt nodded toward the car behind me, but I didn't turn and look.

"He was loading his bags into the trunk, getting ready for his big escape. Kept looking at his watch. I guess he was still waiting for his girlfriend to show. It was pathetic what a drop I had on him.

"So I shouted, *Hey, Addison! Might as well take 'em out again, you aren't going anywhere.* I was sick of this asshole and all the trouble he'd made for me. All I wanted was to cuff him, deliver him to the cops, go home and take a fucking nap.

"But instead of just takin' it like a man, he starts in blubbering, begging me to cut a deal. Payton, you don't know what it was like. This big dopey Jethro on his knees, offering one of his suitcases up, telling me there's a million dollars inside. A million dollars *cash*, Payton. And all he wants me to do is give him a head start.

"But I knew it would have been a waste of time—his

head start maybe would've bought him a day or two but they'd have caught him just the same. And then you'd better believe he'd've turned me in—he'd have done any damn thing he could just to save his neck.

"And as I stood there with my gun drawn and the son of a bitch kneeling and whimpering, I realized that the only fucking thing that was keeping me from taking him up on his offer was that he was going to get caught, and that meant I'd get caught, and that meant I'd lose my job, I'd lose my kid, I sure as hell would never see the million bucks.

"But I'm looking down at this poor fuck's pleading eyes, feeling pity, and I start thinking maybe there is a way it could work. If I coached him every step of the way. Got him out of state and stashed away for a few months until the hunt died down. Got him a new identity, and fucking *drilled* into him every day how to stay under the radar—because it wouldn't be just his safety and liberty at stake anymore, it'd be mine, too, *my* liberty, my *family's* safety, and—

"Ah, fuck," Matt said. "I shot him."

For a while all I could hear were Elena's muffled sobs and the whistle of her breath through her nose.

I cleared my throat.

"Yeh," I said. "All that would've been a lot of work."

"You shittin' me? No way. And wherever he went, sooner or later, he'd blow it. Or someone would spot him from *America's Most Wanted*—that show goes worldwide these days. How'm I suppose to live with that hanging over my head, my family's head?

"One shot…and it all went away. The money's mine, not just one mil but all of it, and no Jethro to worry about screwing everything up. And you know something, Payton, when you step out of bounds like that? It's a shock when the earth just doesn't open up and swallow you. But it doesn't. The world goes grinding on. I tell you, I felt good. I felt peaceful.

"I popped open one of those suitcases and there was nothing inside it but money. Wads of used U.S. currency packed sideways, neat as sardines. Well-thumbed fifties and hundreds. The other two bags were the same. Would you believe, he hadn't even packed a shaving kit? Guess he figured he could always buy one."

He lowered his head and laughed into his chest.

"But I didn't make his mistake. I looked after practical matters. Getting rid of his body. Over the years, you hear of so many guys and that's what trips 'em up. They get caught transporting it or disposing of it. And I thought, out of the blue, then don't touch it, leave it where it was. Let it ride. Wasn't until later, after I'd counted up the money, I got the idea of buying this place."

"But first you had to prep the body," I said. "I saw the Raid and Black Flag shower you gave it to shoo the shoo flies."

"Yeah, had to do that right away. I knew it would mean some coming and going, and there was the fucking garage attendant to deal with. But I'd slipped him a twenty on the way in, when I was following Addison, and I got the impression his palm would stand a bit more greasing."

"Let me guess," I said. "Jeff."

He nodded. "He was more than willing to look the other way—if that's all he had to do—as long as the price was right. And I made sure the price was right."

"Seventy thousand bucks plus free rent and board for him and his girlfriend," I said. "Pretty generous, Matt. But that's where things started to unravel. It was just your bad luck his girlfriend was an old friend of George Rowell's. And that Owl happened to be visiting her when

Michael Cassidy showed up at the apartment. She was running scared after that botched attempt on her life by your drug dealer friend. She ran to Addison's old hideout on Avenue C."

"Jesus Christ," Matt said. "Owl made her right away, I'll bet."

"More than that—he got her to spill her story about the kind-hearted private investigator who cut her a break, sending her off to rehab instead of letting her get collared with Law Addison. I'm sure you didn't give her your real name, but somehow he must've guessed it was you. Addison was a Metro job after all."

Matt shook his head. "Can you beat that? The one guy I take in to make it work for me, and ends up his girl knows Owl. That's fuckin' New York for ya. What're the fucking odds?"

"Astronomical. Too bad no one made book, got a little money down on it."

Matt leaned his head back and stretched his neck with little rotations. "Yeah, well, I did have money down, a load. In fact, I still got a fucking load riding on this."

"How much, Matt? How much did it all finally come to? What was the tally? I'm curious."

He brought his head back in line. His gray eyes pinned me.

"You're curious. You're curious. You're curious. Shit, Payton, you don't need to tell me you're fucking curious. I get it, already. I know you."

"Let me rephrase the question," I said. "How much, and is it worth all that you've done to keep it?"

Matt's eyebrows rose in baffled innocence, furrowing his brow.

"What? What have I done? C'mon, really?"

"You killed eight people."

"Eight? That can't be right."

He started counting them off on the fingers of his left hand. As I watched him, I realized I could raise my gun and shoot him now, that I *should* shoot him now. But I didn't. I watched him.

His thumb was Law Addison stuck in the car trunk.

His forefinger was George Rowell, pushed into traffic so he couldn't put me on the case.

He didn't count Craig Wales' O.D., because that had been an accident, the hot bag meant for Michael Cassidy alone. I didn't argue the point.

His middle finger.

"That guy at the Crystalview."

He didn't remember his name.

"Paul Windmann," I told him.

"Saw his address on your desk, when I was still looking for Cassidy, I thought it was where she was stashed. I only went there to sniff around. But I knock on the door and next thing this guy's waving a gun in my face. It was over before I even knew what happened. Idiot pulled the trigger, shot himself. I just went over there to ask a few questions and he freaked out and got himself shot."

"Another accident then?" I asked.

He kept his middle finger up.

I said, "Then there's the kid you shot over in East River Park, after your play with the drug dealer went bust. Why did he have to die so bad?"

Matt said, "That little cocksucker, you wouldn't believe me if I told you. I didn't believe he had it in him until he fucking showed me. He stopped me when I was coming out of your building. Skidded his skateboard in front of me, then flashed his cell phone up in my face. What's the picture of, but me with my hands on Owl's chest, pushin' as the black car rounds the turn. Before I could grab the fucking phone, he was off in a shot. Like he just wanted

me to know what he had on me. I guess he was planning
to shake me down. But Homey don't play that."

He flicked up his fourth finger, his wedding ring finger.

The pinkie was for Michael Cassidy.

Matt said, "Can't believe she was over at that hotel all
the while. By the time I got there, she was flying so high,
she just let me in the room when I knocked. There was a
gun on the bed. She made it so…easy. I mean after trying
so hard to hide. And then there she was all sort of laid out
for me, ready, almost comatose. It *should've* been easy.
Just pick up the gun and badabing. But I couldn't do it
at first. Maybe 'cause she was a woman, I don't know.
But then I thought of Jeanne and the baby and what this
woman could do to us, and I shot her in the head. Very
final, that is. Very final."

But it wasn't final at all. It wasn't over.

I asked, "And where's Jeff? He went off to meet you
more than an hour ago, and here you are, but no Jeff."

Elena had stopped her sobbing, suspended it long
enough to strain and listen for his answer.

But his answer was wordless. Matt stuck out his other
thumb.

He said, "That's the lot. See, I told you."

My chest heaved out a short laugh-sob, like I was gag-
ging on ash.

"Okay, six then," I said. "But shit, when you're counting
off victims on your fingers and have to move to the other
hand, it's time to admit you got a problem. You may have
stopped drinking, Matt, but you've turned into a murder-
aholic."

As soon as I'd said it, I regretted it. I noticed for the
first time a distinct drunken cast to Matt's expression.
Not that I thought for a moment he'd been drinking—I
didn't—but there are such things as dry drunks, who can
be just as dangerous and erratic as the regular sort.

Matt said, through a ragged smile, "You may be right, pal. But I can kick it. Same as I did with drinking. Cold turkey. Except maybe…one more for the road?"

He looked down at Elena, on her knees, as he held her by the scruff of the neck, propped up against his thighs.

I said, "You're overlooking something, Matt."

I raised my gun and waggled it at him, just to bring it into play. I'd forgotten how heavy it was with a full clip.

He frowned and shook his head.

"What are you going to do? Shoot me?"

"The thought has been trapezing through my mind."

"You won't. I know you, Payton."

"Don't be so sure about that."

"Oh, wanna see how sure I am?"

He was surprisingly fast for such a big guy—or maybe just, as usual, I was too slow. I didn't even see where it came from, but suddenly he was holding a gun.

Blue metal. It looked like the old .38 he'd always kept in his desk drawer at Metro. I'd only ever seen him crack walnuts with it. But now he cocked it, angled it down at Elena's head.

"Drop your weapon, Payton," Matt said.

"Or what, you'll shoot her? Come on, Matt. How stupid do you think I am? If I drop my gun, you'll shoot us both. But if you shoot her, I'll drop you."

"Then do it. Shoot me now. Go ahead. I told you, that's your only play, Payton. Anything else is just me fucking talking you into putting your gun down. And I will. Because I know you. Oh yeah. Better than you know yourself."

"Do you."

"I know your secret, Payton."

"I'm really the Green Lantern?"

Matt shook his head sagely.

"You think you're a detective in a detective story."

His voice bounced off the dank concrete walls and echoed through the shadows of the parking garage. It sounded more ominous than he probably intended.

I said, "I…"

"Payton, you think you live your life by this sort of code of behavior, but you're only fucking playing at it. You and guys like Owl have outdated ideas about what's right and wrong—but him I could forgive, he was a dinosaur, he lived it. You, you're just aping old movies."

I'd about had my fill of this reunion.

"You, Matt? *You* can forgive Owl? You shoved him in front of a car! And why, to stop him from coming to see me? What did you think he wanted to talk to me about? Or tell me? What made you kill him?"

"Actually, I didn't mean to," he said absently. "Kill Owl? Nothing I would've ever fucking dreamed of doing. He brought me up in this business. I *loved* him. But you know, shit happens."

"Shit," I said.

"After the party where Wales bought it, I picked up Cassidy's trail. I followed her to Avenue C, waited for her outside Addison's place, watched that fucking stoop till seven in the goddamn morning, and then who does she come out with but George Rowell? It was like something outta a fucking dream, where you think of an old friend you've been dying to see in forever, and there they are. And there he was. But holy fuck was he with the wrong woman."

"So you followed them to their hotel," I said. "Only you must've been a little clumsy, because he picked up on the fact that he had a tail."

"I wasn't clumsy, asswipe. Owl was good."

"Well, you must've been good, too, because he didn't

know it was you following him. That's what he wanted my help for—flushing out who was tailing him. Nothing more."

Matt seemed to only half-hear me. When he spoke, it was almost to himself. "He figured it out, y'know. At the end. I tried to fake it when I walked up to him, a big smile, what a surprise. But he wasn't fooled. I saw it in his eyes. Somehow he'd put it all together, out of nothing, like pulling it out of the air. He really was the best of all of us, just a great fucking detective. But he never really got it. The way life works when the chips are down. I mean, there I am, looking for a car coming fast down the road trying to beat the yellow, and he's explaining to me the whole time why *he* has no choice, he's got to turn me in. Can you believe it? Never saw what was coming."

"Maybe he didn't want to see."

"At least he went out on the job. That's the way he always wanted to go. Always said so. So he got his wish."

I said, "You've got to listen to yourself."

"I knew you wouldn't fucking understand, Payton. You and that poor old fool. I could never make you see it. You don't know what it's like for me. Especially now. You don't know what it's like to be a father. It changes everything. There was no way I was going to have my family's future threatened by someone's principles."

Like every asshole he'd ever collared, Matt had cooked up a rationale for all his actions, a way of convincing himself he wasn't just doing what he wanted or what he had to but what was right. And who could argue with it? If it came down to me or his beautiful infant son, who was he supposed to choose? I mean, really, what did I expect?

Matt said, "You asked me before, how much and was it worth it. It came to just under four million dollars. Three million seven hundred eighty thousand. Cash. I'd never seen that much in my lifetime. If I hadn't done what I've done, I wouldn't have that to pass on to my family. As soon as I saw all that money in the suitcases, I knew I'd done the right thing. It was such a fucking relief, *knowing* it wasn't for nothing. Knowing it was worth it. Does that satisfy you, Payton?"

"Not really," I said. "Like how'd you manage to buy this place, a property this size in Manhattan for less than four million? How'd you ever persuade the previous owner to take less than market value?"

He didn't say anything, just stared at me with a combination of sheepishness and pride on his face. Then he unrolled one more finger on his freehand.

"You got any other burning questions?" he said.

"Yeh," I said. "Was it you who sicced Moe Fedel on me after all?"

"Uh-huh."

"Hell."

"Uh-huh."

"You had me believing you hadn't."

"You *wanted* to believe, Payton. That's you in a nutshell. You want to believe."

"I don't want to believe you killed all these people."

"Oh fuck, Payton, throw that in my face."

"And what are you throwing in my face? What do you expect me to do, Matt? What choice do I have?"

"You want a choice. Okay, okay. Here goes. A solid half million dollars in cash. Hundred dollar bills. Think about it, Payton. You will *never* see that much money if you live to be two hundred. So really think, okay? And I don't mean think of a clever *Deal Or No Deal* comeback, jack-off. Think what's really at stake here."

He made a good pitch. And he was right. I lived in a world of penny rolls and crumpled one dollar bills. I literally couldn't even conceive of that much money being mine. It defied my imagination.

Ultimately, I had to tell him I accepted his offer. His choice was no choice. The problem was keeping a straight face as I did it.

"So what's it going to be Payton?"

"I don't know. Right now I feel like I'm in your shoes, Matt, faced with the same problem you were, whether or not to latch onto somebody I figure is going down no matter what I say or do. You gotta know it's only a question of time. Seven bodies, man—that's a lot for anyone to sweep under the rug.

"But I guess they won't get you today and probably not tomorrow, and who knows, maybe you'll find some way to pull it off. If anyone can… So sure, what the hell, I'd love a half million bucks. It'll keep the draft out."

"So, what, is that yes or a no?"

"Yes."

"Fuck, then say yes! That's all I want to hear, yes or no."

"Yes."

"Yeah, I got it now," Matt said. "Just one thing."

He nudged Elena, so she toppled over, landing on her side.

"Kill her."

"Wha—no—what are you talking about?"

"Seal the deal. C'mon, why you think I let you keep your gun?"

"Let me keep…?"

"Do this, we're solid. I'll have something on you as bad as what you've got on me."

"You're nuts, Matt."

"Maybe. Choose."

"I'm not going to kill her."

Elena was squealing. Her eyes were wide with terror, flicking from my gun to Matt's and back. I lowered mine.

That was a mistake.

Matt swung his up to point directly at my chest.

"Eh—Payton—eh! Not a twitch. Pray as you like, but don't genuflect 'less you're done."

He lifted the barrel higher and leveled it at my face. He started walking toward me, taking slow steps like a duelist measuring off his ten paces.

You never really see a gun for what it is until you stare down the muzzle of one in someone else's hands, watch it come closer, closer, till it fills your line of sight. You watch, knowing it's about to spit flame, that the split-second explosion will be the last thing you ever see. You know a bullet's coming as soon as you blink, so you don't blink. You freeze. Grow old looking at it. If it's a big gun, you mark how small it looks. And if it's a small gun, *my*, how big it looks. An enormous maw about to swallow your head.

I concentrated on that black hole approaching me. I didn't blink. It became my whole world, my past future present. Funny that something so small could magnify and become huge, big enough to blot out the sun. It seemed to be sucking at me like a puncture hole in a pressurized cabin. I waited for it, knowing the moment I let my eyes shut I was done...

How quiet it was. Except for my heartbeat and Matt's footsteps, there was no sound at all. Which was odd, actually. There should have been another sound, there had been one before, Elena's muffled sobs. Glancing down, I realized I no longer saw her prostrate shape in the periphery of my vision.

Matt read something in my eyes, but he didn't waver, didn't look behind him. Maybe he thought I was pulling some trick to distract him. He gave me too much credit.

When I saw the movement behind him, I forced my eyes to lock on his, did my damnedest to hold him, make him focus on me. Not on the sliver of Sayre Rauth I could see behind him shifting her weight and raising her right arm out in front of her.

She fired. The .22's dainty reports, even in the echo chamber of the parking garage, were like birthday balloons popping. The barrel gave off puffs of confectioners' sugar.

Matt fell against me and I felt the slam of one of the bullets ripping through him. Then another, and a wetness like a sea mist on my face, only hot as molten wax. I clenched my lips against the animal urge to lick it away from my mouth.

She made no song and dance of it. Four times she shot him in the back, one got him in the neck.

I sidestepped his weight against me, shedding him like an overcoat. He landed on his face. I wiped mine on my sleeve.

Sayre lowered her gun, her cunning, little silver gun, the one that killed Windmann, the one I told her she should ditch. Thank god she'd ignored my advice.

She had dragged Elena over to one side, propped her against the concrete wall. I went and untied her, for something to do.

She gulped a free breath, her eyes tearing up. "He kill George," she said, "and Jeff—" She started to cry.

Sayre came over and put her arms around her, helping her to her feet. They walked together to the stairs.

I checked on Matt, but there was no more Matt, only a silent body, a mound of lifeless meat on the ground. I patted his pockets but couldn't find his cell. Finally grabbed a handful of coat lapel and heaved. Rolling him as easy as shifting a flood-sodden sandbag.

I found his cell phone, turned it on. A brightly lit animation appeared on the screen—crisp, vibrant—and the phone tootled a snappy tune. The first stored number was labeled JEANNE. I didn't call it.

Instead I dialed 911. After the call, I slid the phone back inside Matt's jacket pocket and rolled him back onto

his face. I draped the belt with the gold coins in it over
him. They would add weight to the story I'd tell the cops.
Besides, they were his. If any man had earned his spoils,
it was Matt. Then I went down to wait at street level for
the cops to arrive.

The sidewalk was empty, both directions, not even a
derelict or a roving wolf-pack of pumped-up 'bangers
in sight. No sign of Sayre or Elena either. Disappeared
into darkness together, the hard black-blue night.

I looked over at the East River, and the lights of
Brooklyn beyond, and—

Cried my eyes out.

Only the sound of sirens brought me back. Wet goop
was running down my cheeks. The night looked crystal
clear and everything was starry.

The siren's wail didn't sound far off, but its crybaby cry
grew fainter, not louder, more distant, farther away. Not
my ride, someone else's emergency. It was first come, first
serve in the big city.

Me and my dead had to wait our turn.

Get Hard Case Crime by Mail...
And Save 50%!

☐ **YES! Sign me up for the Hard Case Crime Book Club!**

As long as I choose to stay in the club, I will receive every Hard Case Crime book as it is published (generally one each month). I'll get to preview each title for 10 days. If I decide to keep it, I will pay only $3.99* — a savings of 50% off the standard cover price! There is no minimum number of books I must buy and I may cancel my membership at any time.

Name: _____

Address: _____

City / State / ZIP: _____

Telephone: _____

E-Mail: _____

☐ **I want to pay by credit card:** ☐ VISA ☐ MasterCard ☐ Discover

Card #: _____ Exp. date: _____

Signature: _____

Mail this page to:
HARD CASE CRIME BOOK CLUB
20 Academy Street, Norwalk, CT 06850-4032

Or fax it to 610-995-9274.
You can also sign up online at www.dorchesterpub.com.

* Plus $2.00 for shipping. Offer open to residents of the U.S. and Canada only. Canadian residents please call 1-800-481-9191 for pricing information.

If you are under 18, a parent or guardian must sign. Terms, prices, and conditions subject to change. Subscription subject to acceptance. Dorchester Publishing reserves the right to reject any order or cancel any subscription.